IN A TIME OF PASSION AND WAR, FAITH
AND TREACHERY, THEY WERE THE MEN
AND WOMEN WHOSE LIVES WOULD
CHANGE THE COURSE OF HISTORY . . .

Saul—Warrior, hero, and Israel's first king, he forged
a powerful alliance among the Twelve Tribes, but
this charismatic and caring ruler would be led
astray by the greatest enemy of any man of faith:
doubt.

Jonathan—Saul's loyal son, he will befriend a handsome young warrior-musician named David and
follow him into exile rather than carry out his de-
ranged father's orders to murder the man on
whose shoulders rests the future of Israel.

Eri—As armorer to the king, he enjoys immense
prestige and power, but he will give up both to
follow his heart and a destiny that will bring him
unimagined glory . . . or ignominious death.

Tania—This beautiful, royal daughter of the Nile
would offer herself in marriage to her people's enemy and the man who once sought her first husband's death. Yet her elaborate plot for revenge
would exact an unexpected price: the one thing she
values above life itself.

Mered—A vet⬛⬛⬛⬛⬛⬛⬛⬛⬛⬛⬛⬛ a violent
personal⬛⬛⬛⬛⬛⬛⬛⬛⬛⬛⬛s a plan
that wil⬛⬛⬛⬛⬛⬛⬛⬛⬛vid, and
Eri . . .⬛⬛⬛⬛⬛⬛⬛e hands
of their ⬛⬛⬛

Kaptar—As⬛⬛⬛⬛⬛⬛⬛, he left home rather than
endure his mother's marriage to his father's enemy. Now the young Egyptian noble will find himself on a long and treacherous journey to reclaim
his birthright and drive the oppressors from his ancient land.

The Children of the Lion series by Peter Danielson
Ask your bookseller for the titles you have missed

Volume XVII

THE DEATH OF OF KINGS

PETER DANIELSON

 Producers of **The First Americans,
Beneath the Sky,** and **The Holts.**

Book Creations Inc., Canaan, NY • *Lyle Kenyon Engel, Founder*

BANTAM BOOKS

NEW YORK • TORONTO • LONDON • SYDNEY • AUCKLAND

THE DEATH OF KINGS

A Bantam Book / published by arrangement with Book Creations Inc.

Bantam edition / March 1994

*Produced by Book Creations Inc.
Lyle Kenyon Engel, Founder*

All rights reserved.
Copyright © 1994 by Book Creations Inc.
Cover art copyright © 1994 by Bob Larkin.
*No part of this book may be reproduced or transmitted in any form
or by any means, electronic or mechanical, including photocopying,
recording, or by any information storage and retrieval system, without
permission in writing from the publisher.*
For information address: Bantam Books.

*If you purchased this book without a cover you should be aware that
this book is stolen property. It was reported as "unsold and
destroyed" to the publisher and neither the author nor the publisher
has received any payment for this "stripped book."*

ISBN 0-553-56146-4

Published simultaneously in the United States and Canada

*Bantam Books are published by Bantam Books, a division of Bantam
Doubleday Dell Publishing Group, Inc. Its trademark, consisting of the
words "Bantam Books" and the portrayal of a rooster, is Registered in
U.S. Patent and Trademark Office and in other countries. Marca
Registrada. Bantam Books, 1540 Broadway, New York, New York
10036.*

PRINTED IN THE UNITED STATES OF AMERICA

OPM   0 9 8 7 6 5 4 3 2 1

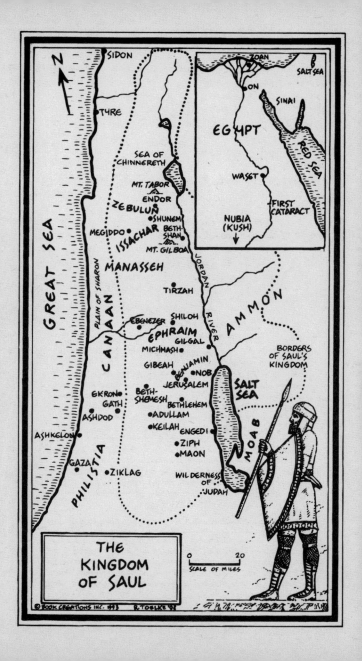

THE
KINGDOM
OF SAUL

© BOOK CREATIONS INC. 1993   R. TOBLKE '93

For God's sake, let us sit upon the ground,
And tell sad stories of the death of kings.

—WILLIAM SHAKESPEARE,
Richard II

THE DEATH
OF
KINGS

Prologue

~~~~~~

The scholar left his rooms in predawn darkness. He was one of only a few people who were astir. As he walked past the market, a tradesman set his brass pots clattering as he arranged his booth for the coming day. A countryman grunted with effort as he hoisted a basket of fresh figs. The scholar exchanged a coin for some of the ripe, brown fruit. The guards at the small gate called the Eye of the Needle, looking forward to being relieved, were red-eyed from their long, lonely vigil. They recognized the scholar and let him pass into the darkness outside the walls.

The scholar was alone as he staffed his slow way up the rocky path. When he stood on the heights looking out over the city of Solomon's glory, the chill of the night was still upon him. He clasped his mantle close about his wrinkled neck and lifted his face to the sky. The morning stars sang together as they had sung when God laid the foundations of the world. The old man loudly voiced his praise. There was only God to hear. The red disk of morning swelled its fiery way upward from the bowels of the earth, lighting the walls of Solomon's great temple in eye-numbing reflection.

The palace was an impressive structure, large enough to house even Solomon's family. Within was the throne of Israel, majesty in carved ivory and gold. There were four other buildings. One was called the house of the forest of Lebanon because of the wood used in its construction. Another was the domicile of the king's Egyptian wives.

The sun warmed the scholar. He sat with his back against the gnarled trunk of an olive tree and breakfasted on figs while he watched a group of young people climb the hill toward him. The newcomers greeted him with respect and warmth. He nodded and spread his hand toward the vista below.

"What do you see?" he asked.

"I see a great city," a young man said.

"The capital of a mighty empire," said another.

"I see the goodness of God," whispered an olive-skinned girl in an awed voice.

In the distance, on a road that wound toward the city, a long caravan emerged from the lowland mists. The students arranged themselves in a semicircle around the scholar so that all could watch the approach of the long line of oxcarts coming from the direction of what was still called by many the Philistine Sea.

"The cargo of the navy of Tharshish," said a young man.

"Gold and silver."

"Ivory."

"Apes."

"The king and his wives will dine on peacocks' tongues."

"There are not enough peacocks in Ophir to provide tongues for all of Solomon's wives."

There was laughter.

"Now the king will be even richer."

"Is not a rich king the symbol of a prosperous nation?" asked the scholar.

"It is true. God has blessed Israel."

"Yes," the scholar said. "God spreads His hand over us, but let us speak of the ways used by God to make this kingdom come into existence and survive." He moved his hand fluidly and gracefully to encompass the city and the surrounding countryside.

"He gave us great leaders, David and Solomon, and He put courage into the hearts and strength into the arms of our warriors," said one student.

"David was great, as is his son," the scholar said, "but there was another, of whom we will speak later. He

was a great man of war. It is true and fortunate that God gave courage and strength to the men of His chosen people, but to fight against whom?"

"The Philistines, the strongest and most fearsome enemy ever faced by Israel."

"Ah," said the scholar, "but were the Philistines the strongest of all possible enemies?"

"Who could have been more fierce than they?" the sloe-eyed girl asked.

"Think on it," the scholar said. "Think back to the time of Moses when God was forced to show His might to enable Israel to come up out of Egypt. Think back to the time of Ramses the Third. Who halted the seemingly irresistible advance of the men from Caphtor? They came in great waves with their high-powered ships, with the iron weapons they had taken from the Hittites, with their hordes of kilted warriors. Who stopped them?"

"Ah," said a young man, "I see your point. Ramses stopped them. Egypt stopped them."

"That was God's plan," the scholar said. "He set a task for Israel, but not the impossible task of facing the armies of a strong Egyptian pharaoh. First He weakened Egypt. He bled her with wave after wave of invaders, and then He left it to the mighty men of old to establish His kingdom without having to drive Egypt from what once had been a part of Pharaoh's empire. He spoke to the prophet Samuel, telling him of the need for a king. He lifted up Saul, tall and proud, and Saul freed the lands of Benjamin and Ephraim from Philistine occupation. He taught Saul the necessity of union, and He gave Saul the ability to teach others so that the Twelve Tribes were molded into a single political unit."

"But Saul divorced himself from God," a young man protested.

"Ah," the scholar said. "Did he, indeed?"

"It was not Saul who brought about this golden age," said the sloe-eyed girl. "It was David."

"Saul abandoned God and in turn was abandoned."

"And yet we owe this to him," the scholar said, nodding down at the shining city.

There was a murmur of protest.

"Yes." The scholar nodded. "To Saul, and the brave men who followed him, and to the armorers, those who wore the mark of the lion, who supplied Saul's army with the iron weapons of the Hittites."

A raven landed on the limb of an olive tree and looked with cocked head at the group below. A soft summer breeze whispered in the grove. The scholar said, "I see doubt in your faces."

"Below us is the City of David," said the olive-skinned girl. "It is not the City of Saul."

"Give glory to shining David," the scholar said, "but do not detract from those who came before him. Let us sit upon the ground and speak of Saul, and Jonathan, of the smith of Shiloh and his son in the days when David was but a boy and the iron sword of the Philistine made Israel bleed."

CHAPTER ONE

Urnan the smith, armorer to the king, pulled his horse to a halt and dismounted among the glory of yellow flowers that crowned the hill overlooking the Jezreel Valley. In the distance the dome-shaped majesty of Mount Tabor rose above the purple horizon. In the time of Deborah, prophet, military leader, poet, and judge of Israel, the tribes mustered on Tabor before going to battle against their Canaanite enemies. It was said that God was there among the altars of the ancients, and on this spring day even a non-Hebrew like Urnan could almost feel His presence.

The armorer had ridden far. He was grateful for the horse, a splendid animal won in battle with the Philistines by King Saul himself. Urnan felt that if Israel—and he, the smith of Mesopotamian descent who had merged his fate with hers—owed anything to the Philistines, it was not so much for the knowledge of how to work iron but for the introduction of the horse. Sooner or later some armorer, perhaps one like Urnan who

5

bore the mark of the lion, would have discovered the secret of bleeding iron from the rocks of the earth, but mere man could not invent the horse. A bony donkey was a poor substitute for the broad-backed animals whose sires had been looted by the advancing Sea Peoples from fabled Cilicia.

Urnan's horse, called Ramses in honor of the humble donkey he had once owned, nibbled yellow flowers and swished its tail. Urnan rubbed his sweat-sodden backside gingerly. The smith had traveled from Gibeah, where Saul had built his citadel, to the shores of the Sea of Chinnereth in the north and then southward along the banks of the Jordan. He peered into the blue distances at the mud-brick walls of the small village of Endor, his destination for the night.

Ramses picked his way surefootedly down the flowered slope and through the fertile fields of the valley. Not long ago these fields had lain fallow when the people of the valley had fled the armies of the five cities of Philistia. But now there was a king in Israel, Saul the Benjamite, and the Philistine had been pushed back onto the coastal plain.

Urnan rode slowly into the village. Although the iron swords of Saul's army had brought security to the lands of Zebulun, strangers were few and were seen with suspicion. His advance toward the central square was watched by wary women and wide-eyed children. As in many villages throughout the lands of the Twelve Tribes, there were few young men in Endor. All the able-bodied men were serving with the king who had unified Israel, Saul.

A white-bearded old man in embroidered robes stood in the middle of the dusty street, arms crossed on his chest, staring at the newcomer. Urnan dismounted and bowed a greeting.

"From the dust on your tunic I see you have traveled far," the old man said.

"I greet you in the name of the king," Urnan said. "I ride in his service and I seek a place of comfort for the night."

The patriarch was soon joined by a woman of equal

years. She stood by his side and peered at Urnan with eyes weakened by age.

"A friend of the king is welcome here," the old man said, "but, alas, our accommodations are few."

"There is the house of the widow Jerioth," the old woman said.

"My needs are simple," Urnan said.

"Follow the street to its end," the woman said. "The house of Jerioth is near the olive orchard."

It was not a grand house, the home of the widow, but the baked and packed earth of the yard was swept clean, and when the woman answered Urnan's hail her clothes showed the wear of many washings.

"I was told that I might obtain food and lodging for the night," Urnan said as he dismounted.

The woman studied him closely. Her eyes were black, and their darkness was matched by a great mane of hair that spilled to her shoulders in tight curls. She was a handsome woman to be without a husband, but it was not unusual in Israel for a widow to be so young. Incessant warfare demanded the blood of men.

"You have the look of a gentle man," Jerioth said. Urnan was silent as she assessed him. Finally she said, "My table fare is simple."

"As are my tastes," Urnan said.

"The stable is over there," Jerioth said, pointing. "I will begin preparing the meal."

"I will be grateful," Urnan said.

After tending to the needs of Ramses, Urnan entered the house. The smell of fresh bread and spices triggered a feeling of hunger.

He ate in a half-reclining position on a couch covered by clean-smelling, homespun cloth while Jerioth stood in wait. The bread was chewy and hot from the oven, the soup hearty, the melon sweet and juicy.

"I am pleased," Urnan said, rubbing his full stomach.

"For the absence of meat I apologize," Jerioth said.

"Not even in the king's citadel do they eat meat every day."

"You will find water for washing in your room," the

woman said abruptly, pointing toward a door leading out of the main room of the house. "If you require anything I will hear when you call."

The room was small, but it smelled fresh and clean. Urnan removed his clothing and washed away the dirt and perspiration of the road. He was drying himself when he heard a knock on the door.

"Would you like some wine?" Jerioth called.

"Yes, thank you. I'll be out shortly."

He saw that Jerioth had removed her outer mantle. Her inner garment was fashioned simply of linen colored a muted shade of red by the dye made of insects taken from the oak tree. Elaborate, white-stitched embroidery decorated the bodice covering her shapely breasts. Her dark, bounteous hair was covered by a hood.

"It is new wine," Jerioth said, extending a cup toward Urnan.

"You will join me?" he asked, lifting the cup.

She nodded, and he sat on the edge of a couch and watched as she lifted her cup to her full lips. Her eyes gleamed black as she looked at him from under long, dark lashes.

Urnan was no longer young and bursting with juices. He was a man entering his middle years. He had loved twice. The sultry and sensuous beauty of the widow of Endor suddenly reminded him of the women he had loved and lost. Shelah, who had been raped and then killed by soldiers under the command of Galar of Ashdod, who now led all of the Philistine armies, had been dark and lithe like this woman. Tania, his sweet Egyptian princess, had shown the same sly forwardness when she first saw Urnan.

The two wives whom he had loved were lost to him, Shelah by death, Tania by distance and the hostility of the Libyan rulers of Lower Egypt. But this one, this dark-eyed, full-bodied woman, was near, and there was an invitation in her eyes. With surprise he felt the beginning of inner heat.

"You are alone?" he asked.

She nodded. "My husband died fighting with King Saul at Michmash."

"Your father?"

"I am like few other women. I am not attached to any man. No father, no husband, no brother, not even a master. I have my garden for vegetables and my cow for milk and butter. I glean the fields for grain. I take in the occasional traveler."

Urnan nodded his approval.

"I do not share wine with all my overnight guests," she said, and a smile parted her full lips to show the gleam of white teeth. "And you?" she asked, refilling his cup.

"I am a smith. An armorer. The rocks of the earth that contain the metal of the Hittites—"

"I know the name. Iron."

"—are scarce. I ride the hills and look for the red of the ore."

"And for whom do you fashion your weapons?"

"For Saul."

She dropped her eyes to her cup.

"Do you disapprove?"

"Oh, no," she said quickly. She smiled at him, her eyes sparkling mischievously, but then her lips went slack. She feared that she was giving him the impression that she was a loose woman, and that was far from the truth. She was a woman alone, but she had known no man since her husband had marched off to fight in Saul's wars. She could not have explained the overwhelming need she felt when she looked into Urnan's eyes. She knew only that her guest was distinguished and handsome and that she was a healthy young woman who had long been without a husband.

What followed was inevitable. It was one of those rare comings together of a man and woman whose hearts keep the same rhythm, as totally inexplicable as first love.

Afterwards Urnan lay in Jerioth's large, soft bed, hands under his head. Her dark hair fell softly on his shoulder. He knew that there was risk in what they had done, although the punishment for mere fornication was not as severe as the penalty for adultery—death by stoning—which was more often applied only to the woman than to the man. But he wondered if Jerioth made it a practice to give her male guests more than food and lodging. Did she have a reputation as a woman of the town?

As if she could read his thoughts, Jerioth lifted her head and kissed him softly.

"What magic have you worked on me?" she asked.

"Perhaps we were both enchanted."

She laughed, a fruity, throaty sound that pleased him. "I had decided not to tell you that you are the only man besides my husband I've known, but I will tell you, even if you don't believe it."

He looked at her for a moment. "I believe you," he said truthfully.

"I prided myself on my purity," she said, "but you swept it all away with a look."

"Perhaps you sensed my loneliness and felt pity for me," Urnan said. "God will forgive you for an act of compassion."

"You flirt with blasphemy easily."

"I am not of the blood of Abraham."

She turned her face away from him.

"Does that make your transgression worse?" he asked softly.

She turned back to him, smiled, and shook her head. "I know so little about you, but I do know that you have loved a woman. Your tenderness and gentleness tell me so." Her voice became grave. "But she is dead."

Urnan nodded.

She looked deeply into his eyes. "She is still here," she said, touching his chest with her gentle fingers. "Tell me about her."

Suddenly Urnan found himself talking about Shelah and Tania. He could not have said which loss was more painful. Shelah had been dead for many years, but she was still in his heart. The loss of Tania was more recent, and he felt a sharp pain in his chest whenever he thought of her.

"Do you pray to the One God?" Jerioth asked.

"Lord, I believe," Urnan said, "help thou mine unbelief."

"Again you come close to blasphemy," she said.

"Yahweh is the God of the Hebrews."

"You are not of the blood, and yet you fight for Israel," she said.

"This is my home," he said.

"Please don't tell me you're a Canaanite," she said.

"No, my ancestors came out of Babylon," he told her, "and before that from old Ur, on the Euphrates. They were all armorers."

She vented her full, throaty laugh again. "Good. I would not want to commit the sin of Samson by loving a Godless one."

"My people had many gods. In old Ur they came down to alight on the top of the great temple to cohabit with the priestess and breed heroes," he said.

"Nonsense," she said firmly. "But you are not a heathen."

"I suppose I am half convinced that Yahweh is God."

She touched his arm. "Abraham came from Ur."

"The founder of my family was an armorer named Belsunu who learned his trade in Ur. Perhaps it was ordained that two men from the old city were to become allied. Belsunu fashioned arms for Abraham."

"How do you know so much about your ancestors?"

He shrugged. "How do you know that you and those around you are the seed of Abraham? Through family tradition. My parents told me all the old tales before they died." He picked up an oil lamp and held it so that the light showed his birthmark, a purple design like the paw print of a lion on his lower back.

"The males in my line all bear this mark. My father had it. My son, Eri, has it, and his son, Sunu. It is said to be the mark that God put on Cain, who was the first worker in metals, and that because of Cain's sin we who are descended from him are doomed to wander the face of the earth and to use our skills to make the weapons that spill men's blood."

She shuddered.

He put down the lamp and put his arms around her. Her lips were soft and her body warm, and for a long time they were silent.

"Your wife, Shelah, feared God?" she finally asked.

"She was devout."

"Then she will stand in a latter day upon the earth, and though worms have destroyed her body she will see God in her own flesh."

"So I have heard from the priests," Urnan said. "Although I'm not sure I believe."

"In the bowels of the earth, in Sheol, your wife awaits," Jerioth said.

She looked at him, and he could see the reflected light of the oil lamp shining like little stars in her black eyes. The grave look on her face made Urnan keep silent and wait for her to continue.

"I have felt your pain," she said. "You worry how the woman you loved is faring in the afterworld."

He shrugged, unwilling to accept the idea of Shelah in another world.

"The king has prohibited what I do," she said slowly, as if making up her mind.

Urnan was confused. "I know of no law against taking in overnight guests."

"No, not that," she said. "You see, I have a talent that is in demand even in God-fearing Israel." She paused. "I am a necromancer."

"You take a risk in telling me that," Urnan said, a reprimand in his voice.

"Not so. Saul's edict is against summoning up the souls of the dead, not against merely talking about it."

"Still, it's dangerous to go around claiming to be a spiritualist."

"I choose carefully those to whom I reveal my dark secret," she said.

"But you know that I come from the king."

"I have looked into your eyes, Urnan the smith,

and I do not see a man who will betray me. I see a man who is in need of my skills."

Urnan smiled. "I agree that I am in need," he said, "but not of a necromancer."

She ignored him. "Let me summon your Shelah. It will ease your mind to hear from her own lips that she waits comfortably and contentedly in anticipation of Paradise."

Urnan was not a man who could unfeelingly take a woman's body. He felt a bond with the lushly beautiful young widow. He worried about her. Saul's edict against necromancy was a serious one; the punishment was exile. If he were to participate he, too, would be breaking the law.

"Yes?" she asked, lifting his hand and touching his palm with her full lips.

"If it will please you."

"Not here," she said, getting out of bed. She pulled a robe around her and tossed his mantle to him. It struck Urnan as funny. It was as if Jerioth was concerned about Shelah seeing them naked and fresh from love.

The widow led him into the main room and seated him on a couch. "Think of her," she said.

Urnan waited, expecting Jerioth to bring out the paraphernalia of candles and black cloaks, but she just stood before him with her head bowed, praying in a whisper.

Without warning he saw Shelah. She was seated across the room, her face in profile. She seemed to be surrounded by a gray mist. She was young, just the way he remembered her. She even wore a garment he recognized. He felt a jolt through his heart; then his heart seemed to stop entirely. Ah, God, Shelah was so beautiful. "My wife," he whispered in a hoarse croak. Shelah turned to face him, her dark eyes searching.

"Can she see me?" he whispered to Jerioth.

Jerioth nodded.

"My love," Urnan said, and the shade smiled a full, gleaming look of joy. "Shelah—"

The spirit's smile faded.

"Are you—how is it—" His tongue could not form the question.

"Spirit," Jerioth said, "if you love this man, speak."

"Do not weep for me, Urnan," the shade said softly. "All is well."

"The spirit can tell you your future," Jerioth said, "but only if you want to know."

"No," Urnan said quickly. Then he smiled. What harm could come from what was most probably a trick? "Yes, tell me the future."

The shade nodded. "For you, husband, I see arduous times, and not only for you, but for all those who are of the seed of Abraham."

Urnan smiled to show his disdain. Anyone could have made that prophecy. Times were always hard. Perhaps it was only the sepulchral tone of the shade's voice that made him shiver.

"You have the love of a woman," the spirit continued, "and the love of your family, and in the midst of your trials you will know happiness."

Urnan looked at Jerioth and smiled. He said, "So this is the wisdom and insight of the netherworld."

"Listen," Jerioth said.

"You cannot be everywhere at all times," the shade said, "and so one you care for will be lost. You will search and what you find will bring you both joy and sorrow."

"Who will be lost?" Urnan asked, leaning forward.

"It is not given to me to know all," the shade said.

Almost, Urnan believed. "My love," he said, "will I see you in the afterworld?"

She smiled, but her answer was long in coming. When she spoke her words were slow and measured. "It is by belief and by choice that I lie in Abraham's bosom. Remember that."

The mist became thicker, the well-remembered face faded, and once more Urnan was aware of the sounds of the village coming in through the open windows.

"I'm sorry," Jerioth said. "Sometimes the spirits

speak at length; at other times . . ." She shrugged.
"But you heard. She is content to wait."

Not knowing what to think, Urnan said, "I think
that I need another cup of wine."

Urnan drank deeply and awoke long after dawn.
There was warm milk fresh from the cow, a hunk of
bread, and a bowl of cooked figs for his breakfast. Jerioth watched him silently as he ate.

"When will you come back?" she asked as he put
on his mantle.

Urnan felt a sudden surge of need. Her willingness
and her lushness had left him with memories and a re-
newed desire.

"As soon as I can," he said.

"Please hurry," she whispered.

When he looked back she waved, and he fought a
strong urge to go back and take her once more to her
warm, soft bed.

God had outdone himself in the making of a day.
The spring air cleared Urnan's head of the remains of
the wine, but not of thoughts of Jerioth and of his curious experience. In the light of day it was easy to doubt,
to wonder if the appearance of the shade of Shelah had
been nothing more than the result of the wine and the
powerful attraction he had felt to Jerioth. Perhaps she
had the gift of his old friend, Kemose the Egyptian, who
could influence others with the power of his will. Perhaps he had merely been a victim of those black eyes
and sweet body. Surely the love he had known in Jerioth's bed had come too quickly and too easily to be real
and lasting.

"Yes," he said aloud, deciding it was merely the
wine and the strange passion the woman of Endor had
engendered in him that had weakened him and left him
prey to her suggestion, nothing more.

CHAPTER TWO

Gibeah, the birthplace of Saul, king of Israel, occupied a strategic position on the main road linking the land of Judah and the city of Jerusalem to the hills of Ephraim in the north. As in most towns in Israel, new buildings sat atop the rubble and ashes of the old. Most recently, war and death had come to Gibeah from the hands of the Philistines. Prior to that, in the time of the Judges, the town at the core of Israel's new unity had been destroyed by other tribes of Israel following the rape of a concubine of a Levite priest by the Benjamites of Gibeah.

The name Gibeah meant hill, or height, and on the heights Saul built his citadel. The pride of a people newly freed from the yoke of the Philistines led them to call the structure the royal palace, but it was actually a fortress copied from a Philistine frontier redoubt. A double wall of stone enclosed an area approximately forty paces long and twenty-eight paces wide. Inside the walls were a large, open courtyard and quarters more suited to a warrior than to a king.

The village clustered snugly around the citadel. Eri the smith, son of Urnan, had built his home atop the stone foundation of an older structure on the outskirts. It was a large home, designed optimistically to house a growing family. One room was set aside for the patriarch, Urnan, who came and went as his duties allowed.

Like Abraham, Eri had two wives, and, just as that situation had presented challenges for the father of all Israel, so it did for Eri the smith.

On a balmy spring morning, Sarah, first wife to the master of the house, was awakened by a gentle touch on her shoulder. She moaned in protest and opened one eye to see a familiar face, that of Baalan, second wife.

"Go away," Sarah said. She resented having been wakened, for sleep shielded her from reality.

"You can't lie in bed until noonday," Baalan said patiently.

Sarah sat up. For a moment she was lost, and then the horror came back. She heard the screams of the dying, saw blood spouting, saw the sword of the Philistine butcher, saw her mother holding out her hands in supplication as a blade pierced her stomach.

"Sarah?" Baalan said.

"It's all right," Sarah said. She was back in the house of the man they said was her beloved Eri, and there before her was the woman who had taken her place in Eri's bed. The usurper. The Ammonite slave. The woman who had given birth to a son, Eri's son.

Resentment soured Sarah's stomach and drained the blood from her face. For years she had found refuge from the pain and the terror, for years she had lived sheltered inside a warm and cozy cocoon. Then Urnan had penetrated that cocoon, and she felt as if she had gone mad. Eri, sweet Eri, so youthful and fair, was no more. In his place was a stranger, a man of strong, wide shoulders and muscular arms and years far beyond the age of her Eri. And beside him was Baalan and her son, Sunu.

"We are baking this morning," Baalan said. "Would you like to help?"

Pleasant memories brought a half-smile to Sarah's lips. Even in the mists of her retreat she had known the smell of bread fresh from the oven and the comforting presence of the woman who loved her and cared for her tenderly. Baalan had tended her as the child she was, never mocking her inability or unwillingness to speak, always loving, always there to guide and comfort.

Sarah tossed her head. In body she was a woman in the full flush of maturity, but her mind and her memories were those of the fifteen-year-old she had been when the merciful blankness descended. Child she had been and child she was, in spite of the Egyptian magic Urnan used to bring back the memories of her life before the Philistines came to Gibeah.

It was the child who spoke in a sullen voice. "Baking is the work of slaves. Please see to my breakfast."

It was still quite odd to want to speak, to be able to speak. The words sounded foreign to her ears, and there were times when she had to pause to think about how to form the sounds with her lips.

"Sarah," Baalan said gently, "there are no slaves in this house."

Baalan had bread and honey waiting for her in the kitchen. The son of the house, four-year-old Sunu, stood before Sarah as she ate. She gave the boy a bite, and his smile was as sunny as the day.

"Let's go into the garden, Mother Sarah," Sunu suggested when Sarah was finished.

The scorching heat of summer had not yet arrived, but the cold of winter was gone. The sky was a vault of God's own blue, and the sun radiated a pleasant warmth. Sarah sat on a stone bench and watched Sunu stalk and capture a scarab beetle.

"See how his legs wiggle," the boy said, extending his hand toward Sarah's face. The beetle lay on its back, its legs waving frantically.

"Get that ugly thing away from me," Sarah said sharply.

Sometimes it was a pleasure to watch Baalan's son,

for he was a happy child, well formed and beautiful. He had run off his baby fat and was beginning to show a length of leg foretelling that he would be a tall man. Of late, however, Sarah began to see Sunu differently. He was Eri's son, his firstborn, and Eri's only heir. Although the smith was not as rich as her stepfather had been, he was not poor. In addition to a small nest egg of coins, there was the house, the workshops, and a stock of weapons, decorative items, and jewelry made by Eri and his workers. Should anything happen to Eri, it would all become the property of the son of an Ammonite slave.

There was, she told herself, a remedy for the situation. Many times Urnan had whispered, "You can have a boy of your own, Sarah. You can have a son."

She was not quite sure of the law, but her reason told her that a son of the first wife, not the son of a slave, would be the heir. She placed her palm on her flat stomach.

"Mother Sarah," Sunu said, interrupting her thoughts. "Someone's coming." He took Sarah's hand and led her to the gate. A tall and sturdy figure in the robes of a shepherd was approaching.

"What is he carrying on his back?" Sunu asked.

Sarah had to search her memory. In her mind she could hear melodic sounds, the plucking of the strings of the *kinnor* as it accompanied the chanting of a priest at temple service. Pleased to be able to remember, she said, "It is a harp."

"He's coming here," Sunu said in delight.

Sarah watched the stranger approaching. He was a goodly man with broad shoulders and the long stride of a countryman. Along with his harp he carried a small bundle slung over his shoulder. In his right hand was a shepherd's staff. When he saw the woman and the boy he lifted his left hand in greeting.

Sarah's heart leaped as he smiled. He was the most beautiful man she'd ever seen. Man? No, a boy on the brink of manhood, like her Eri when she first saw him, but like an Eri created by some divine molder of flesh into a shining dream.

The stranger paused and spoke words of polite greeting that passed over Sarah's head, leaving as little understanding as the buzz of a bee. She was lost in the sight of the dark eyes that sparkled with life, the strong chin with an endearing cleft, the nose proud and perfectly molded. A mane of thick, black hair crowned his head in dark glory.

She could not take her eyes off his face. His lips moved. When his words began to penetrate her daze she discovered he was saying her name.

"You are Sarah?"

"This is my other mother Sarah," Sunu said. "This is the house of my father, Eri the smith."

"Then I am at the right place," the stranger said. "It is Eri whom I seek."

"Eri?" Sarah asked, trying to recover her stunned senses.

"My father is at the forge," Sunu said.

"You called me by name," Sarah said.

"Forgive me, lady," the stranger said. "I am David, son of Jesse. When last I saw you, you were not well. It was the occasion of your wedding."

"My wedding?"

"Mother Sarah doesn't remember things too well," Sunu said.

"You were married in my father's house," David said.

Sarah nodded. She had no memory of the event, but Eri had told her of it.

"I will take you to my father," Sunu said.

"God be with you," David said to Sarah.

"And you," she answered weakly, for the sound of his voice caused her to tremble inside. Once upon a time she had felt that same feeling when a young Eri spoke to her, but now that man was gone, and she missed him.

Eri was working at the forge, a leather apron over his short tunic, his right arm bulging as he struck sparks from a white-hot blade on the ironstone anvil. He looked up only briefly at Sunu and David. Finally satisfied with the blade he was forming, he lifted it from the anvil with tongs and plunged it into a container of blackened water. A loud hiss and a cloud of steam arose. Only then did he put down his tools and hold out both hands toward David.

"My friend," he said. "My good friend."

"I bring you the best wishes of my father," David said. "I, myself, hesitate to impose on you—"

"Nonsense," Eri said. "You are most welcome. Just as your father gave me the hospitality of his house so do I offer mine to you."

"You are kind," David said.

"But what brings you to Gibeah?" Eri asked.

"I have been summoned to the court of the king." David shifted the harp on his shoulder. "It is hoped that my poor talent with song will sooth the king in his—" he paused "—moments of agitation."

Eri nodded. "Do I see the hand of your father Jesse in this?" he asked.

"I come with my father's blessings, of course," David said, "but it was Samuel who suggested it."

Eri said nothing. David was only a boy, and a godly one. Samuel had denounced the king as an enemy of God and refused him the right to formal worship. It would be too easy for an innocent boy to be caught up in the power struggle between Samuel and the king. Eri vowed to himself that he would do whatever was in his power to keep David safe.

Perhaps David's songs *would* be good for the king. Saul had changed since he and Eri, boys together, had tricked the priests of Dagon in the Philistine cities into returning the Ark of the Covenant to Israel. Saul had been a regal figure; he stood a head taller than most Hebrews. He was also a man of prodigious martial skills and courage. With the help of his son, Jonathan, he had driven the Philistine from the land of Benjamin, but success had not been without its price. In the process he had angered the prophet Samuel.

"The king does have his bad moments," Eri admitted. "If anything will ease his mind, your music will."

"God's will be done," David said, bowing his head.

"You've traveled far," Eri said. "Refresh yourself, and by that time Baalan will have food prepared. Then you must tell me of your father and your brothers."

"I remember you now," Sunu suddenly piped up as they were eating. He stared up at David with wide eyes. "You killed a lion."

David's face flushed in modesty.

"Yes, I told him," Eri said. Many years earlier Eri and Sarah had watched David, only a boy, kill a mature lion that was threatening the flock David was tending.

"With your bare hands," Sunu said in awe.

"Not quite bare-handed," David said.

"Tell me about it," Sunu said.

"Later, later," Eri said. "Our guest is hungry. There will be time for stories after the meal."

"Promise?" Sunu asked.

"I promise," David said.

When the meal was finished, Baalan sat beside Eri with her arm around Sunu's shoulders as David told of seeing the lion stalking a lamb and of attacking the beast with his shepherd's staff. Sunu listened with his mouth open and his eyes wide. Sarah's eyes followed every movement of David's lips.

"But weren't you afraid?" Sunu asked.

"When God is with you, what is there to fear?" David asked. "The beast was after my flock. I had no choice."

"I would have been afraid," Sunu said.

"But when you are a strong man like your father you will be brave," David said.

"Yes, and I will kill lions and Philistines," Sunu said.

"Before my son gets too much of a taste for blood, will you sing for us?" Eri asked.

"I would be pleased to, if someone will fetch my harp," David said, looking at Sunu.

Sunu leaped to his feet and ran to the room that had been given to David. He came back carrying the harp carefully, his arms above his head to keep the instrument from dragging on the floor.

In the quiet of evening, as Baalan lit the oil lamps, David's voice lifted in praise of God. *"The Lord is my shepherd; I shall not want."*

Sunu was half-asleep. Baalan, who had embraced the God of Abraham, folded her hands and bowed her head. Eri listened to the words of the young singer and mused.

"Surely goodness and mercy shall follow me all the days of my life—"

Eri looked around, letting his eyes linger on the face of the woman who had sustained him during the long years of Sarah's affliction. Baalan smiled at him and gently shifted Sunu onto her lap. Sarah sat as if she were in a trance, staring at David.

Eri voiced a silent prayer, asking for goodness and mercy for those whom he loved. He and Sarah had seen enough of death and destruction. His hand rose to his neck and the scar left when the slave mark branded on him by the Philistines had been removed.

Give us tranquillity, Lord, he prayed silently. *Keep us together as a family in calm harmony.*

"More, please," Sunu said sleepily when David's voice fell silent.

"No, we have imposed upon our guest long enough, young man," Baalan said. "It's time for you to be in your bed."

"Tell me again about the lion tomorrow?" Sunu asked David.

David laughed. "Tomorrow I must report to the palace to do my duty by our king."

CHAPTER
THREE

Eri greeted by name the two men guarding the inner courtyard of the citadel. In return they saluted him with their spears.

"What have we here, armorer?" one asked, nodding at David.

"The son of Jesse, who has come to see the king," David said.

The guard laughed and David tensed. Eri put his arm around David's shoulders and squeezed encouragingly.

"It takes a brave man to visit Saul when he is in a temper," the guard said. He turned to Eri. "Last week he sent a representative to Samuel to ask once more for the old man's blessings in the war against the Philistines."

"And once again Samuel said no?" Eri said.

"Just this morning the messenger returned. The prophet refused even to hear his petition on behalf of the king. He said that communication between Saul and the priests of the God whom the king has defied is no longer possible."

Eri shook his head sadly. "Where is the king?"

"In the throne room," the guard said. "Jonathan and your father are with him."

Eri nodded. Urnan had not only joined his son as armorer to the king, but had become a friend and trusted adviser as well. Ever since Urnan had come upon Saul, weak and feverish, wandering among the Hebrew corpses on the battlefield at Ebenezer, the fate of Eri's family had been linked to that of Saul. Urnan had carried Saul away from the scene of disaster on the back of the old donkey, Ramses, and Saul had pledged an eternal debt to the smith. Now it seemed that the king preferred the company of the older and wiser father to that of the son.

In fact, it seemed to Eri that Saul trusted Urnan more than he trusted his own son, Jonathan. In his more and more frequent rages Saul could not forget that Jonathan had disobeyed his orders when he and Eri climbed the cliffs to overcome the soldiers at the Philistine outpost near Michmash. Even though the victory of two warriors over many had inspired a great triumph for the king and for all Israel, the memory enraged Saul. What angered him even more was that Jonathan had unknowingly violated the king's order that no man of Israel was to put his lips to food until the battle was over.

Eri led David toward the king's quarters, passing guards who looked at them in silence as the king's voice bellowed through the stone halls. Saul's rages could be frightening, as no one knew on whom his anger might descend.

Eri paused at the door to the throne room. Saul stood in the center of the room. His hair was in disarray, his eyes were filled with pain and anger, spittle spewed from his lips as he railed against Samuel and God.

"Have I not driven the idol worshipers from the lands that you gave to Moses?" Saul bellowed. "Have I not praised your name in word, act, and deed?"

Urnan was standing at the king's side, talking soothingly, trying to calm him.

Jonathan, looking worried, came toward them. "It is not the time to bring a stranger here, Eri," he whispered.

David ignored Jonathan's words, sidestepping him to enter the throne room. He swung the *kinnor* from his shoulder and sat down on a wooden stool. As they stroked the strings his fingers took on a life of their own. The music began softly, then swelled to give body to David's voice as he sang, *"Hail to Saul, tall king of Israel. Hail to the deliverer of his people. Hail to the mighty slayer of the enemies of God."*

At the first sound, Saul turned around and fell silent. As David sang the story of the battle of Michmash, he sank down upon his throne, the crudely worked stone bench that was the seat of power for all Israel.

David finished his song. Jonathan looked at Eri and raised his eyebrows in question. Everyone stared at the king, waiting.

"You sing well, boy," Saul said.

"Your praise fills me with gladness," David said.

"Sing," Saul said.

As David's fingers danced over the strings, movement at the door caught his eyes, and he glanced up to see a girl in white robes, her glory of dark hair piled high atop her head. He looked at her for only a moment, but she remained a vivid picture in his mind.

From all over the palace, guards came into the room to crowd against the walls and listen as David's strong young voice was raised in praise of God. The girl in white came closer. When David paused she smiled and said, "That was very beautiful. Who are you?"

"Lady, I am David, son of Jesse. I am grateful that I please you."

"I am Michal, daughter of Saul, and your songs do please me."

David sang: *"Blessed be the Lord God, the God of Israel, who only doeth wondrous things. And blessed be His glorious name forever: and let the whole earth be filled with His glory."*

Jonathan, standing beside Eri, whispered, "Who *is* this boy?" Before Eri could answer Jonathan said, "Whoever he is, he was sent to us by God."

Eri looked at Jonathan quickly and felt a pang of uneasiness. It was not God but Samuel who had sent David to the king's court.

The girl, Michal, sank to the floor on a cushion at David's feet. Her dark, almond eyes never left his face.

"Give the king thy judgments, O God, and thy righteousness unto the king's son," David sang, to the ripple of music that sounded as sweet as the flow of clear water down a rocky course. *"He shall judge the poor of the people, he shall save the children of the needy, and shall break in pieces the oppressor."*

"Truly, God is good to Israel," Saul said when the song was over. Unashamed of his emotion, he wiped away his tears with the roughened back of his hand.

Michal, too, was touched by the sweetness of David's voice. She caught his eye, and he, boy that he was and shy before Michal's beauty, flushed and looked away, only to have the image of the girl's comely face stay with him.

CHAPTER FOUR

In contrast to Saul's citadel at Gibeah, the home of the Philistine general, Galar of Ashdod, was palatial. Idols of gold and silver looted from the various peoples who had stood in the path of the migration of the Sea Peoples filled the mansion's great marble room. The house was fully staffed by retainers and slaves, including a carefully selected harem of the fairest daughters of Abraham, watched over by Galar's own guard.

Galar's family was an old one, a clan that had gained influence and power by virtue of strong arms and stout hearts in the days when rich kingdoms fell to the men from Caphtor and even mighty Egypt seemed to be tantalizingly within reach. Galar's ancestors knew how to accumulate power and riches, and they passed along to their descendants the ability to retain both. A member of Galar's family sat upon the throne of the city of Ashdod. Galar himself was commander of the unified Philistine army.

Unlike the Hebrews who tended to fight tribal wars

among themselves when not faced by a strong threat from without, the five great cities of the Philistine plain acted as one in military matters to field an army that had, before the defeat at Michmash, dominated the lands of Canaan from the sea to the Jordan, except for isolated pockets of Hebrew resistance.

The general was a man at the peak of physical prowess, tall and agile. A kilt bordered in cloth of gold revealed strong legs developed in the long marches. His short tunic of gleaming white linen covered broad shoulders, a thick chest, a smoothly muscled back, powerful biceps. His olive skin was weathered by years of military service, but his tightly curled hair gleamed darkly without a trace of gray. His nose was like the beak of a bird of prey, strong and sharp. His mouth was that of a man who knew the meaning of pleasure as well as cruelty.

He sat regally upright in an elaborate chair that resembled a royal throne. Before him stood a man whose leather chest armor was covered by a shabby, homespun mantle of sheep's wool.

The supplicant was heavily bearded. His eyes were those of a jackal. His nose was mottled with red, telltale evidence that he liked his wine.

"Before you are killed and your heart thrown to my dogs," Galar said, "what have you to say, pig of the hills?"

"I am Mered," the cringing man said. A Hebrew, he showed no sign of resentment of Galar's insult, and he spoke in a cajoling whine. "I am sure, great general, that a man of such majesty and generosity would not order death arbitrarily for one who has come to perform a service."

Behind the Hebrew two men of Galar's personal guard moved forward. Galar had only to lift one finger to halt them.

"What service can a pig of the hills offer that would interest me?" the general asked.

Mered looked over his shoulder. "If I could have your ear in privacy for a moment, great one."

Galar motioned with one hand. The guards

thumped their spear butts on the marble floor in salute and retired, closing the great bronze door behind them.

"Speak," Galar said.

"Great one," Mered said, "I am a captain of hundreds in the army of King Saul."

Galar's face wrinkled in disgust and disbelief. An army led by men such as this could never have inflicted the disaster at Michmash upon the Army of the Five Cities. Michmash was an ulcer on Galar's pride. He had been away when two lone Hebrews climbed what were thought to be impregnable heights to kill many Philistine soldiers and inspire the other pigs of the hills to attack with a fierce and surprising determination, and without Galar's leadership, the retreat had turned into a rout. The losses were so great that even now, months later, the army was not back to strength.

"Go on," Galar said impatiently.

"From my position inside Saul's citadel it would be possible for me to supply you, great general, with information regarding Saul's plans and movements."

"The Army of the Five Cities can crush the Hebrews without the aid of traitors," Galar said, ready to call the guards.

Imagining the weight of a Philistine blade at his neck, Mered spoke quickly. "Would it have been helpful at Michmash to have known that most of the men in Saul's command had to fight with staves?"

Galar's eyes narrowed. This pig of the hills was a walking insult. However, Galar was a practical man. It would have been *very* helpful to know the strength of the Hebrew army.

"Am I to believe that a Hebrew, one who claims that there is only one god, would betray that god and his own people?" Galar asked.

"I have been done a great wrong," Mered said. "I have given long service to my people. I have killed my share of the enemies of Israel, and I have been loyal. My reward for my sacrifices was to have Saul's cousin, Abner, elevated in rank above me. In all justice the post of commander of the army should have been mine. Instead, because Abner is a Benjamite and of Saul's blood, he is my superior. I think you will agree, General, that there comes a time when a man must look out for himself."

Galar tried to hide his distaste. A spy was odious, but perhaps this pig could be useful. "What do you ask in return for this, ah, service?"

"Silver," Mered said.

"Of course," Galar said.

"And safe conduct when you destroy Saul's army."

Safe conduct to the nearest slave camp, Galar thought. Death would be too kind for the likes of Mered. "Yes, of course," he said.

"And position over those who denied me my right," Mered said.

A slave, master of slaves, Galar mused. He nodded. "Perhaps you can be useful. I suppose you have figured out a way to get word out of this so-called king's stronghold?"

"I have, my lord," Mered said.

Galar was feeling more optimistic about Mered's offer. Although, like most soldiers, he had nothing but contempt for traitors, he had to admit Mered had a certain amount of courage to have ventured onto the plain alone and let himself fall into the hands of a Philistine patrol.

"Do you know a smith named Urnan?" Galar asked.

"I do, my lord. He is not only armorer to the king, but one of his closest friends and advisers."

Galar savored the information. "Your first assignment," he said, "is to keep me informed of the whereabouts of Urnan the smith. Deliver him into my hands and you will be rewarded."

"Yes, my lord," Mered said. "In the meantime, lord, I am but a poor man. If you could see fit to improve my condition I would be most grateful."

"Guards," Galar shouted.

Mered drew back in fear as the bronze door opened on protesting hinges and the two men-at-arms marched in to halt with precision, clicking the butts of their spears on the marble floor. But he sighed in relief when Galar said, "Give this man twenty shekels of silver and safe escort to the mountains." Galar looked back at Mered. "The smith," he grated. "Remember the smith."

"Yes, my lord," Mered said as he bowed and backed out the door.

As he thought of Urnan, Galar grew more and more angry, remembering how at Michmash he had ordered Urnan's slow death, had left him hanging on a tree to know pain and thirst. Somehow Urnan had escaped and killed Jobal, the man who had thrust a sword into the belly of the smith's wife so many years ago at Shiloh. Now and again one had to give credit to the pigs of the hills. Urnan the smith must have had the help of his god, or some god, to come back from slavery and avenge himself on the slayer of his wife.

For a moment, but only a moment, Galar wondered if the smith had ambitions against his own life. True, it was Jobal who had killed the smith's wife, but Galar had been in command of the troop and had sold Urnan and his son into slavery. Surely, if the smith had hated long enough and strongly enough to survive to kill Jobal, he might harbor the same hatred for Galar.

It was foolish, however, to think that such a pig of the hills could ever threaten the commander of the Army of the Five Cities.

CHAPTER
FIVE

Aiah, wife of Mered, captain of hundreds, greeted her husband warmly when he returned. With loving care she took his travel-soiled mantle, removed his sandals, and washed his feet.

"How did you find your uncle's family?" she asked, for Mered had not told her that he was going to visit Galar.

"They were all well," Mered said.

"Praise God," Aiah said.

As she dried her husband's feet she looked up at him with a smile. He was the central pillar of her life; she had become his wife when she was no more than a girl. Over the years a genuine fondness had grown between them; his happiness was her happiness. And she was grateful to him, for she had done the one thing that would have justified his taking another wife: She was childless.

"And did you miss me?" Mered asked with a smile.

"Why would I miss an old he-goat like you?" she teased.

"You wound me," he said, putting his hand to his heart.

She knelt beside his stool and put her arms around him. "In truth, husband, the house is empty without you."

Mered wanted to tell her that soon things would be different, that soon he would no longer be a mere underling in Saul's kingdom. When the army of kilted Philistine warriors overran Gibeah and put an end to the pitiful little dreams of a disunited people, she would wear the finest linen and jewels befitting a queen.

He began to act on his plans. "Did the girl, Sarah, visit you while I was away?" he asked.

"Such a sweet child," Aiah said with a smile.

"And has she totally regained her senses?"

"By God's own miracle," Aiah said.

From the time that Eri the smith had brought his family to Gibeah from the hidden workshops in the desert south of Judah, Aiah had been touched by the plight of Sarah. As Sarah came back to the real world she found a mother figure in the kindly, buxom Aiah. Many times Aiah had held the confused girl and whispered reassurance to her.

"Do you ever speak with Sarah about the work of her husband?" Mered asked.

Aiah shook her head. "The poor child is still sunk deep in her own miseries. I'm not sure she even knows what Eri does."

"I want you to continue to be her friend," Mered said.

"Of course I will. Why do you tell me?"

"She confides in you. I have heard her tell you intimate details about her life. Encourage her to talk about Eri's work and what is said when the king's son or other members of the court are visiting."

"You're asking me to spy on our neighbor?"

Mered laughed. "I can't quite picture you as a spy, my love." He patted her arm. "Let us just say that I want you to become a close observer of what goes on in the home and workshops of the armorer. It is for the good of the kingdom. Our king is sometimes distracted, and it is up to men like me to keep things functioning smoothly. The more I know the better I can serve my king." He still saw doubt in her eyes and continued.

"For instance, the king is often lax in communicating his plans in sufficient time to allow us, the men who move the army, who have to worry about sufficient arms and food, to prepare. If you learned that Eri's shops were turning out an unusual number of blades, arrows, spear tips, then I would know that Saul was planning to march into battle, and I could make my own preparations."

"I will do as you wish, husband," Aiah said.

When next Sarah visited Mered's house, Aiah listened, as usual, with great understanding and sympathy. When the girl whispered of her love for Eri, for a younger Eri who was gone, replaced by a mature man, a stranger, the older woman felt like weeping.

"Go to him in the night," Aiah advised.

"But he has a wife," Sarah protested.

"And Baalan is a good woman," Aiah said. "She looked after you during the time when the devils possessed you. She loves you."

"Don't ask me to love her," Sarah said. "She has taken the bed of my husband. She has given him a son."

"Then there is only one thing for you to do," Aiah said, feeling an ache in her barren womb. "Give him a son of your own."

Sarah discovered that if she closed her eyes and pretended it was a young Eri who possessed her, she could give the urges of her body free rein. Eri, making up for years of self-enforced abstinence, came to her bed to tell her of her beauty, to kiss her firm breasts and run his work-hardened hands over the smooth contours of her hips. But she could think only of Baalan and Baalan's son.

"Eri," she said one night when he was lying atop her, spent and sated, content to feel her softness and warmth under him, "I've been thinking that since I am well, you no longer need a second wife."

"Baalan loves you very much," Eri said.

"But she is only a slave," Sarah said. "We no longer need her." She hesitated. "I am fully capable of running my own house now. You have no need for a second wife, and I have no need for a slave. Send her away."

Eri pulled away from her and sat up. "The laws of God say that she is my wife," he explained.

"I will remind you," Sarah said angrily, "that I am the daughter of Sapha, that I am the ward of a very rich and powerful man."

There were times when Sarah became confused, mixing the past with the present, and Eri had learned that it was best to reestablish reality.

"Sarah," Eri said softly, "Raphu is long dead. His possessions and his riches were looted by the Philistines."

Sarah turned her back to him. "You don't love me," she said.

"You are my wife, the love of my youth, my present love," Eri said.

"If you had loved me you would have taken me to your bed long ago so that I could have given you a son instead of that slave."

"I could not," Eri said. "I made a vow. To have known you physically as a wife while you were off somewhere in a world of your own would have been a lonely undertaking, and not honorable."

"You say you love me. I would be more convinced of that had you not taken a slave girl to your bed."

Sadly, Eri turned her to face him. He moved an oil lamp closer to the bed so that he could see her face and she his. "Listen carefully," he said. "I do love you, and I respect you, but Baalan is also my wife. You will always have a special place in my heart as the love of my youth and my first wife, but there will be no more talk of sending Baalan away. This is her home. I am her husband and Sunu is my son. He was promised greatness by Samuel himself."

Sarah looked at him with disbelief.

"Samuel is a prophet and beloved of God," Eri said. "His prophecy is of divine origin."

Sarah was wise enough to say no more. When the absence of her monthly shame told her that God had answered her prayers, she told Aiah the news first.

"It will be a son," Aiah said.

"I pray so," Sarah said.

Aiah laughed and hugged her. "I know it will be a boy because you want a son so badly."

Sarah smiled happily. When she had a son of her own, a son much more beautiful than Baalan's Sunu, then she would be able to convince Eri to send the slave and her imp away. In the meantime, she could make Eri realize that Baalan was not the paragon he considered her to be. To Sarah it seemed that in Eri's eyes Baalan could do no wrong. Baalan was the perfect mother, the most accomplished cook, the most efficient manager of a household.

It was simple to cause trouble for the Ammonite, as simple as adding extra salt to a pot of lentil soup so that when it was served to Eri it tasted like brine, as simple as smearing soil on one of Eri's tunics freshly washed by Baalan. Sarah could not understand why, when Eri made a face and pushed the soup away, when he donned his clean tunic and saw the great stain on the front, he did not immediately berate Baalan.

Frustrated, Sarah came to think that only the motherly Aiah understood her. Only Aiah agreed with her that it was unthinkable for Baalan's son to be heir to Eri's possessions. Mered was also very considerate. He was always asking Sarah about her family. Was Eri well? Was Urnan planning another journey in search of iron ore? Was Eri working long hours?

Sarah, pleased by the attention, began to take more interest in the activities of the men in her household and to report them to Mered.

Thus it was that Mered learned that Jonathan had been ordered by Saul to move the army to the north. Even Jonathan, so young, so inexperienced, had been promoted over Mered. Mered was still a captain of hundreds, while the king's son had been made captain of thousands. A nomadic herder in Mered's pay carried a brief message to a Philistine outpost on the edge of the plain. A rider carried the message to General Galar.

Galar's first thought was to meet the Hebrew army in the lands of Manasseh or Issachar, but after more serious consideration he decided on another course of action. At the moment the Hebrews were strong, strong because they were united. He would send the Army of the Five Cities to the south to strike into Judah. In doing so, he would smash the fragile alliance that Saul had forged among the Twelve Tribes and cut the nation in twain.

CHAPTER
SIX

Urnan was riding south from Jerusalem toward Gedor, from where he planned to strike out into the Wilderness of Judah. The brief pleasures of spring had been replaced by summer's searing sun. Sweat plastered his thighs to the contours of Ramses' broad back. As the sun came nearer the zenith Urnan sought shelter and found it in the shade of a grove of sycamores on a slope above the narrow road.

He was lying down, using his sleeping robes as a pillow, thinking pleasant thoughts of the widow Jerioth, when the valley below him was suddenly filled with the thunder of iron-shod wheels. Some peculiarity of the landscape muffled the sound of the Philistine chariots until they burst around a rocky outcrop no more than an arrow's flight from where Urnan lay.

He leaped to his feet and put his hand over Ramses' nose to quiet him. Each of the half-dozen gleaming chariots was drawn by two horses moving at a The horses were ornamented in the Egyptian with gaily colored fabric coverings on neck and back. The drivers leaned forward to control the long reins. In each vehicle stood a kilted archer, bow held at the ready, quiver with a supply of arrows secured to the chariot's side at his right.

Urnan nodded grimly. The narrow gorge had steep slopes on either side that would provide good cover for Hebrew soldiers. The Philistines, familiar now with Saul's battle tactics, were sending their chariots ahead to scout the defile for signs of ambush.

The advance force disappeared around a ridge to the east. Behind them came the Army of the Five Cities.

They came with pennants flying, with a rumble of wheels and a creak of leather as cavalry followed the main body of charioteers. With the clank of metal and the dull shuffle of hundreds of feet, heavy infantry in blue kilts striped with red and white filled the narrow valley from end to end, marching four abreast along the road. The plumes of horsehair on their helmets had been dyed blue to match their kilts. Leather cuirasses protected chests and backs and left brawny, sun-browned arms bare. Each soldier carried two spears in the same hand that clutched a round leather-and-bronze shield. A short iron sword completed the armament.

As unit after unit passed below the grove where Urnan was hidden, it became evident that this was no mere raiding party. Saul's scouts had reported that the main contingents of the Philistine army were still in their respective cities on the plain and along the coast. His move to the north was designed to take advantage of the confusion that had followed the debacle at Michmash. The Army of Israel was moving toward the Plain of Sharon, and the king was unaware that Galar was moving into the land of Judah in force.

Galar.

The general's party rode in the center of the extended army. Galar was mounted on a splendid horse adorned with cloth of gold. His silver breastplate and helmet gleamed golden in the sun.

Watching him, Urnan was astounded by the power

of his hate. It had been many years since Galar of Ashdod gave the order to destroy Urnan's home, murder his wife, and take him and his son into slavery, but the memories came back in numbing force as Galar passed so close that Urnan could see his lips move as he talked. His hand clutched his sword, then relaxed. He was one man against thousands. He would wait. One day he would have his revenge on Galar.

Urnan waited for a full half hour after the rear guard passed through the valley, then turned his mount's head not southward toward Gedor, but to the north. The land that God had promised to the descendants of Abraham was a small land, and the area in which Saul had established his dominance over the invaders was even smaller. Distance was not great, but in the jumble of hills that formed the backbone of Israel, travel was measured in days.

Urnan rode hard and reached Gibeah on the second day. Eri was with the army, marching with Jonathan. Only a small garrison manned the king's citadel. First Urnan warned Baalan and Sarah; then he used his authority to order the garrison to mount sentinels should Galar change direction and threaten to bring his destruction to the heart of Saul's land.

Sarah's face paled when Urnan gave his warning, but Baalan was firm in her promise to take the entire family to a well-concealed cave in the nearby hills if they suspected that Galar's army was moving north.

Urnan allowed Ramses to rest overnight and was on the road before morning's light. He came upon the rear guard of the army to the east of Aphek and was given escort to Saul's tent. As he pulled Ramses to a halt and dismounted, he heard the sweet sound of David's harp.

The king sat on a camp stool beside a fire. He had removed his armor and was at his ease in a flowing white robe. David sat nearby, harp on his knee. The captains were there along with Abner, the overall commander of the army. Urnan nodded to the heavily bearded Mered, lifted his hand in greeting to Eri, who sat with the king's son, Jonathan, and bowed his respects to Saul.

"My friend," Saul said, rising to embrace him, "what has interrupted your mission to the south?"

Urnan could feel all eyes on him. As the king and his captains listened to his story, there was a growing sense of tension and excitement.

"You are sure it is the Philistine army, not just a raiding party?" Saul asked.

"Two hundred chariots passed within a stone's throw of me," Urnan said. "There were at least five hundred horsemen."

"Infantry?" Saul asked, his eyes blazing with eagerness.

"Thousands. So many I could not count."

"Yahweh is good!" Saul shouted, rising. "Galar's line of march was taking him deeper into Judah?"

"Toward Bethlehem," Urnan said.

Saul stood a head taller than those who clustered around him, but it was not his height alone that gave him his aura of majesty. He lifted his hands toward the darkening heavens. "Now, by God's will, the reluctant ones in Judah will be taught the value of unity."

Saul's army moved largely on foot, but it had the advantage of knowing every fold and bend in the countryside. With Jonathan's unit in the forefront, they marched southward. As they passed from the lands of Benjamin the army grew in number, for news that the Philistines were on the prowl in Judah was spreading.

David had become Saul's armor-bearer. He was learning the art of war from a master of hit-and-run tactics and was looking forward to the inevitable battle when the army overtook Galar's force. He had equipped himself with an old bronze sword with which he practiced late at night after most were asleep. But that he was still only a boy was obvious when he couldn't hide his disappointment when Saul gave him his first order.

"You will go to your father's home," Saul said.

"I beg you, sire," David began. His face was dark with frustration.

"I have come to love you like a son," Saul said.

"If you love me you will not shame me," David said.

"It is no shame to protect something of more value than one more sword among many." Saul smiled fondly. "Am I of some use in the land of Israel, boy?"

"You are, sire," David replied. "You are Israel's heart and her strong right arm."

"If I am of worth," Saul said, "then do as I ask, and do not make me risk someone on whom I rely. When this fight is over and the Philistine dog is driven back to his kennel on the plains, I will send for you, and your songs will once again soothe me."

With great reluctance David left the army and traveled toward the house of Jesse.

Jonathan's scouts located the main body of the Philistine army near Shocho, west of Bethlehem, and each commander busied himself and his men in maneuvers, seeking the most advantageous position. The opposing forces were almost evenly matched, for Galar had not been able to restore the Army of the Five Cities to its pre-Michmash strength, and Saul's army had been increased by men of Judah who had, indeed, been shown the need for unity by the Philistine invasion.

CHAPTER
SEVEN

The scroll room in the temple of Amon at Waset, Egypt's Southern City and the home of ancient kings, contained hundreds of rolled papyri. It seemed to Kaptar that his uncle was determined to have him read all of them. On a glorious day when the marsh along the river was filled with fat, foolish waterfowl begging to be taken, the smell of the ancient scrolls and of the oil lamps was odious. To be imprisoned in the library was a fate beyond the comprehension of a lad who, at twelve summers, was just two years shy of official manhood.

It took no imagination at all to think of at least a score of activities preferable to squinting in the dim light while running one's finger along the lines of hieroglyphs that told the history of the Two Lands. He would have much preferred to be in the metalworking shops amid the smells of superheated charcoal and white-hot metal. Fashioning a fine blade from a crude casting of iron, feeling the weight of the hammer, the pull of it on the biceps with sweat soaking one's headband and running down one's bare back, gave one something tangible to hold and admire. And it gave him a feeling of closeness with his long-lost father, Urnan the smith, who, like Kaptar, bore the mark signifying that he was one of the Children of the Lion.

Actually, if hard-pressed, Kaptar would have admitted with some reluctance that there was a certain magic in learning about the past, even from ancient scrolls.

"To know who you are," his uncle Kemose had told him more than once, "you must know from whom you came."

Kaptar had the blood of kings in his veins. True, they were weak kings quite unlike the giants of old who had worn the twin crowns of the Two Lands. It would have given him greater pride to be able to say that he was descended from one such as the great Ahmose, who drove the Hyksos invaders out of the Two Lands, or the second Ramses, whose monuments adorned the land from the delta to the far south.

Kaptar's royal bloodline came from his mother, Tania, who was cousin to Kemose, high priest of Amon at Waset, and to Paynozem, who sat on the throne of Egypt at Zoan. But these were kings who had allowed Egypt to be split into competing factions and to fall partially under the rule of aliens.

The boy's musings were interrupted by the entry of the high priest. He rose quickly to show proper respect for his uncle.

"Sit," Kemose said.

The high priest was an impressive man of uncommon height. In his priestly robes he seemed to reach almost to the high ceiling of the library. His hands were large and showed signs of hard work unsuitable for a prince of the Two Lands and a high priest of Amon. His gnarled and misshapen knuckles were, in fact, a symbol of the weakness that had overtaken Egypt, for Kemose had been seized by Philistines and set to work like a common slave at a copper mine on the island of Kittem.

"Today you are studying the period of history prior

to the reign of the third Ramses," Kemose said. "What have you learned?"

With his hands at his sides and his eyes turned toward the images of the gods on the ceiling, Kaptar recited, "I have learned that there were weak kings in those days of old before Ramses III rallied the nation to its magnificent stand against the peoples of the sea. Before Ramses there was a period of decline and chaos that was broken for only a short time by Seti II."

"And have you discerned a reason for the weakness?" Kemose asked.

"It seems to me, Uncle, that too many ambitious men forgot the advantages of unity and aspired only to power for themselves. The army was made up of mercenaries, foreigners held great influence at court, there were greedy pretenders to the throne as well as those who hoped to gain riches by backing them, and—" He paused and looked at Kemose thoughtfully.

"Go on," the priest said.

"And—forgive me, Uncle—arrogant priests who hungered for power."

"You have read well. Were those the only factors in the downfall of the thirteenth dynasty?"

"The nation was infiltrated by immigrants from the west, the south, and the east," Kaptar said. "After the brief respite during the reign of Seti II, the Two Lands disintegrated once more into petty kingdoms and principalities."

"As in the days of the beginning."

"Yes, before Narmer the unifier and Menes the consolidator."

"Your impression of the time of chaos?" Kemose asked.

"It is written that every man was deprived of his rights and that the Two Lands had no king for many years. There was no law. The lands were in the hands of nobles and the rulers of towns. War and death were the rule for the great and the small, as men slew their neighbors. The throne was seized by a foreigner, a Syrian. It is written that he set the whole land tributary to him. He brought Libyan hordes into the country and plundered it."

"Tell me, nephew, why do we study the past?" Kemose asked. "Is it just because history tells interesting stories?"

"If I may quote you, Uncle: Know the mistakes of the past lest you repeat them."

"And what lesson is taught by the period of lawlessness following the thirteenth dynasty?"

"The ruin of the Two Lands came from the west as Libyans plundered their way across our frontiers, took possession of the rich fields along the river, and were allowed by the weak kings to settle in the delta on the banks of the Canopic branch of the Nile."

"Good, good," Kemose said. "Now draw me a comparison between the times before Ramses III and the current reign of my brother Paynozem, may he live."

"For our ears only?" Kaptar said.

"For your mind," Kemose said.

"Paynozem, in Zoan, calls himself king of the Two Lands," Kaptar said, "but the empire is gone. The Peleset were driven back from Egypt's borders by Ramses III, but they settled in Canaan, once an Egyptian province. The kings who followed Ramses III took his name, but had not his abilities. The post of high priest of Amon at Waset became hereditary, and under the weak Ramessids, power was consolidated in the Southern City so that it became an independent principality. The unity of the kingdom was ended. In the time of your father, Pesibkhenno II claimed to be king of the Two Lands, but it was an empty boast, for the Libyans had once more taken control of the delta by peaceful conquest. Today, as then, Egypt's army consists largely of Libyan mercenaries. Your brother Paynozem, high priest before you, married Pesibkhenno's daughter and moved his throne to Zoan. He claims to rule the Two Lands."

"And does he?"

"Uncle, he is a tool of the Libyans. Between his throne in Zoan and the Southern City, here at Waset, lie the most heavily populated Libyan nomes."

"And is there danger of the throne, at least of Lower Egypt, being seized once more by a foreigner?"

"At the sacred city of On, a Libyan named Buyuwawa calls himself king, and he has installed his son, Musen, as a priest of the temple and commander of the mercenary army."

Kemose nodded. It was Musen who had caused Paynozem to exile Kaptar's father, Kemose's friend Urnan, from Egypt. Nothing rankled Kemose more than the fact that he had been unable to stop the exile of Urnan the smith and that he was not powerful enough as king of Upper Egypt to mount an expedition into the former lands of the empire to locate this Child of the Lion.

"Uncle," Kaptar said, his voice serious, "will Egypt ever be one great nation again?"

"That depends," Kemose said cautiously.

"On what?" Kaptar asked.

"On many things, but the most important is the man who will rule Egypt in the future. We have great need of a strong leader." Kemose studied Kaptar's eager face for a long time, then smiled and said, "You have read well. So well that I think a reward is in order. I had thought to mount a hunt into the desert—"

Kaptar's face beamed. "For lions?"

Kemose smiled fondly. "To face a lion is a man's task."

Kaptar's smile faded.

"But perhaps a boy verging on manhood would be of some use on such an expedition."

"Thank you, Uncle," Kaptar said, bowing. "How may I help you prepare for the hunt?"

Kemose was amused by Kaptar's eagerness, but he kept his face straight. "I suppose you might use the skills you inherited from your father to see to it that my weapons and yours are well honed."

"It will be done."

"And choose your charioteer."

"I will take the Nubian, Jeku."

"An excellent choice." Kemose chuckled. "If your

arrows fail, Jeku is large enough to strangle a lion with his bare hands."

Kaptar laughed with his uncle.

"We do not want to make this an affair of the court," Kemose said, "so go about your preparation quietly."

Kaptar nodded. To go into the desert with dozens of vehicles and the mob of followers who took every opportunity to be near the man who occupied the seat of power in Upper Egypt was to frighten away any beast within two days' journey of the city.

Four chariots left the stables before dawn. The horses were held to a walk until they were clear of the city. They followed a narrow, switchback road out of the fertile valley and up to the top of the cliffs, where they halted. Across the river the temples of the kings glowed in the dawn light. Kaptar looked out over the stark grandeur of the desert. Somewhere in the near distance there was a flash of movement, and Kaptar tensed.

"It is only a jackal," said the giant Nubian at his side.

Kaptar had never faced a lion, and he knew that it was unlikely that he ever would without traveling far from Waset. Once, the magnificent beasts had been plentiful in Upper Egypt. The scrolls in the temple library recorded many successful hunts by the kings and princes who had once ruled the Two Lands. Since the advent of rule by the priests of Amon, lion hunting had fallen out of fashion. The priests were more interested in serving the gods than in proving their manhood by slaying animals, which was just as well because lions had become scarce in the deserts near Waset.

Yet there was hope. No one had mounted a hunt in Kaptar's memory. If the gods willed it, and if he had faith, perhaps some solitary old male, or even a pride of lions, would have migrated downriver from beyond the cataracts, and he would have the opportunity to face danger and prove his bravery with a lion skin as trophy.

At midmorning Kemose, in the lead chariot, startled a gazelle from a dry ravine. With a whoop the high priest's charioteer lashed his horses into a gallop. Sand flew from under the wheels of the chariot, and the horses strained to keep pace with the fleet animal. Kemose drew his bow. Kaptar held his breath as the arrow flew through the air.

The sleek little gazelle seemed to freeze in midleap before it crumpled to the sand in a heap. The big Nubian roared out his approval as he steered Kaptar's chariot to the scene of the kill.

"We will dine well tonight," Kemose said.

"A fine shot, Uncle," Kaptar said.

"Now you will lead. The next shot will be yours."

"I pray that my aim will be as true as yours."

"It is the hunt, as much as the taking, that makes the heart beat faster," Kemose said.

With the sun still a handspan high in the western sky, Kemose ordered his servants to set up a dry camp in the lee of a rocky outcrop. He smilingly granted Kaptar's request to be allowed to scout ahead while there was still light. Jeku sighed, for it had been a long day and he was obviously ready to sit and listen to the sizzling of a gazelle roast over the fire that Kemose's servants had kindled.

"Have heart," Kaptar said. "By the time we get back the meat will be ready."

Jeku drove south, parallel to the distant river, while the sun moved toward the horizon. Aside from a jackal who watched them curiously, the desert seemed to be without life.

"It is time to turn back," Jeku said.

"A bit longer," Kaptar begged.

Jeku clucked and flicked his lash to within an inch of the horses' rumps. The sun hid itself behind the rise as they entered a dry ravine, and slowly the walls of the canyon closed in on them. The only sound was the wheels of the chariot hissing softly in the loose sand. Suddenly Jeku reined up.

"What?" Kaptar asked.

The Nubian pointed to something in the sand.

The enormous tracks caused Kaptar's heart to pound. "Lion?" he whispered.

"A female," Jeku said.

"How do you know?"

"From the size. An immature male at best, for the prints are small."

"That's small?" Kaptar croaked.

The Nubian laughed. "In my homeland a man meets a lion on foot, with nothing more than a spear, and when a maned male leaps he fills the sky."

Kaptar shivered with excitement. "One day I will face a lion in the Nubian way."

Jeku chuckled. "When you are a man," he said. "In the meantime, if this one has not gone far away, it would be best if you took it in the Egyptian way."

The chariot moved slowly. Suddenly a deep-chested, coughing roar reverberated up and down the narrow ravine. The horses pranced in panic. Jeku's hand was firm on the reins and calmed them.

"A male," Jeku whispered. "Very close."

Kaptar readied his bow, selected an arrow. He saw the lion first. Blood pounded in his temples. His throat was dry. "Look."

"I see."

There were two of them, male and female.

"By the gods," Kaptar said softly. "So beautiful."

The lions were no more than fifty paces away, standing together on a ledge high above Kaptar's head. The male was huge, and his mane was as black as night. The female snarled, showing long, yellowed fangs. Kaptar drew his bow.

"Hold," Jeku said.

Two cubs tumbled out into the open and, sensing the alertness of their parents, froze.

Kaptar let the tension out of his bow. "I cannot," he said.

"Take the male. It is the female who hunts."

Kaptar shook his head. There was a magnificence in the stance of the black-maned male, and a lithe beauty in his mate. The cubs, as if sensing that the danger had passed, tumbled into a mock fight.

"Your heart is big," Jeku said, clucking the horses into motion. There was just room to turn the chariot between the rock walls. The horses' hooves skittered on loose rock.

Kaptar was looking at the horses when he heard the same chilling roar that had first announced the presence of the lions. At the same moment, a dark form launched itself from the rocks above. Kaptar's reaction was swift. He drew and fired an arrow in one motion and heard it thunk solidly into the exposed belly of a lion as it soared over his head.

Its claws slashed at Jeku, ripping away the covering on his head. The force of the blow sent the big man sprawling over the edge of the chariot's box. He tried to catch himself and managed to hang on to the edge of the box with one hand as the horses leaped forward. A wheel smashed against a rock. The chariot lurched, and Jeku fell to the ground, senseless. The harness ripped, the shaft of the chariot snapped, and the horses fled down the canyon as the lion, a young male, landed, whirled around, and roared in pain and defiance.

Kaptar had regained his balance and was in the process of pulling another arrow from his quiver when the lion charged. He drew the bowstring to a point beside his right cheek. Time stopped. He saw the great cat lift off the ground, saw the awesome maw open, saw massive front paws and wicked claws stretching toward him. He heard the twang of the bowstring as he released it, the hiss of the arrow. The cat came hurtling through the air. Kaptar leaped aside but managed to seize a hunting spear as the lion smashed down on the chariot. Kaptar hit the ground off balance, rolled, and was back on his feet, grasping the spear in both hands.

The lion, frothy red foam spewing from its maw, looked for its tormentor, saw the still form of the Nubian, and leaped toward him.

Kaptar screamed a warning when he saw the lion going for Jeku. The animal turned, crouched low, roared. Kaptar, his spear poised, waited. The cat was not long in coming. It launched itself while still five paces away, and Kaptar looked up to see it fill the sky, just as Jeku had described. Kaptar felt very small. The shaft of his spear looked very thin and fragile.

The lion impaled itself on the spear, claws slashing the air in front of Kaptar's face as the point pierced its heart. Then the shaft broke with a loud snap, and the lion's body fell on Kaptar. He closed his eyes, expecting to feel the slash of claws, the sharpness of teeth.

All was still except the lion's rear legs, which twitched and jerked in death. Kaptar could barely breathe. Fur muffled his face. An animal stench filled his nostrils. He pushed with all his strength, and the lion rolled limply to one side, its hindquarters across Kaptar's legs. He finally freed himself and staggered to his feet.

The Nubian stirred as Kaptar approached. His eyes rolled and widened as he sat up and took in the scene with a dazed expression. Blood was running down the side of his head.

"You're hurt," Kaptar said.

Jeku felt his head gingerly. There were two long, deep grooves made by the lion's claws. "I'll be all right," he said.

A sound from behind caused Kaptar to turn suddenly, fear surging through him. He had killed one lion. There were two others.

A pebble bounced down the rocky slope below the ledge on which the lion family stood. One of the cubs was scrambling back onto the ledge. Two pairs of yellow eyes stared unblinking at Kaptar. He moved slowly to the chariot and took out his second hunting spear. The lions watched him intently. The male opened his mouth to show his fearsome teeth, while the female made a small sound that sent the two cubs scurrying out of sight. Then the two adults turned and disappeared.

"Go in peace," Kaptar said. "Be fruitful."

Jeku was inspecting the chariot. "We won't be riding back to camp in this. If, young master, you will go fetch the horses, I'll begin the task of claiming your trophy."

The horses had not run far before their broken harness had tangled. They awaited Kaptar's approach, snorting in fear.

By the time he returned to the scene of the kill, Jeku was almost finished skinning the lion. The horses pranced and snorted, but with much encouragement and soft assurances from the Nubian one of them accepted the wet, rank skin of the lion across its withers. Jeku sat in front of the heavy skin. Kaptar rode the other horse.

In the camp that night Jeku sawed music from a peculiar, one-stringed Nubian instrument while Kemose's servants danced in honor of Kaptar.

Kemose handed a cup of wine to Kaptar. "If you are old enough to kill a lion in the Nubian fashion you are old enough to enjoy the charms of the grape." He paused. "But I suggest you don't tell your mother."

Kaptar grinned. He loved his mother, the beautiful princess Tania, but she refused to see that soon her son would no longer be a boy, but a man.

When Kaptar got to his feet to join the retainers in song and dance and celebration, the world swam around him, and he was not sure that Kemose was right about the wine. But as he cavorted and leaped his head cleared. The moon rose over the eastern horizon to light the desert, and in the distance he thought he heard his uncle say, "Perhaps he will be the king who will save Egypt."

CHAPTER EIGHT

Musen, son of the Libyan lord Buyuwawa, had two ambitions. The first was to see himself—or, at worst, one of his descendants—on the throne of the Two Lands.

Musen was the king's army commander, but he was more than a soldier. At his father's insistence he had been trained by the priests and was as well educated as any scribe of the temple. He had taken it upon himself to learn as much as there was to learn about the country he called his own. He did not have the blood of the ancients, but he was Egyptian-born, and he felt that Egypt belonged to him as much as to the weaklings who had allowed the departure of glory from the Two Lands. He knew his history. Non-Egyptians had occupied the throne more than once in the past, and because history had a way of repeating itself, it was quite possible that he or his could do the same.

Musen's other aspiration was related to the first. The throne of Egypt descended by tradition through the bloodline of royal women, so for Musen to become king he would have to marry into the royal family. Which royal family to choose out of those who made pretensions to the throne? As it happened, the same blood ran in the veins of Paynozem and the ruler at Waset, in Upper Egypt. Therefore, a union with the princess Tania, cousin to both Paynozem and Kemose, the high priest of Waset, would be a positive first step.

He had first seen the beautiful Tania when she was the wife of the armorer Urnan, friend of Kemose, and he could not forget her. It was impossible to erase the memory of the splendor of her body, the richness of her hair, the secret fire that flickered in the depths of her ebony-dark eyes.

But there were other memories, unpleasant memories, reasons why Tania would never willingly consent to marry him. To capture her husband, who had been supplying loyal Egyptians living in the delta with iron weapons to use against the Libyan lords, Musen had taken Tania captive. In rescuing his wife, Urnan had killed several of Musen's men, an act that the Libyan could neither forgive nor forget. To Musen's regret, Urnan had then been allowed to escape from Egypt. But he knew that Tania blamed him for the loss of her husband.

Musen's father, Buyuwawa, shared his son's dream of seeing one of his seed on the throne of the Two Lands. Thus it was Buyuwawa who approached Paynozem, the king, an audience prefaced by the delivery of gifts of gold and gleaming gemstones, of fat cattle and stores of food from the rich farmlands under the control of the Libyans.

Paynozem's court at Zoan was, on the surface, a match for the splendid and glorious establishments of the great kings, but anyone who knew art and architecture would have been able to penetrate the sham easily. The great Ramses II had built in stone. Hosts of craftsmen had labored in dozens of stone quarries. Nile barges wallowed under the weight of rough-cut building blocks. Skilled artisans polished the stones and incised the decorative hieroglyphs to ensure that the name of the king would live forever.

Paynozem's architectural statements were made in mud brick, not enduring granite. Brightly colored ornamentation on the outside and decorations adorned with sheets of gold thinner than the most delicate papyrus disguised the true nature of his palace. In its great rooms Nubian dwarfs gamboled with trained apes for the king's amusement. Every village in Lower Egypt had been scouted for the most shapely, most sensuous, most tractable young girls to give pleasure to the king through their talent for the dance and other activities. His Libyan allies had contributed sultry Semitic beauties to his harem of wives. But no one was more aware of the precarious nature of Paynozem's throne than he who sat on it.

Paynozem now knew that it had been a mistake to abandon Waset, leaving his brother, Kemose, in power. Kemose was bound by tradition. Kemose believed that Egypt was for Egyptians and was not to be shared with the nomads from the deserts of Libya. Paynozem had moved the court to Zoan in an effort to unite the Two Lands, but the effect was the opposite. Now there were two kings in Egypt, the brothers Paynozem and Kemose.

When Buyuwawa asked Paynozem for an audience, the king immediately called in his counselors and spent hours speculating about what the old Libyan wanted. They decided it would be necessary to hear the old man out.

The Libyan lord arrived amidst much pomp. Fully armed units of his army led the procession, doing a precision drill with their spears and swords and shields. Watching them, Paynozem was forcefully reminded that Musen had, with one order to his mercenaries, the means to topple the throne. Troops of acrobats and magicans put on a show that brought hoarse cries of delight from the masses on the streets leading to Paynozem's palace. Suggestively dressed dancing girls swayed and swirled in front of Buyuwawa's litter. Four splendidly muscled Nubian slaves carried the litter and were followed by other slaves bearing golden gifts.

When at last the procession was over, Paynozem sat

on his carved and gilded throne, and Buyuwawa, respectful of his age and rank, sat slightly lower on a chair that had been designed for use in Paynozem's tomb. Behind each man stood half a dozen trusted advisers. Musen was among the Libyan delegation.

First Buyuwawa read a prepared hymn of praise for the great king. Paynozem listened with a fixed smile and shifted uneasily when Buyuwawa finished.

"Paynozem, Great King Who Will Live Forever," Buyuwawa said, "you have been informed, I'm sure, of the latest clash between your loyal army and the forces of the pretenders at Waset."

Paynozem nodded. He hadn't actually heard of any recent battle, but he wasn't surprised. Quite often trouble sprang up in the area where villages loyal to the priest of Amon at Waset abutted those who were under the control of Musen's army.

"How long, great king, are we to allow the priests at Waset to defy the great god who sits the throne of the Two Lands?" Buyuwawa asked, spreading his hands in frustration, an anguished expression on his face. "You have the means at hand, great king, to put an end to the division of the Two Lands, if you will only use it."

The Libyan spoke Egyptian with a strong accent, and Paynozem had some difficulty understanding. "I would use any means if I were sure that the outcome would be more satisfactory than another endless civil war," he said.

"It is your destiny, great king, to rule all of the rich lands of our country," Buyuwawa said.

Paynozem nodded.

"My son, Musen, has built an army second to none," Buyuwawa said. "And he is ready, great king, to march on Waset and to subjugate the pretenders. You have but to give the word and the hands of those who oppose you will be delivered in a pile to rot in the fields of the delta."

"My loyal friend," Paynozem said, "I have discussed this subject with my advisers." He frowned. "They do not agree with your son's assessment that he could best the forces of my brother on the field of battle." His eyes smiled, although his lips did not, as he said, "After all, Lord Buyuwawa, Musen's army would be facing Egyptians, not Nubians or foreign mercenaries."

Buyuwawa ignored the insult and started to speak, but Paynozem continued. "Perhaps you are not aware that diplomatic negotiations are continuing in an effort to convince the priests at Waset that unification under the legitimate king of the Two Lands would be best for the nation. Our hopes are high for success."

"And if your diplomacy fails?" Buyuwawa asked.

"My contributions to the Army of Egypt more than equal yours," Paynozem said. "Diplomacy is more effective when it is backed by a strong army."

"You have the loyalty of your Libyan subjects," Buyuwawa said. "My son and I are first among them in paying tribute to you, great king."

"For which," Paynozem said wryly, "I have rewarded you well in lands and titles."

Buyuwawa nodded. "Of our allegiance there is no doubt, great king, but—"

"But?" Paynozem asked in a voice filled with suspicion.

"As you know there is a Libyan majority in certain nomes to the south of Zoan," Buyuwawa said. "Loyal subjects all, but they often ask why the king seems to favor those whose ancestors were born along the Nile over those whose forebears were men of the desert."

"The king gives equal rights to all who obey his laws," Korna, Paynozem's Seal-bearer and Master of the Horse, interrupted.

Paynozem lifted his hand for silence. He, more than anyone, realized the necessity of keeping the friendship of Buyuwawa and his Libyans. "What can the king do to assure his loyal Libyan subjects that he treats all with an even hand?"

"May I speak frankly?" the Libyan asked.

Paynozem nodded.

"It has been suggested that an alliance between my

family and the family of the king would assure the small
people of the king's regard." Buyuwawa cocked his
head, waiting for the king's answer.

Paynozem felt the blood rise to his face, but he had
long experience at hiding his emotions. How dare the
foreigner suggest that a woman of royal blood be given
in marriage to a Libyan barbarian! The old man was
acting as if he, a mere local chieftain, had equal status
with the head of state of a sovereign country. Diplomatic marriages had long been a matter of policy, but
only between the royalty of great nations. A woman of
the family of the king of the Two Lands would never,
never be given to a mere functionary with the blood of
the Libyan nomads.

Paynozem was saved from his anger by Korna, who
stepped forward and bowed. Paynozem did not know
that his maternal uncle, his dependable adviser, had
conferred with Musen before this meeting.

Said Korna, "I ask the Living God not to refute the
suggestion by the honorable Lord Buyuwawa without
considering all possibilities."

"Speak, Uncle," the king said.

"As it happens," Korna said, "the possibility of an
alliance such as Lord Buyuwawa suggests does not in-
volve any member of the court here at Zoan."

"I do not follow you," Paynozem said irritably.

"General Musen, son of Buyuwawa, will explain,"
Korna said.

Paynozem looked toward Musen, who stepped forward. "If I may make a suggestion, great king."

Paynozem waved one hand. His anger was gone.
He resigned himself to the inevitable. He was in no position to deny a request from Buyuwawa and Musen. He
had already decided that he would offer a daughter by
one of his Libyan wives. The girl was only eight years
old, but the marriage, if any, would be ceremonial.

Musen spoke in a strong voice. "A union between
your army commander and the princess Tania, your
cousin, would serve two purposes, great king. First it
would assure our people that you hold them in regard.

Second, it would lay the foundation for cooperation between you, great king, and your brother."

Tania. Paynozem barely managed to keep from leaping to his feet.

"Great king," Korna said quickly, "there is some merit to Musen's suggestion."

"And does General Musen have reason to believe that Princess Tania would favor his suit?" Paynozem asked coldly.

"May I submit, great king, that the decision would be made not by Tania but by the high priest, your brother," Korna said. "You and I both know your brother as a rational man, who, it must be said, has the interest of Egypt at heart. I have heard from the lips of Kemose himself that he, like you, deplores the state of warfare that exists between the upper and lower portions of the Two Lands. It is my belief that Kemose would welcome a means of lessening the tension."

Paynozem believed, although he held his tongue, that his brother would do one of two things if he were confronted with a request to give his cousin as a wife to a Libyan. Kemose would either laugh at the proposal or lose his temper and kill the man who suggested it.

The king's mind was working swiftly. He had been considering a conference with his brother but had not yet devised a suitable excuse. He made a decision.

"My friends," he said with a smile, "I praise you for your collective wisdom. Because my loyal Libyan subjects and my uncle, my trusted adviser, all agree on this course of action, I must accept it as being an astute approach to our problem. I myself will travel to Waset and offer to my brother the boon of peace through a union of north and south."

For the moment Paynozem was content. It suited him to let the Libyans believe that he was stupid enough to overlook the obvious fact that a Musen linked in marriage to the royal family would become one more claimant to his throne—and, because he was backed by the army, the most dangerous of all. Paynozem would dutifully go to Waset. He would speak with his brother. He would, before the public and the Libyans, offer the political union to Kemose. But in the privacy of Kemose's palace, in the dark of night, he would tell him that it was time for the Two Lands to work as one, that it was time for the Two Lands to fight as one.

Against the Libyans.

CHAPTER NINE

In the heat of the afternoon Urnan and Eri sat in the shade of a gnarled olive tree on a slope overlooking a peaceful valley near the small village of Shocho, to the west of Bethlehem in Judah. As a defense against the summer heat Eri had trimmed his thick, black beard, leaving only a dense stubble clinging to his chin and cheeks. Anyone could have seen the family resemblance in the faces of the two men, who had strong noses, well-shaped chins, wide-set brown eyes, and the high cheekbones of their Mesopotamian ancestors.

From beyond the ridge behind them came the sounds of an army in encampment. The clear, solid ring of hammer on anvil arose from one of Urnan's mobile shops. A donkey brayed a long, coughing protest, and a passing raven dipped down over the summer-browned vegetation on the floor of the valley as if in anticipation of the day when he would feast on the fruit of battle.

Of the Philistine host there was no evidence, but Eri could sense their presence. They were there in the

63

thousands, beyond the far ridge, with horsemen and chariots and the stolid ranks of heavy infantry that had conquered powerful cities and even pushed mighty Egypt to the breaking point.

Urnan was half dozing with his back against a sun-heated stone. Hearing the sound of hooves, he opened one eye and saw a horseman top the ridge and ride toward them. Eri lifted an arm in greeting to Jonathan.

The king's son dismounted and rubbed his rump, grinning wryly as he massaged sore muscles. "The grand army of the Lord God Yahweh," he said, "always alert and ready for action." He secured his mount's reins to a bush and sat down on a flat boulder.

"Galar seems no more eager for a fight than we," Urnan said.

Jonathan flicked sweat from his forehead with his forefinger and sighed. "I don't know what Galar is waiting for. My father, I fear, waits in the vain hope that our hairy holy man, the great Samuel, will send his blessings. Or that God will speak to him as He speaks to Samuel." Jonathan's voice was bitter.

"We did not have Samuel's blessings at Michmash," Eri said. "Nor did we need them."

Jonathan stared at the ground. "Blasphemy other than my own frightens me," he said, only half jokingly.

"Your horse has been ridden hard," Urnan said.

"I took a few men around behind Galar's position," Jonathan said. "He has extended himself by marching this far into Judah. He's left behind a rear guard, but it's a unit composed of older men and those who are ill or wounded. I advised my father that we could destroy it with one quick night march and leave Galar isolated."

"And?" Urnan asked.

"And my father said that we have the advantage of the ground here, that we know the country better than Galar, and that we must not squander our energies."

"You don't agree?" Eri asked.

"Who am I to question the tactics of Saul?" Jonathan asked. "He has the fruit on the tree to prove the wisdom of his leadership."

The three friends lapsed into a comfortable silence.

The sound of a shofar arose from the Hebrew camp. Echoes rang on the warm, still air. Urnan closed his eyes again.

"In God's name," Eri said quietly.

A solitary warrior was standing on the ridge of the opposing slope.

"Look," Eri said.

Urnan opened one eye, followed Eri's pointing finger, and sat up abruptly.

The man was no ordinary Philistine, although his uniform was that of a heavy infantryman—kilt, breastplate, brass greaves, shield, ribbed and tasseled helmet. And a spear like nothing they had ever seen.

"Not much left of the tree from which that weapon was made," Jonathan said in awe as he stared at the spear, which was as thick as a sapling and was capped by a huge, sharp, fearsome iron tip that gleamed in the afternoon sun.

"Is he as big as he looks?" Eri asked.

"Bigger," Urnan said.

"Taller by half than even Saul himself," Jonathan said.

"I would bet that it takes more than one man just to carry his armor," Urnan said.

Suddenly the giant spoke. His voice matched his stature. Big, deep, commanding, it reverberated from every rocky slope.

"Men of Israel. Pigs of the hills," the giant roared, brandishing his huge spear. "Hear me. I am Goliath. Goliath of Gath. I come with a challenge to you. Send your champion. Send your bravest and strongest man to do combat with me. From this single combat will come victory for either the Army of the Five Cities or the rabble of Saul."

"Oh ho," Urnan said.

"Is there a pig of the hills who has not the heart of a slut of a Hebrew woman?" the giant demanded in his thunderous voice.

So loud and powerful was Goliath's challenge that within moments several hundred soldiers of Saul's army stood on the crest of the ridge, watching as the giant

paced back and forth, back and forth, his strides long
and ponderous. So imposing was Goliath's bulk that Eri
expected to hear a thud of contact each time his sandaled foot touched the ground.

"I see you, pigs of the hills. But I see no man who
will face me," Goliath roared.

On the crest of the hill there was a stir. The soldiers
parted to reveal Saul, standing tall and proud in his
armor, sword ready at his side.

"I like this not," Jonathan said, rising quickly.

Urnan and Eri followed the king's son as he
climbed to the top of the ridge. Goliath of Gath continued to roar out his insults and challenge.

"Big, isn't he?" Saul asked when they reached his
side.

"I suggest that we send a phalanx of archers down
the hill to see if they can find a crease in his armor,"
Jonathan said.

"No, that won't do," Saul said quickly. He waved
his hand toward his troops. "Look at their faces."

Some of the men were terrified; others gaped in
awe.

"It has taken me years to teach them that they are
more than the equal of any Philistine," Saul said. "If
this challenge is not met they will see this giant in every
Philistine infantryman they face."

"Then I will meet this boastful heathen," Jonathan
said.

"Not you," Saul said.

"And not you," Jonathan said to his father.

"Who else but me?" Saul asked.

"It's true, Father, that you are the greatest among
us both in courage and in strength, but you must consider what would happen should, by some chance of
fate, the Philistine best you."

Saul kept his eyes on Goliath. "See how he moves.
His strength does not match his great size. He is slow,
overburdened by his armor and his weapons."

"I have no doubt that you could kill him," Urnan
said, "but Jonathan is right. You are the heart and soul
of this army, sire, and if your foot should slip at the

wrong time or if the fates were unfavorable, losing you would accomplish exactly what this big Philistine promises, defeat for the Army of Israel. Look at them." He waved his hand to indicate the soldiers who were still gaping fearfully at the Philistine.

"Then they would not stop running until they reached the hills of Benjamin, and the Philistines would drag them out of their holes one by one," Jonathan said. "It must not be you."

"Who, then?" Saul asked, recognizing the wisdom of his son's words.

"As you say, the Philistine is slow and clumsy. There must be a man agile enough and brave enough to find his weakness."

Saul nodded. He cupped his hands to his mouth and bellowed, "Hear me, men of Israel. This I promise you. To the man who silences the Philistine jackal who howls in the valley will be given great riches. He will be given one of my daughters in marriage, and his house will be free in Israel to the end of his days."

The soldiers looked at Saul, then looked away guiltily.

"There will be no volunteer this day," Eri said.

"Don't look at me," Urnan said with a wry smile. "I am a craftsman, not a warrior."

Goliath of Gath paced back and forth, repeating his challenge, salting it with stinging insults. When at last the sun was just above the western hills, he slowly climbed the slope and disappeared. The soldiers of Saul stood staring after him for a long time before turning to go back to their tents. They walked with their heads down, not daring to look at one another.

CHAPTER
TEN

Near Bethlehem, in the house of Jesse, there was much prayer. The Philistine beast was loose in the land and Jesse, a man of God, knew full well that a rift existed between Samuel and Saul, the only man who stood between the enemy and his home and his flocks. The good man prayed for the king and asked God to give strength to his arm and courage to his heart, but he also prayed for Samuel.

According to stories brought by travelers from Benjamin, Saul had usurped the ordained function of the priest by offering sacrifice himself when Samuel was late; moreover, Saul had disobeyed Samuel's injunction to destroy everything that lived in the lands of the Amalekites. But Jesse was not convinced that Saul had deliberately abandoned God. Nor did he believe that God had abandoned the king. If God were against Saul, how then had Saul defeated the mighty Philistine army at Michmash? Samuel was a prophet, and beloved of

68

God, but he was only a man and man could err in his judgment.

Hadn't Samuel shown very odd behavior when he visited Jesse's house? One by one the priest had called Jesse's strong sons before him. None of the three seemed to please him. After questioning, Jesse admitted that he had one other son, a boy who was tending the flocks.

"Fetch him," Samuel had said.

Jesse knew that his son, David, was of a beautiful countenance, and ruddy with health, but he *was* only a boy. Why, then, had the priest lifted a horn of oil and anointed David as if he were choosing the boy for some purpose known only to himself and, perhaps, to God?

So it was that Jesse prayed for the king and the army and for his three sons who were with Saul at Shocho.

He longed for word of his sons' welfare. Calling David before him, he said, "I fear that your brothers did not take adequate bedding for the cold of night. Go to Shocho and deliver warm fleeces to each of them."

"I will do as you wish, Father," David said, trying to hide his elation.

"But you must return immediately," Jesse said, "bringing me word of your brothers."

"I will," David said, but in his heart he hoped that there might be something, such as the start of a great battle, to give him an excuse to stay.

He packed the fleeces, along with bread, dates, and cheese, on the back of a donkey. His muscular, sun-browned legs bore him swiftly toward the west. He arrived at Saul's encampment just as Goliath of Gath positioned himself beside the dry streambed that cut through the valley of Shocho and began his daily series of taunts and insults. David secured the donkey and climbed to the crest of the ridge to see what was happening. Standing among the soldiers, he looked down into the valley in wonder.

He had never seen so huge a man. The Philistine's biceps were as thick as David's waist. He listened in disbelief as the kilted warrior insulted not only the men of the army but all of Israel's women. When the heathen began to blaspheme against God, he felt his face flush. Expecting someone to move quickly to meet the Philistine's challenge, he looked around. He saw only fear and gloom.

When he could stand it no longer, he went down into the camp, his face burning with shame for his people. He looked up when he heard his name being called and saw the familiar face of Eri.

"As I remember," Eri said, "the king ordered you to go to your father's house and stay until the battle was over."

David smiled. "My king ordered me to my father's house, true, but he did not say for how long. I am here on the orders of my father, to bring warm night cloaks to my brothers."

"I would imagine that they're up on the ridge watching the daily exhibition by the great Goliath," Eri said.

"Why aren't you?"

"I've seen it before," Eri said. "The man has a small imagination. When you've heard his stock of insults once, that's enough. He tends to repeat himself."

"Yet no one goes into the valley to stop him?" David said.

"It's true that there have been no volunteers yet," Eri said, "but there will be. Saul has made the prospect attractive. The man who kills the giant will be showered with gold. He will marry one of Saul's daughters, and his house will be free forevermore in the house of Israel."

"He will pay no taxes?" David asked.

"That's the promise of the king."

David stared thoughtfully for a moment before his brothers appeared. Shammah, next youngest to David, asked, "Have you seen the giant who defies Israel?"

"I have," David said. "What will be given to the man who slays him?"

"The king is willing to pay much gold to the man who kills him," Shammah said. "And he will give the hero one of his daughters as a wife and make his house free of taxes in Israel."

Eliab, the oldest brother, interrupted. "Why are you here, David? What about our father's sheep?"

"I have left the flocks in the care of a keeper and brought warm night cloaks for all of you." He turned as Urnan joined the group and accepted the smith's clasp of his shoulders in greeting.

"Urnan," David asked, "is it true what they say will be done for the man who slays the giant?"

"Gold," Urnan said. "A princess of Israel for a wife, and a tax-free house forever."

"Who is this uncircumcised Philistine, that he should be allowed to continue to defy the army of the living God?" David demanded. Eri lifted his eyebrows at the vehemence of David's response.

"David," said Eliab, his brother, "you must get yourself back to the flocks."

"I must see the king," David said, turning and running toward Saul's tent.

He looked very young, even younger than he really was, as he stood before the king and bowed his head in respect.

"You have disobeyed me," Saul said.

"Not so, sire," David said, "for I have obeyed my father, and what did I hear even as I arrived but blasphemy against God and calumny against Israel and all of her people?"

Saul nodded, then cast a glance at Abner, his army commander.

"No soldier of the one God should fear this Philistine," David said.

Saul lifted his eyes toward heaven, holding his tongue. Too many days had passed, and unless something was done quickly the army was going to melt away in the night as men ran in fear from the Philistine might embodied in Goliath.

David looked angry and determined. "I have decided, sire, to kill this Philistine," he said.

Saul's head jerked down. "You're just a boy. Not only is Goliath a giant, he has been a man of war from his youth." The king shook his head. "What you ask is not only foolish, it is impossible."

David lowered his head in dejection. The king stepped forward and put his hand on David's shoulder. "When you are a man you will fight as a man. Now you are a boy, and dear to me as a son. I would miss your face and your songs."

"Sire," David began, but Saul raised his hand to silence him.

"Go back to your brothers and make your farewells," Saul said, "then return to the safety of your father's house."

Eri stepped forward. "Once when I was traveling in Judah with Sarah, I watched from a hilltop while a boy killed a lion. That boy, younger than this one who walks so sadly away from you, was armed with nothing more than a shepherd's staff. If someone had asked me if I thought such a lad could kill a lion I would have said that it was not only a foolish but an impossible idea."

"Was it David?" Saul asked, looking at Eri.

Eri nodded. "He seized the lion by his mane and slew him."

A dark anger flashed in Saul's eyes. Eri recognized the signs of an emotional storm in the making and fell silent, following David out of the tent.

When they were gone Abner put his hand on Saul's shoulder. "Letting the boy fight the Philistine would serve a purpose," he began. He stepped back as Saul's eyes flashed. "Wait, listen to me," he said cautiously. "The whole army is ready to flee from this one man, but here is a mere boy willing to stand up to him. Losing a lad as talented as David would be sad, but perhaps it would be for the good of all Israel."

"I will not risk him," Saul said. Every muscle in his body was tensed.

"Saul, my cousin," Abner said, "in every battle you send men forward to die, because that is your duty. If by sending this boy to die on Goliath's great spear you put heart into this army, if his death shames some seasoned warrior into marching down the slope to slay the giant, perhaps that would be God's will."

Saul was weeping silently. "It's hard, Abner," he said.

The general nodded. "I will summon David."

"You will wear my own armor," Saul said to David.

"Thank you, sire," David whispered.

The king himself helped dress David in the royal armor, placing a brass helmet on his head. David lifted the king's sword and hefted it. "Sire," he said, "I cannot go into battle weighted down with all this."

He removed the armor and handed the helmet back to Saul. "The Lord delivered me from the danger of the lion's paw," he said, "and from the jaws of the bear. He will keep me safe from harm as I face this Philistine."

Tears ran down Saul's cheeks, but he made no move to stop the boy who walked proudly toward the top of the ridge. Saul had hoped against hope that God's hand was in this, that David was a messenger from Yahweh and held God's righteous power in his hand, but not even Yahweh would send an unarmed boy against such a terrible enemy. Still, Saul did nothing, for he knew that Abner was right: David was to be a sacrifice on the altar of Israel. His death would buy courage for the army.

Goliath was still bellowing and ranting when David, his staff in hand, reached the top of the ridge. The shepherd wore only his short mantle over a gray tunic. He ran lightly down the hill and reached the dry streambed, bent, chose five stones that had been smoothed into roundness by eons of running water, and put them into a leather bag at his waist. Carrying his staff, he advanced toward the Philistine.

Goliath lumbered toward the center of the valley, his lips parted in a snarl of anticipation. When he was close enough to see David's face, he halted. "In the name of Dagon, god of all, have they sent a boy against me?" he thundered. He raised his head and shouted insults at the Hebrews lined up on the crest of the ridge.

David stood silently. Even at a distance of fifty

paces, the giant was a fearsome bulk outlined against the sky.

"Well, boy," Goliath said, "since you seem to think that I am a dog to be beaten with a stave, I must kill you, I suppose, although I would prefer that it be the bones of the one who calls himself king of the pigs of the hills that I leave to the fowl of the air and the carrion-eating beasts."

So saying, Goliath moved forward with surprising speed, lifting his great sword. Behind him, from their side of the valley, the hordes of the Army of the Five Cities shouted for blood, but from the onlooking men of Saul's army, there was only an eerie silence.

David had more than the staff. He had his faith—and that, coupled with the arrogant confidence of youth and the strength he gained from his indignation toward the giant who dared mock the God of Israel, was an advantage not taken into account by the Philistines who were so certain of victory.

As the giant plodded toward David his footsteps seemed to shake the ground. He growled low in his throat like an animal. David gave no ground; with casual slowness he knelt to lay his staff down. Straightening, he opened the leather bag that was hanging at his waist and took out a shepherd's weapon, the sling he had used to protect his flock. He glanced up and squinted, studying the scowl on the face of the approaching giant. He calmly fingered the smooth stones he had taken from the bed of the dry stream, selected the best, and held it up between thumb and forefinger to examine it. Satisfied, he dropped the stone in the leather pouch of the weapon and hefted it to test the balance.

Meanwhile, with great strides, Goliath was rapidly closing the distance between them. The men of both armies were silent, waiting for the boy to turn and run. They gasped in amazement when, instead of fleeing, David began to run forward, whirling his sling in a circle over his head. At a distance of no more than ten paces from the giant he let the smooth stone fly.

Goliath, puzzled by what seemed an irrational action, lifted his great sword. A laugh rumbled upward from his massive chest, only to turn into a choking rattle as David's stone sank deeply into his broad forehead just below the protective brim of his helmet. The giant swayed like one of the great cedars of the northern mountains in a windstorm, then fell slowly, so slowly. The sound of his armor-clad body crashing to the hard earth seemed even louder in the hush that had fallen over the opposing armies.

Unbelieving, the men of both armies waited for Goliath to rise and smash the upstart boy. Instead, David walked over to the giant's body, bent down, lifted Goliath's great, gleaming sword, and hoisted it with both hands.

"Ahhhhh," moaned the host of the Philistines as the blade arced down. "No!" they cried as Goliath's head, severed from his body, rolled along the ground. David removed the giant's helmet, dug his fingers into the sweaty, tangled hair, and lifted the blood-soaked head high in the air.

From the Army of Israel came a roar, and men sprang down the slope screaming war in the name of God and country. Israel and Judah fought together, smashing into the massed Philistine forces atop the opposite ridge and pounding them mercilessly. Before Galar could bring his chariots and cavalry into position the Army of the Five Cities was in flight.

Long after the battle, when the exhausted men of Israel returned from chasing the fleeing Philistines, David found the king standing with Abner.

"Sire, I have put the armor of the Philistine in my brothers' tent," David said. "I pray that this meets with your approval."

"It is yours by right of conquest," Saul said, studying David. Goliath's severed head, almost as large as David's torso, dangled from the boy's right hand, dragging on the ground.

"So does death come to one who mocks the One God," David said, lifting the head and then letting it fall heavily to the dust.

"Go wash," Saul said, "and then come to my tent

for your evening meal, for this day you have served Israel well."

When David was out of hearing Saul turned to Abner. "In truth, who is this boy?" he asked in awe.

"He is the son of Jesse," Abner said.

Saul shook his head. "That I know. But who has sent him to us?"

CHAPTER ELEVEN

The great city of Waset, where the priests of Amon ruled, was three-quarters of the distance between Paynozem's court in Zoan, in the delta, and the First Cataract of the Nile. Paynozem had traveled that length of river once before, going north to meet his bride and, he thought at the time, to reunite the Two Lands; on that voyage the current of the great river had given speed to the royal barge. Now, as he journeyed southward to visit his brother in Waset, sail power and the muscle power of slaves battled the force of the waters that gave Egypt life. When one traveled upstream the days were long.

At the great bend the Nile swept eastward toward the sea, only to turn abruptly away. The narrow, fertile bands of green on either bank expanded into what was, for that often harsh land, a broad and beautiful plain. The royal barge steered to the western bank, where it was moored while preparations were made for Paynozem to enter the city. The king had forgotten the splendor of the sacred architecture that lined both sides of the river. Compared to this seat of southern power, his own court at Zoan was paltry. He felt a growing resentment. Why had he abandoned the ancient glory of the Southern City, the place of his birth?

To Paynozem's distress, he had to wait two days for the arrival of the cargo barges carrying the royal chariots; the splendidly matched horses to pull them; the carefully chosen bodyguard of men, all of one height and size; the gifts for his brother and his cousin; the offerings to Amon, god of the city. So he was pleased when Kemose appeared beside the moored barge early in the morning, without any warning. Their meeting was one of brothers, not of rulers of competing kingdoms. They shared fruit and meat and saluted each other with the strong beer of the south as they lifted golden goblets.

"While I recognize the need for ceremony and pomp to befit a visiting king," Kemose said with a smile, "I must admit, brother, that I could not contain my curiosity and my need to see your face."

"I, too, was impatient," Paynozem said, "not only to see your face and the face of my cousin Tania, but to see the city."

Kemose nodded. "Perhaps a quiet tour, brother, in anonymity?"

Paynozem smiled, remembering how it had been when they were boys conspiring together to outwit the surveillance of the palace servants. "Do we dare?"

"Kings can dare anything," Kemose said.

The two rulers made only a token attempt at disguise, and no one who saw them rumbling through the streets and along the great avenues of the city doubted that they were men of greatness and power. With Kemose holding the reins of a chariot bedecked with the insignia of an officer of the Army of Amon, they rode along the long avenue of ram-headed sphinxes from the northern temple complex. Between the paws of each sphinx was a statue of the third Amenhotep, the great builder. Massive pylons inlaid with gold, silver, and malachite served as a backdrop for a portrait colossus of the ancient king that towered tall without reaching the height of the obelisks gleaming in gilded splendor.

The brilliant sunlight emphasized the beauty of the bright, polychrome decorations of the temples and made the carved inscriptions on gates, columns, walls, and pylons stand out in greater relief.

With only a half-dozen attendants the brothers boarded boats and returned to the western bank, where, to show off the greatness of the city's past, Kemose directed the boatmen to land them on the causeway leading up to Amenhotep's funerary temple. There, twin seated colossi guarded the architectural tribute to the great king's memory.

The brothers were silent, each deep in his own thoughts, as they stood before the images of Amenhotep. Kemose, glancing at his brother, saw on his face a look of awe. Perhaps, Kemose thought, his strategy of exposing Paynozem anew to the consecrated monuments to those who had gone before was accomplishing the intended purpose—reminding Paynozem of his obligations to Egypt.

Beyond the temple rose the stark and barren hills wherein lay the looted tombs of Amenhotep III and other great kings of the past. Those empty tombs, Kemose knew, belied the surface glory of the stone monuments. In a time of anarchy and chaos the priests had lost control of the royal necropolis in the valley behind the cliffs. Kemose himself had seen the results, had participated in the removal of the mutilated and looted mummies of kings to another, safer site. He remembered well his anger and frustration when he had first entered a sacred tomb and seen the barbaric, unthinking destruction by criminal looters of the tombs of gods who had once walked the earth.

The history of the Two Lands was long. Periods of greatness and decline alternated. Great kings such as Menes, Ahmose, Amenhotep III, and Ramses II had lifted the nation to sublime heights only to be followed by weak kings who were overwhelmed either by alien hordes or by the greed of ruthless power-seekers from within.

More than anything Kemose wanted to see the Two Lands reunited, to see the twin crowns resting securely on the head of one man, a man of wisdom and strength. He knew that Paynozem was not that man, and he was honest in admitting to himself that, in all probability, neither was he. Eternity was long and the gods were patient. Perhaps it would be Paynozem's son, or his grandson. Perhaps it would be his nephew Kaptar who would grow into the warrior king and merge the Two Lands into a great empire once more.

Kemose had faith that one day a great king would not only leave the hands of the Libyans of Lower Egypt to rot in the sun, but would march out of the Nile valley to eliminate once and for all the Libyan threat. Such a man would ascend the Nile past the cataracts and restore Nubia to its rightful place as an Egyptian province, and he would punish the petty kings and the remnants of the Peleset who pretended to be the equals of the kings of Egypt while ruling over their flimsy little satrapies in Canaan and Syria, lands that, like Libya and Nubia, had been given to Egyptian rule by the gods themselves.

Tired, the brothers returned to the royal barge at twilight. The heat of the day had dampened their clothing, and the desert winds on the western bank of the river had ground sand into their skin. Kemose accepted his brother's invitation to freshen himself. He admired the beauty of the Libyan slave girls who assisted him, but refrained from accepting their giggling invitations to pleasure. Dressed in royal linen from Paynozem's own wardrobe, he joined his brother on the foredeck where the evening meal was served under the stars. They ate heartily, drank deeply, and lounged back in casual fellowship, sated, comfortable in the coolness of the evening.

"Although it has pleased me greatly to see you again," Kemose said, "I must confess that I harbor great curiosity about the purpose of your visit."

Paynozem raised himself to one elbow on his couch. "I had thought, brother," he said, "to discuss the future of the Two Lands in the presence of learned advisers, but perhaps it would be best, after all, if I test your feeling in private."

Kemose nodded, but flags of warning were going up

in his mind. A subtle change in tone of voice indicated that the man had ceased to speak as a sibling and was now the king.

"You are aware, I'm sure—no one is more cognizant of the state of affairs than I—that the local lords in the Libyan nomes south of my capital and around the great oasis hold enough power to sever the delta from Upper Egypt."

Kemose spoke carefully. "I do not spy on my brother, but, yes, I have heard that the Libyans hold the balance of power in Lower Egypt. I have heard, indeed, that they control your army."

"Not entirely," Paynozem said.

"Why, then," Kemose asked, "does your bodyguard not wear the insignia of the Army of Lower Egypt?"

"You press me," Paynozem said testily.

"That was not my intention. I am merely discussing a subject you yourself began."

"I have troops loyal to me who can keep the lower delta and my capital safe," Paynozem said.

"But then there would be a hostile nation ruled by Libyan lords—led, most probably, by Buyuwawa and his son Musen—between us," Kemose said.

"I fear so." Paynozem leaned forward and spoke earnestly. "I erred when I moved the throne to the delta, brother. I should have stayed here, at the seat of power. We should have fought side by side, as brothers and not rivals, against the foreigners." He held out both hands to Kemose. "But perhaps it is not too late."

"You have come to propose war?"

"First things first," Paynozem said. "Would you consider a coregency, brother? You and I side by side on the throne of the Two Lands?"

"I would consider traveling to the netherworld if it reunited Egypt and returned her to her former greatness," Kemose said with emotion. "You propose war, then. I from the south and you from the north against the Libyans."

"Yes, war in the end," Paynozem said, "but not with careless haste. The Libyans are strong. If we are to have a chance of winning, of driving them back to their sand burrows in the western deserts, I must first regain control of my own army."

"How do you propose to do that?"

"It will be a slow and careful process. I will gradually move officers loyal to the throne into positions of authority, while leaving Musen in command. I will shift units made up solely of Libyan mercenaries into areas where they will be least effective and most vulnerable."

"This sounds like the work of years," Kemose said.

"The sphinx does not measure time," Paynozem said. "He endures, as Egypt has outlasted the Asiatic shepherds and Syrians and the greed and ambition of traitorous nobles, and as it will outlast this latest threat."

"Perhaps my *ka* will live as long as the sphinx," Kemose said. "My flesh will not. If you do not propose war against the Libyans, what?"

Paynozem stood and began to pace the deck of the royal barge. Finally he turned to face Kemose. His anxious face was illuminated by torches. "The first step is to lull the Libyans into complacency. For this purpose I propose an alliance with them."

Kemose chewed his lower lip thoughtfully.

"An alliance by marriage," Paynozem continued, "the purpose of which is to make Buyuwawa and Musen believe that I am stupid enough to give Musen access to the throne through the blood of our royal family."

"If you plan to give one of your daughters to this Libyan, why did you feel it necessary to consult me?" Kemose asked.

"It is not my daughter that I have in mind."

Kemose, guessing the identity of the proposed bride, protested, "You must be jesting."

"I do not jest about such serious matters. I propose that both Upper and Lower Egypt put out a hand in friendship to the Libyans by giving Musen the hand of our cousin, Tania, the granddaughter of our father's brother, in marriage."

Kemose laughed heartily. "I want to be present, brother, when you suggest this madness to Tania. Have you forgotten that our little cousin has a sting like the horned asp of the desert sands?"

CHAPTER TWELVE

Musen arrived on the outskirts of the Southern City just ahead of the cargo boats. His barge was only slightly less ornate and luxurious than that of Paynozem. In the royal procession that wound its way through curious crowds to the palace, Musen rode just behind the king in a chariot designed not for ceremony but for war, a fact Kemose did not fail to note as he waited on a dais to greet the king and offer him the blessing of Amon. Nor did he miss the fact that Musen's escort was a small but impressive group of well-trained and superbly armed Libyans.

Paynozem's royal guard was composed of hand-picked Egyptians whose height did not vary more than a finger's width. They marched smartly with shields and short spears held at salute toward Kemose.

Kemose had made it a point to have his own palace guard dressed in battle gear, not the ornate and decorative uniforms of ceremony; and once the visitors had been greeted and given thronelike seats on the platform before the palace, Kemose gave the signal to his army commander to begin a show of strength for the benefit of the visitors.

With rumbling wheels and flashing, knife-studded spokes, war chariots burst into the huge square two abreast to roar past the platform in what seemed to be endless profusion. Behind them came horsemen leading precisely marching hosts of tawny-skinned Egyptian infantry. It could have been a scene painted on the wall of the tomb of one of the great kings, for men such as these had established the empire.

Kemose leaned toward his brother. "Such men have marched to the far reaches of Nubia and Syria," he said, loud enough for Musen to hear. "And will again," he added after a significant pause.

To the left of Kemose sat Tania, dressed in a brilliant white pleated gown that emphasized the sable blackness of her hair and her kohl-accented eyes. At her side, looking on in awe at the pomp and ceremony, was Prince Kaptar, also dressed in white, his short kilt showing his sturdy legs. At his waist, pressing against the birthmark on his hip in the shape of a lion's paw, hung the short sword he had made himself.

Kaptar, like Kemose, had examined the northerners carefully, and he was not impressed. His uncle Kemose, he felt, was a much more striking man than Paynozem; and he didn't like the sharp-faced countenance of the Libyan. As for their display of military precision, any unit picked at random from the ranks of his uncle's Army of Amon could readily match the visitor's carefully chosen troops.

The sun made an arc in the sky equal to two spans of an outstretched hand before the last soldiers of the Army of Amon marched out of the square to resounding cheers from the huge crowd. At a signal from Kemose, slaves with litter chairs ran forward and a new procession was formed to carry the visitors to the temple of Amon to pay due respect to the god. As high priest Kemose officiated in the ceremony.

At the end of a long day governed by strict protocol, when the visitors were lodged in a section of the palace reserved for distinguished guests, Kemose walked through darkened corridors to the women's quarters and presented himself to Tania.

Tania had changed into a filmy nightdress that showed the dark orbs at the tips of her breasts and the womanly vee below. A handmaiden was brushing her hair. Her son, Kaptar, without his sword but still wearing his ceremonial kilt, lounged on her bed, chattering away in excitement about the day's events.

"I have been expecting you, Kemose," Tania said.

Kemose knew that what he had to say would not please his cousin, and, in truth, he dreaded her reaction. He had always been fond of the youngest member of his family. He knew her well, and he respected her fire and her intelligence. He had given her in marriage to a man who had been his best friend, the Mesopotamian armorer, Urnan, with whom he had escaped slavery, traveled the northern sea, and worked to arm loyal Egyptians. Ironic that Urnan had been deported from Egypt by the very men, his brother and the Libyan, who now came to ask that Urnan's wife be united in marriage with Musen.

"I gather that the Libyan worm has inched himself into a position of power in my cousin's court in the north," Tania said.

"He has," Kemose said.

"And I would guess that this state visit is not merely a social occasion, nor would your brother make the long journey from the delta because of desire to see his beloved family."

"The Libyan has shifty eyes," Kaptar piped up.

"Speak when you are spoken to," Tania said quickly but not unkindly.

"The boy is a good judge of character," Kemose said.

"There is something on your mind," Tania said.

"My brother has come to me with two proposals, one overt and one covert."

"And they are?" Tania asked.

"In private, he has told me that he desires the reunification of the Two Lands, and we have discussed means of accomplishing that goal."

"A worthy ambition," Tania said, her voice rich with sarcasm. "He wants to wear the double crown himself, of course."

"Since our desires will not be achieved today or tomorrow we can only pray to Amon that he who rules a nation made one again will carry our own blood, be he Paynozem's son or—" He did not finish the thought.

Tania looked quickly at Kaptar. The blood of the royal house flowed in his veins.

"Possibly," Kemose said, nodding.

"I think I understand now why your brother brought the Libyan with him," Tania said. "He could hardly be suspected of plotting with you against Buyuwawa with Musen along to keep an eye on him, could he?"

"About the other request," Kemose said. "I have tried to find a reason for denying it, but try as I might I cannot come up with a diplomatic way. My impulse is to tell Paynozem and Musen to take their carefully drilled little escorts, their gifts, and their gold-covered barges and go as swiftly as possible to either Lower Egypt or the nether regions, whichever is nearest."

"As bad as that?"

"I'll let you judge, cousin," Kemose said. "Paynozem asks your hand in marriage."

Tania made a face of disgust. "Paynozem chose to secure his little throne in the north by marrying the daughter of Pesibkhenno," she said. "Does he think now to seize power in Upper Egypt in a manner which did not work well for him in the north?"

"He asks your hand not for himself," Kemose said. He prepared for the explosion.

Kaptar knew what he meant and immediately leaped from the bed with an angry oath.

"I will not have such language," Tania said calmly.

"How dare he ask you to become the wife of that Libyan pig?" Kaptar shouted.

.

"Patience, my young warrior. I have said that I wish to refuse," Kemose said.

"Don't be hasty," Tania said softly.

Kemose stared at her in surprise.

"That Libyan pig tried to kill my father," Kaptar said, aiming an angry kick at the chair. "And Paynozem sent him into forced exile."

Tania said, "All that is true."

"He hurt you," Kaptar said, his face flushed with anger.

"It was not more than I could bear," Tania said.

"Mother, I will not allow you to even consider such an abhorrent act," Kaptar said. "In two years I will be a man. Then I will kill Musen myself."

Tania put her hands on her son's shoulders. "You may, you may indeed, but in the meantime, my young warrior who killed a lion . . ."

Kaptar would not listen. With one angry look at his mother he ran out of the room.

Kemose couldn't take his eyes off Tania. He felt as if he were looking into the eyes of the jackal god, the prince of the dead. She smiled a dark smile.

"Do not think I have forgotten. In the night, when sleep does not favor me, I remember all the pain Musen caused me when he broke into our house and tortured and threatened me, and the grief I felt when I learned I would never see Urnan again."

Her dark eyes glittered with a hard light. "I have prayed to the gods to send me an opportunity to avenge myself on Musen. Now it has come. If we are ever to reunite Egypt under a line of kings from our bloodline, would it not be helpful to have a spy not only in the enemy camp, but in his bed?"

"You would do this for your country?" Kemose asked, astounded. This was a side to his cousin's character that he had never suspected.

"Not only for my country," she hissed. "For myself." She laughed, and the sound sent shivers down Kemose's spine. "I will not kill him, not for a long time. Not until I have given him pain and humiliation many times greater than that which he caused me."

*   *   *

The announcement of the impending union between a princess of Upper Egypt and Lord Musen was
the occasion for a night of drinking, eating, and enter-
tainment lively enough to engage the interest of even a
jaded king.

Kaptar, dressed as a prince, the braided wisp of
hair that was the symbol of young royalty hanging from
one side of his shaved head, watched in horror as his
mother fawned over the bearded, swarthy Libyan who
sat by the side of King Paynozem as if he were of equal
rank.

In the following days, while the court prepared for
the wedding, Kaptar absented himself from the palace,
but he was at the temple to watch his uncle perform the
ceremony that, in his mind, cost him his mother.

As he watched, his shame grew. He had tried to
convince himself that it was patriotic and brave of Tania
to sacrifice her honor on the filthy altar of the Libyan's
desires, but he couldn't. Tania was his mother. It was
one thing for a beautiful princess of Egypt to take a
handsome young courtier to her bed. Such freedom for
pleasure was the right of a royal princess without a husband, but to allow the swarthy, foreign pig of a man who
had cruelly deprived Kaptar of his father into her bed
was too much to bear.

Kaptar had been told that he was expected to accompany his mother to the city of On, where Buyuwawa
ruled in defiance of Paynozem. That, he decided, he
could not do.

"My mother is dead," he whispered to himself in
the dark of night, fighting back his tears. Even now he
knew that his mother was nude in the arms of the hated
Libyan. He imagined her, with long, lovely limbs, flat
stomach a plane leading down to her dark femininity,
breasts as firm and shapely as those of the young girls in
the women's quarters. His anger threatened to boil over
when he thought of her loveliness exposed to the eyes of
the Libyan barbarian. He ran to his quarters, where he
packed a few necessities, put on the rough garments he
wore when he worked in the forge, and strapped his

sword to his side. As a last act he hacked the royal braid from the side of his head.

The night was far gone as he made his way through quiet, deserted streets, finally taking shelter in a mud-brick shed on the waterfront to wait for dawn. He was awakened by the arrival of workmen crying out to each other and the sound of cargo being loaded onto a dhow at the docks. He shivered with the morning chill and drew his robe closer. When he stepped out of the shed he came face to face with two rivermen.

"What have we here?" the larger of the men asked, with a smirk that showed blackened teeth.

"You carry a fine sword, young master," the other man said, wiping his nose with the back of his hand. "I'll have it, if you don't mind."

"As it happens I do," Kaptar said, leaping away from the man's outstretched arm. He grabbed the short sword, remembered how he had killed the lion, and went into a fighting crouch.

The larger man pulled a stave from a stack of cargo and raised it. Without hesitation Kaptar darted in and slashed through the thin robe of the attacker. Blood gushed out, and the man dropped his weapon to clutch his belly.

"The motherless one has killed me," he bellowed.

"You'll live," Kaptar said. "Get yourself to a physician soon so that he can stitch you together."

"You will be cursed of the gods," the smaller man said, drawing a long, curved knife from the depths of his robe.

"I have done you no wrong," Kaptar said, backing away. "I ask only that you let me pass."

"You have killed my brother," the man said, feinting with his long knife. As he lunged toward Kaptar's stomach, he found his extended arm spouting blood from a stump where his hand had been. The hand lay on the stone of the quay, the curved knife still clutched in its fingers. The man screamed in shock and fell to the ground.

Drawn by the screams, other workmen appeared.

Kaptar turned to flee, but they blocked his way. His back to the wall, he held his sword at the ready.

A gray-bearded man dressed somewhat better than the others lifted his hands. "Leave the boy alone."

"He's a butcher," someone cried.

"Tend those who are wounded," the graybeard said. "The boy is blameless. I saw what happened. He was attacked by these two brigands."

"You have my gratitude, sir," Kaptar said.

"Come," the old man said. He put his hand on Kaptar's shoulder and led the boy toward the dhow at the wharf.

"This is your boat?" Kaptar asked.

"Thanks to the generosity of the gods."

"And where do you sail?"

"To the south. To the cataracts."

"I have some gold, only a little," Kaptar said. "It is yours if you will allow me to sail with you."

Kaptar's one thought was to put as much distance as possible between him and the mother who had betrayed him and everything she had taught him to believe in. Beyond that his plans were vague. His one wish was that the next two years would pass swiftly. He firmly believed that some magical transformation would come to him when he reached the age of manhood. Then he would go north, find Musen, and kill him.

CHAPTER THIRTEEN

In the open courtyard of the royal palace at Gibeah, Saul sat on a hard bench with his back against a wall. The weather was turning and there was a chill in the air. The sun warmed his face but not his heart. Once again he had driven the kilted hordes of the Philistines back to the coastal plain, but as he sat alone his thoughts were not those of a victor.

The victory in Judah had been complete. The carrion-eaters of the earth and the sky sated themselves on the Philistine dead. The journey of the Army of the Lord northward to the land of Benjamin was a continuous victory march.

After each victorious battle the people lined the streets of towns and villages in the hundreds, cheering the man who, by deed and stature, had earned the right to be called king. Women sang of the mighty Saul who had slain his hundreds, and although Saul had never sought the acclaim of his people, the words were sweet to his ears.

The boy from Benjamin, smallest and poorest of the Twelve Tribes, had not gone into the cities of the Philistines in search of the sacred Ark of the Covenant to attain personal glory. The young man who had led hit-and-run attacks on the Philistines did not fight for fame or for advancement beyond the leadership of those who wished to follow him in his continuing war against the occupying forces. It was true that he had sought out the prophet Samuel, but not in search of a crown; he had offered Samuel silver in exchange for help in finding his father's lost donkeys. Samuel had chosen him to be king. Saul had not asked for the title, nor had he welcomed it.

In the beginning Saul's ambition was limited to serving God, and he felt that he had done so by tricking the Philistines into returning the Ark to Israel. Later he came to believe that through his own actions he could attain freedom for himself, his family, his village, his tribe, and the people of Israel, in that order. He was more than willing—eager, in fact—to admit that he could not have achieved any of his victories without the help of God, for he was a devout man.

There were those, and he suspected that Samuel was among them, who said that he was not as sincere in his worship of the One God as he could have been. Some Yahwehists criticized him for naming one of his sons Esh-baal, which meant "Baal exists," and another Meribbaal, "Baal rewards," but those names were, after all, in the tradition of the land given by God to the descendants of Abraham. As far as Saul was concerned, it was coincidence and the nature of the language, not blasphemous design, that his sons' names contained letters spelling out the name of the ancient and evil idol of the Canaanites.

But it was not because of those names that the king of Israel was in religious exile, cut off from the comfort and support of the priestly establishment and barred by long-haired Samuel from participation in the formal ceremonies of worship. Saul felt that Samuel had personal reasons for undermining the man who had freed Israel from the invaders. While it was true that Samuel was a prophet and beloved of God, he was only a man and, thus, subject to such weaknesses of man as envy and pride. Even while Samuel was anointing and later reconfirming Saul as king, Saul had sensed a certain hesitation in the prophet, a reluctance, perhaps, to abdicate his own position of leadership to a younger man. Certainly, Saul thought, Samuel had overreacted when, for very practical reasons, Saul had spared the life of the Amalekite king and allowed his own soldiers, who had marched long and fought hard, to claim the spoils of victory by sparing the finest animals in the Amalekite herds from Samuel's injunction of death to everything that moved.

Perhaps the prophet had greater reason to be angry when Saul usurped his priestly duties in order to prevent his army from dispersing. Samuel was seven days late for the appointed time to hold a formal sacrifice to the One God, and Saul had performed the ritual himself. But not even that warranted the excommunication of a man who had always served God with all his heart, all his soul, and all the might of his good, right arm.

Saul had never asked to be king, nor had he prayed to God for such distinction, but God had given him the body of a fighting man and the heart to go with it and had rewarded him. It was natural for Saul to want the same distinction for his sons. His dream of an Israel secure within its borders—and those borders were those of old Canaan, the land promised to Abraham by God—was very much alive, in spite of Samuel's continued efforts to shatter that vision. The work yet to be done to assure Israel's heritage required a strong leader. He dreamed less of empire than of a united, secure Israel, and he saw a dynasty established by Saul the Benjamite as a means of guaranteeing the nation's security. If only Samuel's stiff-necked intransigence would not become an obstacle to the ascension to the throne of one of his sons.

Into Saul's dark thoughts, as if sent by the forces of evil or by Samuel himself, came the captain of hundreds, Mered.

"Are you in health?" Saul asked when Mered sat

down on a bench opposite him. Any man who fought
with Saul could sit with him and address him as a military peer, not as royalty.

"Yes. And you, sire?" Mered asked.

Saul did not bother to answer. He merely shrugged
his great shoulders and looked upward into the blue eye
of the sky.

"I have come from Tirzah, in the north," Mered
said.

"And the army?"

"The Philistine is confined to the coastal plains,"
Mered said.

"Bless God," Saul said.

"Even now Abner moves southward with the army,
which is, of course, fading away as the men go to their
homes for the season of cold."

Saul nodded. That was to be expected. With the
spring, after the planting of crops, the soldiers of the
One God would be ready once more to smite the enemy.

"In Tirzah, as in all towns and villages in Israel, the
women sing of the might of Saul."

Saul waved a hand in acknowledgment.

"They say that Saul has slain his thousands,"
Mered said, his pouting lips forming what passed for a
smile. "And that David has slain his ten thousands." He
watched Saul closely for his reaction. His reward was a
convulsive movement of Saul's shoulders and a baleful
glare from suddenly cold eyes.

"The court musician has come far," Mered continued. "It astounded me, sire, that when he decided to
end the boastings of the giant from Gath he was really
no older in age than a child."

"A handsome lad, indeed," Saul said, having
fought down his anger. "He was dwarfed by my armor."

"His shoulders have grown broader," Mered said.
"I sometimes get the idea that he feels the king's armor
would be a better fit now."

Saul frowned. There were times when he wasn't
sure of his feelings for David. He had come to love the
boy as a father loves a son, and to depend on his songs

for ease from his pain, but he, too, had heard the women singing the praises of the boy-man who had killed Goliath and who had quickly become one of the most renowned fighting men in Israel.

"In fact," Mered continued, "if you will forgive me for saying so, sire, I worry that young David harbors dreams not only of marrying a king's daughter or of wearing a king's borrowed armor."

Blackness possessed Saul. It rose up in him in a silent storm, blocking all reason, consuming him. Every muscle in his body tensed.

"You did not see, sire, but I was there, and I saw, how your son, Jonathan, removed his own robe and put it on David's shoulders after the slaying of the giant. It was as if, and I shuddered to think it, your son was offering this callow boy the garments belonging rightfully to the heir to the throne of Israel."

Saul was in torment. He had seen Jonathan's gesture and had been chilled by it, as if it were some evil omen. Day by day he could see the affection between Jonathan and David growing. They were all turning against him, even his firstborn son. But in truth that defection had begun before David appeared at court, when Jonathan had disobeyed the orders of his father and his king not once but twice.

And there was Samuel. Samuel had never been content to step aside and let him rule Israel. From the very beginning the prophet had sent roving bands of religious fanatics to exert pressure on him and keep him subservient to the will of Yahweh as expressed by Yahweh's spokesman on earth, who was, of course, Samuel.

It was obvious to Saul that Samuel did not want to see him bring his work, the unification and strengthening of Israel, to fruition. Saul believed implicitly that God's promised empire would come, and he believed just as strongly that Samuel would do anything within his power not only to prevent Saul from sharing in the glory of Israel's triumph over her enemies but also to bar Saul's sons from the throne.

He thought of David. What sort of man was he, this

killer of lions and Philistine giants who had advanced rapidly from court musician and armor-bearer to national hero and, soon, the son-in-law of a king?

He knew that some people said that David had been sent by God to drive the evil spirit and the demons from the king's soul. David was the shining hero. Saul, a man in the power of devils, was an object of pity.

"First I freed Benjamin and Ephraim from the yoke of the Philistine," Saul said, speaking not to Mered but to the sky, the heavens, to God. "I have molded the Twelve Tribes into a mighty force in the name of God. With God's help and guidance I have brought Israel to the brink of a golden age."

"All that is true," Mered said, nodding.

"And my reward from men is to be cut off from worship of my God, to be mocked by my son, to be betrayed by those whom I have called friend."

Mered put his hand over his heart. "You will always have one friend, sire. To the death, if need be."

"Of all of them I loved him most," Saul said. "I made him an officer. I gave him command of hundreds, and then made him captain over captains. I should have known, when he took my son's robe without question, as if it were his due." He shook his heavily maned head. "I should have known."

"He is popular with the people," Mered said, "and with the priests, as well. He is a devout Yahwehist."

"And who is not?" Saul demanded.

"No one is a more dedicated man of God than you, sire," he said quickly. "And your sons, as well. In fact, because of his deep friendship with David, I would say that Jonathan is more pious than ever." He was silent for a moment. "When David has taken a princess to wife, he will be close to the throne."

And if my son, Jonathan, does not care to fight for his birthright, Saul thought, *he will be very near indeed.*

Saul rose and pulled his robe close. "It is growing cold," he said. He left Mered in the courtyard and went to the throne room, to wallow in his black misery.

Suddenly he heard the sound of trumpets, the mourning, spine-tingling call of rams' horns, the clatter of chariot wheels. He looked up, ready to climb to the ramparts to greet the first of the returning army, then dropped his head in agonized indecision. David and Jonathan would be at the forefront, perhaps riding in the same war chariot, tall and strong, both fair to the eye.

Jonathan who had disobeyed him.

David.

"Saul has slain his thousands, David his ten thousands."

Once again in his memory he saw Jonathan spreading his robe over the shoulders of the boy. In the dark, unreasoning rage that possessed him, he imagined his son and heir allied with the man who had become his most popular general. In that bleak moment it was not beyond his twisted mind to believe that Jonathan and David were plotting against him to seize the throne for themselves and the priests.

What a fool he had been to promise his eldest daughter to David in marriage. How could he avoid fulfilling that promise? *Think,* he told himself. *You cannot allow a traitor to become your son-in-law.* Out of the corner of his eye he caught a flicker of movement and looked up. David and Jonathan stood side by side in the doorway.

"Father," Jonathan said.

To Saul the sound of his son's voice was almost unbearable. His head was one solid mass of pulsating pain. Were they right, those who said that devils possessed the king?

"Sire," said David, standing straight and proud beside Jonathan, "we have cleansed the north of Philistines."

With a hoarse cry of pain and rage Saul seized a javelin from a weapon rack on the wall. With all his mighty power, he hurled it straight at David.

CHAPTER
FOURTEEN

As Sarah's stomach grew, so grew her resentment toward Baalan and the boy, Sunu. Baalan's even-tempered and loving attempts to soothe her merely made her more contemptuous of the slave-girl usurper. It was inevitable that her loathing for Baalan and Sunu would color her feelings toward Eri. Although Eri was a rich and influential man he could never be, in Sarah's eyes, as wealthy and powerful as had been her adoptive father, Raphu. In her childish mind it did not matter that Raphu was dead. Raphu had not married a slave girl; therefore he was superior to Eri. Nor was Eri totally of the blood of Abraham. His mother was Hebrew, but his father was descended from some horrid, foreign race in a distant heathen city.

Still, her child would be Eri's legitimate heir, as she often said to Aiah.

It seemed that Eri was never home. He traveled often to the armory in the desert. If Eri was not coming from or going to his armory he was away in the north or the west with the army commanded by his two friends, Jonathan and David. Although there had been no great pitched battles involving entire armies since the bloody encounter in Judah, the war against the Philistine oppressors went on. To escape Baalan, and the loneliness, Sarah was a constant visitor in the house of Mered.

Mered was a frustrated man. He was still certain that the mighty Army of the Five Cities would be triumphant in the end, but his usefulness to the Philistines had been diminished by events. With the emergence of David as a military leader, Mered's sources of information were no longer as valuable. He still had one advantage. Through the silly child who was married to the armorer, Eri, he had some access to information regarding the movement of the army. By careful questioning, Mered could determine Eri's destination. Sarah was too self-absorbed to be suspicious. In fact, she was pleased by his attention.

It angered him that he did not have a source close to David, and he decided that his interests would best be served by David's death. Knowing Saul's doubts and jealousies he knew his goal was attainable.

If only the king's arm had been more accurate or David had been less agile in evading the iron-tipped javelin, Mered's plan would have worked. So he continued to plant seeds of doubt in Saul's often fevered mind.

Since the incident of the spear David had absented himself from court, although Jonathan had assured him that Saul had not been himself when he attacked him.

One day, Jonathan, fresh from a small victory over the Philistines, brought some spoils in the form of food and golden cups to his father.

"And my general?" Saul asked. "I have not seen his countenance of late."

"David sends his love and his respects," Jonathan said, "and may I take this opportunity to remind you of your promises to him?"

Saul laughed. "What little gold and treasure I could

give him would be dimmed in brightness by that which he wrests from the treasures of the Philistines."

"It is not riches of which I speak," Jonathan said. "Is it not time, Father, to remember that you promised a royal bride to the man who slew Goliath? And David is anxious for his royal bride."

Saul fell silent. His eyes grew black. Mered felt a glow of inward satisfaction that his plan was going so well until Saul nodded. "It is time," he said. "Let it be known that David shall have the hand of my eldest daughter in marriage."

The army was far to the north, engaged in a small clash with a Philistine force, when Saul gave his daughter Merab's hand in marriage to a Meholathite named Adriel. It would be weeks before David heard that the king had broken his word.

CHAPTER FIFTEEN

Urnan returned from a trip into the east, beyond the Jordan, to find the home he shared with Eri and his family abuzz with the news that Saul had broken his promise to David.

"It doesn't seem right," said Baalan angrily. "David delivered Israel from the threat of the giant of Gath, and he has fought so well. The Philistines are no longer free to raid into Israel whenever it pleases them. It was a solemn promise, was it not, that Saul made to the man who killed Goliath?"

"So it seemed," Urnan said.

"When I grow up I'll kill a score of giants," Sunu said, waving a small wooden sword fashioned for him by his doting grandfather.

"Twoscore," Urnan said.

"Maybe even this many." Sunu held up all five fingers of his other hand.

"At least that many," Urnan said. Turning to Baalan, he asked, "How is Sarah?"

Baalan shook her head.

"Still spending most of her time in the house of Mered?"

Baalan shrugged. "I try."

Urnan put a hand on her shoulder. "I know how hard you have tried," he said. "Perhaps she'll act a bit more like an adult when she's a mother."

Baalan nodded. "Father of my husband," she began hesitantly. "I have a small request."

"What is it?" he asked. "I know of no woman who has more right to make requests of me."

"You flatter me."

"Not at all. You have been a good wife. You cared for Sarah when she was helpless. You've given her nothing but love in return for coldness since her recovery. And, most importantly, you've given me a fine grandson." He patted her on the back. "Make your request. I will grant anything within my power."

"I presume too much."

"Let me be the judge of that."

"What I was about to say regards affairs beyond my reach."

"Perhaps beyond mine," Urnan said, "but now you've made me curious."

"I was wondering if perhaps you could speak to the king."

"About what?"

"About David."

"You mean about the king's having broken his promise to David?"

"Yes."

"As a matter of fact, little one, I had halfway determined to do just that without your prodding." Urnan chuckled. "If Saul could hear the women of Israel he would soon realize that David is not without his supporters."

"The king is a man. Even if he did hear the women speaking he would not listen. He will listen to you because you are his friend."

Saul did listen. Urnan and he sat side-by-side on a bench in the sun. First they talked about the continuing war. Urnan reported that the Hebrew cities across the Jordan were very impressed by Saul's having freed Israel of the occupying forces.

"Let them show their approval with more than words," Saul said. "Let them send me men so that we can drive the Philistine into the sea."

"There are many who would fight," Urnan said. "I was told not once but many times that the men of that country would be proud to follow such generals as Saul and Jonathan."

"And David?" Saul asked, turning to glower at Urnan.

"And David," Urnan said.

Saul lifted his face to the sky as if in prayer, but his eyes were open. "I have not kept my word to David."

Urnan made a noncommittal sound. He counted himself a friend to Saul, but one walked softly with Saul lest his shallowly banked temper be kindled into blazing fire.

"Like many others, you think I was wrong?" Saul asked.

"Yes," Urnan said.

"I am troubled," Saul said softly. "What do you think I should do? I can't undo Merab's union with the man from Meholah."

From behind them a sweet, feminine voice spoke. "You have another daughter."

Both men turned quickly to see Michal, resplendent in blue linen, dark of hair, smooth-skinned, almond-eyed, fair of face. Her full lips had a natural tint of red, and they were smiling teasingly.

"Did you not hear me, Father?" she asked.

"I heard." Saul ran his fingers through his beard. "Why do you remind me of the obvious? Are you suggesting that you would take David as a husband?"

"From the time I first saw him, from the time I first heard his voice lifted in song, I imagined that I would be his and he mine."

"You are young," Saul said.

"Old enough to be a wife, according to the laws."

"We will speak no more of this passing fancy," Saul said.

"Please, Father," Michal said softly. "It is no fancy, for I do love him."

Saul's face darkened. Seeing it, Michal bowed to him, then backed away and into the palace.

"What say you?" Saul growled to Urnan.

Urnan shrugged. "She is your daughter, sire. It is your promise that is at stake."

Saul rose and paced back and forth on the stone pavement. As he walked, hands behind his back, Mered appeared and saluted him.

"Hold," Saul said.

Mered stopped and bowed. "Sire?"

"It has been suggested that I give my younger daughter, Michal, to David as a wife."

Mered nodded.

"Don't stand there silent, man," Saul bellowed.

"I was not aware, sire, that you were asking my opinion," Mered answered.

"What say you?"

"That would be one way of making good on your promise," Mered said.

Saul glowered. "Leave me," he said, "both of you." He held out his hand toward Urnan. "Forgive my bluntness, old friend. It is just that I feel a need to be alone with my God. I will pray over this suggestion and see if He will speak to me as He speaks to Samuel."

Urnan rose and turned to go.

"Eat with me when it is time, Urnan," Saul said.

"With pleasure," Urnan said.

Mered, too, moved away, but when he glanced back, he saw the king beckon.

"Will I give the boy my daughter?" Saul asked.

"She is your daughter," Mered said.

"Don't play at words," Saul growled. "Give me your thoughts."

"The promise of Michal's hand can become a snare for David," Mered said carefully.

"How so?"

"It is customary to ask a bride-price," Mered said.

Saul nodded.

"And if the bride-price you ask of David serves to set the Philistines against him . . ."

Saul waited in expectant silence.

"Let us say that the price for the hand of the fair Michal is the death of one hundred Philistines," Mered said. "In his eagerness to meet that price David might, unfortunately, become overeager. His actions will be like sticking his hand into a nest of wild bees. Surely the stir he makes will bring the entire Philistine army down on him."

"Send a trusted messenger to David," Saul said. "Let him say to David that I, the king, love him, that I have delight in him, and that he will be my son-in-law. When this has been said tell him that I want no dowry more than this, that he of the strong arm and brave heart further avenge Israel on her enemies by slaying one hundred Philistines."

"And what proof will you ask, sire?" Mered asked.

Saul mused for a moment. His lips smiled, but his eyes were cold. "Ramses totaled the dead of the Sea Peoples by cutting off their hands," he said. "But what is to prevent an unscrupulous commander from cutting off the hands of his own fallen?"

Mered nodded and answered the king's cold smile. "You are wise, sire."

"Let David count his vanquished enemies by severing their foreskins," Saul said. "Let him bring me the foreskins from one hundred dead Philistines. Then he can marry my daughter."

Mered bowed and backed away, grimly triumphant. In his eagerness to become a member of the royal family David would surely become impatient and reckless, and such a man did not last long on the battlefield.

Mered was to have one more moment of satisfaction. Since he had been detached from active duty in the army and made a member of Saul's staff at the palace, one man had competed with him for Saul's ear. Urnan the armorer could claim the king's attention because of past association and longstanding friendship, and Mered had thus far been unable to drive a wedge be-

tween them. Saul had said that a trusted messenger
should be sent to David; he would approve of Urnan.
Urnan believed that the king should keep his promise to
David and was, therefore, to be counted as one of
David's supporters. It was ironically fitting that such a
man should be the one to deliver the message that
would be David's death sentence.

CHAPTER SIXTEEN

Tania, Princess of Egypt, was not a woman to weep. It was more in her nature to be angry with the gods than to mourn. She could appeal to Amon, the chief deity of Upper Egypt, in full faith that he would favor her prayers. The gods were as much Egyptian as she. But the sorry depths to which the Two Lands had sunk, the loss of her beloved husband Urnan, and the disappearance of her dear son Kaptar—all that was proof that the gods did not always favor Egypt or Egyptians.

What was to be her future? It was difficult to believe it might include Urnan. Even if he had survived the journey to the far edge of the former empire where war was a way of life, it would have required miracles for him to survive the ensuing years, much less to find a way back to her. But she had faith not only that Kaptar was safe and that he would return, but that her nation would endure too, although she would not live to see the Two Lands reunited.

She could do nothing more to hasten the finding of

107

her son. Kemose was mounting a search for the boy. But she could do something for herself and for Egypt. Tania's revenge on the man who had driven the husband of her heart from Egypt began on her wedding night.

To please his bride, the Libyan had engaged musicians and purchased handmaidens for her. The finest cook in Lower Egypt prepared meals for the princess, and Musen was pleased to see her eat heartily. As his boat sailed down the Nile, her interest in the passing countryside, that narrow stretch of fertile black soil on either side of the river, matched Musen's own, but they saw the land from different viewpoints.

"One day, wife," Musen said, "a son of ours will rule this rich land from Nubia to the sea. It will be one nation again, prosperous, with a contented citizenry."

"All of them speaking the language of Libya?" Tania asked, with a flattering smile.

"We respect the learning of Egypt," Musen said.

"Well you might, since your countrymen neither read nor write," Tania said.

"Perhaps I can, over time, induce you to change your opinion of my people," Musen said. "After all, they are your people now, and they are as much Egyptian as any who might claim to trace his ancestry back to the time of the building of the pyramids."

Tania held her tongue. It was in the night that Musen was punished for the anger in her heart. She played the part of a dutiful wife. She prepared herself for her husband by bathing in scented waters, by anointing herself with perfumed oils, and by dressing in diaphanous, clinging garments that gave tantalizing glimpses of her very feminine body. She smiled. She whispered flattering words into the Libyan's ear. And when he came into her she was no more responsive than one of the newly dead.

It was folk legend among the Libyans that the passion of Egyptian men was but as the glow of embers when compared to the fire of a Libyan. Indeed, Musen believed that Libyan men were more developed than the paler, weaker men of the native race and, therefore, that his ability to please the woman he loved was never in doubt. He had known Egyptian women, and he had been able to make them moan and flail about as wildly as one of his Libyan servants. That he was incapable of generating passion in his Egyptian wife was unthinkable. As the days and nights passed, as the barge floated slowly and comfortably northward, his need to kindle Tania's passion became an obsession.

It was not until they were within one day's journey of Musen's city that the Libyan's frustration became so acute that he lashed out at her.

He was tired. He was perspiring. He was gasping for breath, and yet she lay calmly, serenely, her beautiful face composed in a warm smile.

"By the gods, woman, don't you feel anything?" he demanded.

"I feel my husband's passion fading," she said, pretending concern. "Is it something that I have done? You know that my only desire is to please you." She had forced herself not to cling to him, not to lift herself to him. She was a vital woman and he was not an inept lover, but she kept telling herself that this rude barbarian had destroyed her happiness with the man she loved and was threatening to destroy her country.

For Musen to admit his distress would have been a sign of weakness. He forced himself to complete the act, hating himself for his grunts of pleasure, hating her for her limp, unmoving acceptance.

Never again would he question her behavior.

To Tania's amusement and satisfaction Musen's intrusions into her bedchamber became less frequent, but she did not want him to stop coming to her altogether. When he was in her bed and she teased him with touch and look and smile and with soft hands smoothed with perfumed oil, he became talkative; it required little effort to extract information from him. Under her spell he talked readily about the dreams he shared with his father of a Libyan sitting upon the throne of the Two Lands. He didn't hesitate to show his contempt for Paynozem and even for Kemose, mistaking her interest in his affairs to mean that she had switched her loyalty from her cousins to him.

It was only when Tania was satisfied that there was nothing more to learn about her husband's plans that, one pleasant night, she awaited Musen's appearance in her bedchamber fully clothed, without makeup, her face pale. She carefully chose a time when he had been away for several days, and she knew his need for her would be so great that his body would shake with the force of his lust.

"You are not prepared," he said, with a hint of irritation.

"Sit with me and comfort me," Tania said. "I am unwell."

"I'll call a physician," he said.

"No, please. It is only a woman's illness. It will pass. Your company will be of great pleasure to me. Come, sit with me."

Musen sat beside her. She touched his hands, his face, his neck, tantalizingly ran her soft fingers down inside his tunic, all the while telling him how ill she felt. When he left her his emotions were raging between frustrated anger and irresistible need. Finally he sought satisfaction with a slave girl, a coupling that relieved his tension but left him feeling hollow and incomplete. Even though Tania was unresponsive she was the most desirable woman he had ever known.

More and more often her health foiled his needs. She had been too long in the sun and her head ached frightfully. A tooth pained her. It was the time of the moon for her coloring. She was exhausted by having directed the affairs of the palace.

He begged. He groveled before her, and the more he showed his weakness the more she resisted his advances. Not that she was ever unpleasant. She wept and whispered that she wanted to please him, that she berated the gods for making her so weak and unhealthy as to give her husband pain. And now and again, sometimes after the passage of two or three appearances of the full moon, she gave herself to him with just a hint of received pleasure, just enough to make him long for more.

Tania wrote often to her cousin of her hopes and

fears and what she observed in Lower Egypt. *"My dear cousin,"* she wrote, *"while it is true that a Libyan is not yet seated on the throne of Lower Egypt, the Libyans are the power behind Paynozem's throne."*

"Fortunately for us," Kemose wrote in his next letter, *"at the moment the power behind the power behind the throne is an Egyptian woman from the Southern City in whose veins runs the blood of kings."*

As she studied the Libyans and increasingly saw the power they wielded, Tania grew more despondent.

"I pray that I am wrong and that you, cousin, and the brave men of Upper Egypt will prove it so, but it is becoming more and more evident to me that one day Egypt will be ruled, as it was in the day of the Shepherd Kings and the Syrians, by foreigners. You know that I would do anything in my power to prevent such a disaster, and I know that you will do the same, you and all true men of Egypt, but Musen's army is a powerful force, and Paynozem is nothing more than a figurehead."

This was a situation she could not abide. As she continued to torment Musen, whose helpless lust for her made him an easy victim, she realized what she had to do. She had continued to make him beg for her favors, but their relationship was becoming more and more stormy. Although the Libyan allowed her to shame him, when he was sated with her he was capable of turning on her. Time, Tania knew, was on Musen's side. If she continued to humiliate him the results could be tragic.

"I will remind you," he said on more than one occasion, "that there are others of royal blood in Egypt. Moreover, it is only Egyptian tradition, not mine, that places importance on the bloodline of the royal wives."

Tania had always taken an interest in the legends and stories of the past; now one tale gleaned from the thousands of years of Egypt's history began to haunt her. Like Tania, a royal princess of old had felt the need to take revenge on her husband. She had done so by giving her body to any man who desired it. Her fee for her favors was a pebble. Thus it was that even as the king continued to accept her connubial offerings, she was building a sizable pyramid with the stones with which peasants and common workmen paid for that which the king considered to be his alone. The pyramid was, and would be as long as the lore of Egypt survived, a monument to the king's shame.

Tania's monument to Musen would not be as lasting. The symbol of Musen's humiliation would be flesh and blood.

She selected carefully the man who would father her son. He was, of course, Egyptian, his blood untainted by that of the foreigners. He was a strong and handsome man, one of the few native Egyptians in Musen's army. He was not an officer; he was not educated; he was the son of a farmer. But he was Egyptian. It was time to inject new blood into the royal family.

Since her marriage, Tania had used time-proven methods to prevent the seed of Musen from taking root in her. Now that she was unprotected she had to keep Musen from her bed.

It was as if the gods favored her plan. She took the young Egyptian soldier to her bed shortly after her monthly flowering and with the following moon there was no staining. At selected times during the next moon she gave herself to the young soldier, letting her passions run free under the loving weight of Egypt. She lifted to meet him, moaned with the sweetness of it, loosed upon the appreciative young man all the feelings that she had been keeping in check for months.

When the second moon passed she did not wait for Musen to come to her bed. She went to his. At first he was unresponsive. During the long period without her his resentment had grown, but her touch, the softness of her body against his, made him forget. For weeks she was all that he could ever have hoped. Scarcely a night passed that she did not come to his bed, and she gave herself to his demands with such a willingness and a heat that all his frustrations belonged to the past.

She was demure and feminine when she kissed him one night. Her voice was full of pride. "You are to have a son," she said.

He had almost given up hope. She was not young, and she had given birth only once. He had decided that she was barren, and had she not come to his bed, had she not changed, he would have been forced to take another wife.

"You're sure?" he asked.

"The red bird did not fly with the half-moon," she said.

"A son," he whispered. Then frowned. "How can you be sure it will be a son?"

"Could you, wild bull of Libya, get anything other than a son?"

He laughed. She laughed with him. It would be a son. It would have to be a son, and when he was born she would once again surprise Musen, who was now actively preparing for a Libyan—at least one he thought to be half-Libyan—on the throne of Egypt.

CHAPTER
SEVENTEEN

A whirlwind of death descended on the Philistine plain. A lightning-fast unit of captured enemy chariots led the way, laying waste the farms and homes of Philistine and Canaanite alike. The one purpose of the advance force was to find and hold isolated units of the Army of the Five Cities until the main body of David's strike force, with the general at the head, could encircle the enemy.

Eri and Jonathan were at David's side when the crack unit first ventured out of the hills. After a spirited fight, with a Philistine frontier blockhouse in flames and the dead lying sprawled on the parched earth, the smith and the king's son looked on in amused amazement as the mightiest fighting man in Israel lifted the kilts of soldiers who had fallen by his own hand, sliced through breechclouts, and with great care began to gather the bride-price named by Saul.

One evening after the second foray down to the

plain, Eri and Jonathan found David sitting forlornly in front of his tent.

"What in God's name is that terrible smell?" Jonathan asked.

David, his face flushing with shame and frustration, reached for a leather bag that lay on the ground by his side and pulled open the drawstring. The stench intensified.

"I think the king has set me an impossible labor," he said. "They decay faster than I can collect them."

Jonathan turned and called out to a soldier who was passing, then took the bag from David and gave it to the soldier. "Take this far away and leave it for the jackals," he said. Turning to Eri, he went on, "My friend, we face here a crisis of truly cosmic proportions. What can we do to help our lovesick companion?"

"The only solution I see is for him to drive a hundred Philistines to within a short march of the king's palace, slay them all at once, and deliver the goods before the heat can turn them," Eri said.

David shook his head in mute misery.

"What we need," Jonathan said, "is the services of the priests who prepare the dead for burial in Egypt. Then the bride-price could be delivered in mummified form."

"My father says that they produce uncanny results," Eri said, "that the mummified dead look almost as if they were still alive. I would imagine that a good practitioner of the art could preserve the round, graceful shape of the objects that have so caught David's fancy. Certainly the tribute to Saul would be more pleasing to the nose and probably much more artistic."

Jonathan leaped back and took up a wrestling stance when David made as if to rise, but relaxed when the general sat back down and put his head in his hands.

"What is it that the Egyptians use?" Jonathan asked.

"My father says that their methods are a closely guarded secret." Eri put his hand on David's shoulder. "But maybe salt would preserve them long enough. What do you think, Jonathan?"

"It may be worth a try," Jonathan said.

"Go on, have your little joke at my expense," David said, grinning as he got into the spirit of his friends' jesting.

"No, seriously," Eri said, "salt and perhaps spices might cure those bits of flesh."

"I'm ready to try anything," David said, "but salt and spices are not among our most plentiful commodities."

"True," Jonathan said. Suddenly his face lit up. He snapped his fingers and smiled. "Is it not the time of new wine in the Philistine plain?"

"Indeed," Eri said, licking his lips. The farmers of the plain made delicious wine.

"Then your problem is solved," Jonathan said.

"How?" David asked.

"Leave it to me," Jonathan said.

When next a Philistine outpost was destroyed by David's charioteers and infantry, Jonathan fought alongside Eri and David for a time, and then, when the outcome was assured, he disappeared. When he returned, carrying a large skin half-full of liquid, David was gathering his booty. He waited until David was finished before opening the wineskin.

"If you're going to do what I think you're going to do," Eri said, "let me have that skin first." He drank deeply.

"Trying to drink all the wine of the plain is going to solve my problem?" David asked. His hands were bloody.

"In God's name, David," Jonathan said, wrinkling his nose, "go wash your hands."

"You said—" David paused, thinking that he was being mocked again.

"I said I had the solution," Jonathan said, extending the wineskin. "Drop your precious little objects into the bag, one by one."

David frowned.

"Just do it," Jonathan said. "I guarantee that when

you appear before my father the merchandise will smell only of wine."

It was as Jonathan promised.

Not since the days of old, when Joshua led the Army of Yahweh to victory after victory while claiming the land promised by God, had Israel been so great. The strongest enemy ever faced by the descendants of those who had followed Moses up out of Egypt was reeling from defeat after defeat. The mighty Army of the Five Cities had been split into isolated units in an effort to guard the fertile plain whose farms and orchards were vital to the continued prosperity of Philistia.

One hundred foreskins did not make a large package. With Jonathan at his side David appeared before the king and spilled out onto the stone floor the pale, wine-shriveled bits of flesh that constituted the bride-price. Saul's face was set; his eyes glittered. David watched him closely.

"As you requested, sire," David said softly. "Here is the price you asked in exchange for the hand of Michal."

Saul nodded. His eyes narrowed. "So I have said, so it will be," he intoned. "Leave me now, all of you."

The warriors bowed, turned, and headed for the door.

"Jonathan," Saul said, "a moment."

Jonathan looked at his father and was worried. The king's eyes burned with anger. He was pacing the floor, unable to control his own body.

"Do you not know," Saul demanded, "that the greatest obstacle between you and the throne of Israel is the man whom you call friend, the man with whom you fight against the Philistines?"

"Not so, Father," Jonathan said. "No man is more loyal than David."

"Fool," Saul spat out. "It is whispered in Judah that he has been chosen to be king by Samuel and the priests."

Jonathan shook his head. "I know him, Father. He would die for Israel, and for you."

"Ha," Saul said. "You say that he is loyal, and yet, I warrant, he gathered spoil from those killed by you, and by others. Not even the man who slew Goliath could have killed one hundred Philistine soldiers so quickly."

"With respect, you are wrong, Father," Jonathan said. "Any man who was with us will swear that David was meticulously honest in his count."

Saul stopped pacing and stood by his son, his anger replaced by a haunted sadness. "You are determined, then, to disobey my wishes?"

"I am your humble servant," Jonathan said. "Perhaps I don't understand what you want of me."

"I want you to be king after me," Saul said.

"If that is God's will and yours, it will be my duty."

"It is my will, and God's will, for God gave me the strength and the inspiration to deliver His holy Ark from the Philistine cities. He put the power into my sword arm to slay our enemies. He led Samuel to anoint me king. It is His will that my name will live in the person of my sons and my sons' sons." He leaned forward until his face was inches from Jonathan's. "But there are times when God's will is circumvented by those who claim that He speaks to them and them alone. My spies tell me that David is loved by the people, and that all of the priests sing his praises. This is not the work of God, but of Samuel and his acolytes. If His order is to be preserved you must do this for me, and for yourself."

Jonathan bowed his head.

"You must kill David."

Jonathan's face went white. For a moment he could not speak. "Is death, then, to be David's reward for doing what no other man in Israel had the courage to do? Is betrayal by his friend to be his, rather than those things that have been promised him?" He shook his father's hand off his shoulder. "Ask me to drive myself onto my own sword until the haft rests against my stomach, but I beg you not to ask me to do what you asked."

Saul slowly shook his head.

"You are the king of all Israel, Father," Jonathan said. "While it is true that the women sing David's praises, so do they sing of mighty Saul." He managed a faint smile. "They even devote some verses to me, the king's son. But they know who is king. They know who took up the fight after the disaster at Ebenezer, and who is responsible for making the hills of Israel free again. The people are loyal to you, in spite of what the priests say, Father, and no one among them is more loyal than David."

"Leave me," Saul said wearily.

"I beg you to keep your promise to David," Jonathan said. "I have spoken with my sister. She wants this marriage."

Saul sighed. "And do you want it?" he asked.

"With all my heart."

Saul waved his hand weakly. "I will contest you no more," he said. "I leave it to you and your sister to arrange this fearful union."

Although it was decidedly improper, Michal sought out David late one afternoon and found him alone in a small courtyard near the quarters he shared with Jonathan. She heard the sound of his harp before she saw him and slowed her pace to listen. When his voice joined the chords of the harp, her heart leaped. She stood quietly in the growing shadows of the evening and listened.

"Behold, thou art fair, my love; thou hast doves' eyes within thy locks. Thy two breasts are like two young roes that are twins."

Michal flushed with a mixture of embarrassment and pleasure.

"Thou hast ravished my heart. How much better is thy love than wine! and the smell of thine ointments than all spices!"

David's voice trailed off. The music of the harp softened. He sighed and, as if sensing her presence, turned his head. He leaped to his feet. "Lady," he said.

"Please don't stop," she said, moving toward him, her shapely hips swaying under her linens.

He stood stiffly, speechless.

"The song you were singing," she said. "Did you write it?"

He shook his head. "It is an old song."

"I had thought that it might be for me," she said, her voice disappointed.

"It is for you, most surely," he said, "and much better than any poor words that I could write."

"You are not so modest about your prowess with weapons," she said, frowning. "Yet your music becomes you more than your ability with a sword."

Behind her the sun burst into a red glory as it sank below a thin line of clouds on the horizon. She became a graceful silhouette against the glow.

"Sing for me," she said, seating herself on a stone bench.

He sat, strummed the harp, then hummed a sweet, poignant melody, an ancient tune that many men had sung in praise of beauty. He began softly, as if fearing that ears other than hers might hear.

"Thou art beautiful, O my love, terrible as an army with banners."

She gave a frown of disapproval.

"Turn away thine eyes from me, for they have over-come me," he sang. *"Thy neck is as a tower of ivory, thine eyes like limpid pools. How fair and how pleasant art thou, O love."*

Warming to his song, he leaned toward her, drinking in the scent of her, worshiping her with his eyes. When the harp was once more silent she stood and came to him. She took his hand in hers.

"Hold me," she whispered.

"It is not proper," he murmured, but he could not help himself. He laid the harp down and stood, and she pressed her body to his. His arms wrapped around her small, perfect form, and he felt the warm softness of her breasts against his chest.

Her lips touched his. "Will you forgive my immodesty if I say that I have loved you from the first day I saw you?"

David stood silent, awed by his good fortune.

"Have you nothing to say?"

"Only that I love you."

"But you wanted to marry my sister, she whom my father gave to another."

"It was not I who selected her," David said truthfully. "She was promised to me only because she was the eldest."

"But you thought she was more beautiful than I."

"Now I have had the chance to look more closely," he said, brushing his lips against her smooth cheek. "And you are more beautiful than sunlight on the golden hills of Judah."

"Are you sorry that it is I and not my sister who will be your wife?"

"No," he said quickly. "God knows that I speak the truth when I say that I will never regret that it is to be you."

He kissed her, and there arose such a trembling in his body that his teeth chattered as if from cold. He was suddenly held prisoner by an overwhelming physical need for her body.

"You want me so badly?" she whispered, awed by the strength of his arms, by his devouring mouth.

"How can I wait?" he asked, fearful of what he felt like doing.

"Wait we must," she whispered. "It will not be long, my love."

It was a joyous time. There was a feast of fat things in Gibeah. The rites of marriage were consecrated by a local priest. During the ceremony Saul sat in gloomy silence. Only once did he look at David, and when he did let his eyes fall upon the shining countenance of his new son-in-law, it was a baleful glance that chilled the blood of those who saw it.

CHAPTER EIGHTEEN

Sarah pushed her huge stomach ahead of her into the garden. A restlessness was upon her. Behind her the house of Eri the armorer was quiet. Baalan was resting, Sunu was at his nap, and the servants were escaping from the heat of the day. The courtyard was partially shaded by two ancient sycamores, but she was not content to sit under a tree on a stone bench. The heat came at her like a drawn sword, moistened her skin under her loose night robe, and suddenly knifed through her engorged stomach.

She clasped the mound of impending motherhood with both hands and screamed as she struggled toward the bench.

Baalan was with her within moments, and as another convulsion took her, she clasped Baalan's hand tightly.

"There is nothing to fear," Baalan said. "It is your time."

Baalan assisted the village midwife in the long and difficult labor that ended just before dawn.

"Hush," said the village's senior midwife, an old woman who had seen the birth of more than fivescore additions to the tribe of Benjamin. "You are not the first to feel the pain of motherhood."

If Sarah heard she paid no heed. Her screams filled the room and reverberated throughout the house, causing the housemaid to snicker with satisfaction that the high and mighty first wife was suffering so.

There was no man in the house when the top of the baby's head showed for the first time. Baalan exclaimed in pleasure at the thickness and blackness of the child's hair.

Baalan's hands were steadier, so the midwife instructed her to ease the child's shoulders free. Soft flesh tore. Blood gushed. Sarah screamed as she gave one last heave. The midwife quickly cleared the child's mouth with one finger and suspended it by its heels. Her gnarled hand swatted the red, wet, tiny buttocks, and a reedy yowl of protest announced the new life.

Baalan turned the child eagerly to see its sex and felt a stab of sorrow.

There was still no man in the house of Eri.

"Give him to me," Sarah demanded. "Let me see."

"Patience," said the midwife harshly. "There is work to be done." She handed the baby to Baalan and began to tend to the mother.

"I want to see my son," Sarah whined.

"Be still," the midwife said, "and push."

It was only when the afterbirth had been removed that the old woman moved aside to let Baalan approach. The baby had been washed and swaddled in clean linen.

"Look at the beautiful black hair," Baalan said.

Sarah was holding out her arms. Baalan placed the child beside its mother. Sarah clawed at the baby's coverings.

"Sarah—" Baalan began.

Sarah gave one sharp scream when she saw the baby's tiny pubes. She turned her head and tears ran down her face.

"She's a beautiful little girl," Baalan said.

"Get her out of here, you whore," Sarah said with so much venom that Baalan's face went white in shock.

Sarah's good friend Aiah was a frequent visitor while the new mother was confined. Sarah felt a need to vent her disappointment to a sympathetic ear, but it seemed that either Baalan or one of the servants was always present. As soon as Sarah was able to walk the short distance between the house of Eri and that of Mered she made her way there with the child in her arms.

"My two beautiful little girls," Aiah said warmly, taking the baby and cooing tiny, wordless things at it.

"Give it to one of the servants," Sarah said. "I am weary of its constant demands."

Sarah's bosom had blossomed. She felt top-heavy, and she hated the warm, sticky feel and the smell of the mother's milk that leaked from her breasts.

"You must not speak of your child like that," Aiah said, shocked. "God has been good to you to give you such a beautiful little girl."

"God has punished me and rewarded the Ammonite whore and her son," Sarah said.

The baby was nuzzling against Aiah's empty, stringy breast. "Look," the old woman said. "She roots like a newborn lamb in search of her mother's teat."

Sarah sighed wearily.

"Sit here," Aiah said. "The little dear is hungry."

Sarah obeyed. Although the whole process was degrading, at least the baby's nursing eased the swollen tautness of her breasts.

"I would have given my all for such a child," Aiah said, as she watched with a smile on her face.

"If it were allowed, I would give this one to you," Sarah said.

Aiah made a sign to God. "Watch what you say. Don't tempt Him. He might hear and take the child from you."

Sarah began to weep. Aiah sat next to her and wiped the tears away. "I did so want a son," Sarah said.

"Next time," Aiah said.

"Will there be a next time?" Sarah asked, her voice shaking. "When Eri is at home he seems to have little time for me. He spends it with the whore and her son. With each season that passes he becomes more fond of the boy. He teaches him the arts of war and the magic of his craft. He has not touched me since—"

"You have been with child," Aiah said. "If he has not made demands on you it was out of respect for your condition."

"He goes to *her* room at night," Sarah said. "I wish she were dead. I wish she were dead, and her son with her."

Neither of the women had noticed Mered entering the room. He cleared his throat, and the two women turned. Aiah greeted her husband with a smile and hurried off to fetch him some wine. Sarah wiped her tears away with the back of her hand.

"Be sure you mean your wishes, child," Mered said to her with a fatherly smile, "lest they be granted."

"I do mean it. She has taken what is rightfully mine, and her son will be heir to my husband's possessions and his name."

"Eri has not seen the child?" Mered asked.

"If it had been the whore who was giving birth, not even his precious friends and his love for war would have kept him away," Sarah said.

"How long has it been since he's been home?"

"Two full moons have passed."

Mered shook his head. "You don't know where he is? There have been no messages?"

She shook her head.

"What would you give to the man who freed you of the burden of Baalan and her son?" Mered asked.

"I have nothing to give, save my gratitude," Sarah said.

"And, should the blood of this woman and her child stain the earth, would it also color you?" Mered asked.

Sarah shifted the baby from one breast to the other. The child's hunger was lessening, the eager gulps slowing. She felt a chill. She could tell by the look in Mered's eyes that he was not asking an idle question.

"I don't know," she said.

"As I thought," Mered said, turning away.

"Wait," Sarah said. "Would there not be a way without blood?"

Mered's face was pinched, his pouting mouth pursed. "As Jacob was sold into slavery, so might they be."

Sarah thought for a moment, then nodded.

"You will remember your true friends?" Mered asked.

"With all my heart," Sarah said.

Baalan didn't like to have her house filled with servants. She limited her household staff to one housemaid and a man who was on call to do odd jobs. She had been a slave and she knew that there was satisfaction in a job well done. She also liked privacy and she enjoyed doing things for her son herself.

She and Sunu had just finished the evening meal. Sunu was licking his fingers, having enjoyed more than his fair share of honey cakes, when she heard a commotion from the front of the house. The housemaid screamed. Baalan leaped to her feet, started toward the sound of disturbance, and ran head-on into a thick-chested, powerfully built man.

"What are you doing here?" she demanded.

She felt tendrils of fear. The man's face was hidden behind the folds of his headdress, which was of the style worn by the desert nomads. She turned to run to Sunu, only to be seized from behind.

"Get the boy," someone said in a raspy voice.

Sunu ran to his mother's aid and began pummeling the legs of the man who was holding her. He did not cry out but continued to struggle until he was jerked roughly off his feet and thrown over the shoulder of another hooded man. His small fists pounded the back of his captor until, with an oath, the man spanked his upturned bottom heavily and said, "Be still."

The kidnappers were in and out of the house within

minutes. A cart drawn by two shabby donkeys waited in the rear garden. Baalan, gagged and bound, was tossed into it. Sunu, similarly trussed, was thrown in next to her. As the cart passed out of the gate she saw Sarah there, the baby in her arms, laughing.

Eri lay on his stomach in the cover of a clump of bushes atop a hill and watched the Army of the Five Cities pass. David, at Eri's side, counted chariots, his lips moving.

"This is more than a probe in force," he said.

Eri nodded. He had noted the banners of Ashkelon, Ashdod, Ekron, Gaza, and Gath, all five of the great Philistine cities.

"Look," Eri said, "there's the personal flag of Galar."

"God is kind to us."

Eri, who often expressed his unsure allegiance to Yahweh with the words "Lord, I believe, help thou mine unbelief," laughed nervously. He wasn't quite sure how good God was being to send the entire Philistine army toward Jerusalem when Abner and the core units of the Army of Israel were in Benjamin to allow the soldiers to prepare for harvesting their crops.

The fast-moving force led by David and Jonathan was outnumbered by even that small portion of the Army of the Five Cities that was now stretched out on the narrow road below them. And they had the dreadful feeling that behind this advance force lay the power and massive threat of the main body of Galar's army.

"I will ride to Gibeah," Eri said. "Perhaps you and Jonathan can hold them away from Jerusalem until Saul and Abner can get here."

When David smiled he looked very much the young shepherd boy he was when Eri first saw him. He put his hand on Eri's shoulder. "My friend, at the making of arms you are unsurpassed, and you have few betters at the wielding of them, but leave the strategy to me."

Eri grinned sheepishly. "Sorry."

"It was a worthy suggestion," David said. "It may become necessary, but let us not be hasty."

The corps of dedicated warriors of Israel was camped beyond the next range of hills around a source of sweet water. Jonathan saw David and Eri ride into the camp and came to meet them as they dismounted.

"My scouts report the dust of the movement of many men," Jonathan said.

"Only the dust?" David asked.

"I have sent out other men."

"Good," David said. "Send one more, your best man, to determine how far behind the column that raises dust is the main body of Galar's army."

"His entire army?" Jonathan asked.

David nodded grimly. "With the dawn tomorrow we will have heavy work."

"We can hold them at the entrance to the vale before Beth-shemesh until my father can bring down the army from Gibeah," Jonathan said.

"Will you hear me, my friend?" David asked quietly.

Jonathan nodded, and David squatted and drew in the dust. "Here is the body of cavalry. Here the chariots. You will hit the horsemen here." He stabbed the dirt with his finger. "Here you will destroy the cavalry."

"But the chariots—"

"I will be here," David said, touching a spot that represented a steep ridge overlooking the road toward Beth-shemesh. "While you destroy the horsemen with your archers who will be deployed along both sides of the entrance to the vale, I will deprive Galar of his chariots. After that we will consider what is to be done about his infantry."

Jonathan looked at Eri.

"You have doubts?" David asked.

"How can we doubt when we are outnumbered no more than twenty to one?" Eri asked.

"And to split our forces," Jonathan said. "Doesn't that leave us even more vulnerable to being wiped out piecemeal?"

"That is exactly what I intend to do to Galar," David said. He rose and slapped dust from his hands.

"Do you want to see Philistines in Beth-shemesh and in Jerusalem?"

Jonathan and Eri were silent.

"Trust me," David said.

The Philistine cavalry rode toward the narrow entrance to the valley in a column of twos, four hundred strong. On the semiarid slopes, behind bushes and rocks, Jonathan's archers lay and prayed silently. At the blast of a ram's horn the archers leaped to their feet and sent a hail of iron-tipped shafts flying down the slopes. A wounded man bellowed hoarsely. The high-pitched scream of a horse was lost in the chaos as horsemen fell and animals bolted. No more than a score of horsemen kept their seats and attempted a panicked retreat, only to ride into another hail of arrows.

An injured horse coughed as it struggled to its feet. The Philistine wounded watched flashing blades as Jonathan's men swarmed down the slopes, bows slung over their shoulders, to deal out merciful oblivion to man and beast. Then the only sound was the panting of the victorious Hebrews until, from around the shoulder of a ridge, came a roar as David attacked the chariots.

Eri had chosen to go with David and sat behind a large boulder on the ridge overlooking the road. He tested his strength against the boulder, felt it move slightly. He was ready. All around him on the rocky slope were other men, ready to unleash nature's weapons against the oncoming Philistines.

The lead chariot rolled past Eri's position, and he counted as the vehicles of war passed, the knifed hubs of their wheels striking sun sparks at his eyes. Over the rumble of the wheels he could hear the drivers as they called out to the horses or to the archers riding the chariots with them. His count was beyond one hundred when he heard David's cry and saw huge boulders bounce down the slope to block the head of the road. He looked quickly to his left in time to see a second fall of rocks pound down the slope at the other end of the defile. The lead chariot was crushed by the avalanche of rocks. Behind the barrier drivers swore, tugged at their reins, and tried to turn to flee as arrows rained down death from the sky.

Eri pushed against the boulder in front of him, and it started to roll slowly down the hill. From the slopes on both sides of the road boulders rolled and bounded down. The chariots were trapped between two barriers of stone, helpless to avoid the crushing death that descended upon them.

"Now," Eri yelled, standing and raising his sword. He leaped down the slope with the men of Israel on either side of him. All the chariots were immobilized or smashed. Many of the men were dead or wounded. Eri leaped to the hub of one vehicle, probed under the driver's hastily lifted shield with his blade, felt it penetrate, pulled it back. Blood came at him in a spouting flood as he backhanded the archer in the face with his shield. A stunning blow with a mighty swing of his sword left the archer's head hanging by nothing more than a flap of flesh.

Eri stood with his shield dangling at his side. He was breathing hard, exhausted by the brief but fierce fight. On the floor of the valley nothing lived. A man gave a victory yell and the army took it up, filling the gorge with their voices. Suddenly Philistine infantry began to pour over the rock barrier at the south end of the defile. David's voice rang out an order. The Hebrews scurried up the western slope, disappearing among the boulders and over the crest. The Philistine infantry swarmed up the slope after them, bent on avenging the death of comrades, and ran into a hail of arrows. But the odds were too great for David's force. The rear guard loosed one final flight of arrows and ran for the crest of the ridge.

The Philistines were intent on salvaging their chariots and weapons when the two units of David and Jonathan's force struck the supply carts and camp followers at Galar's rear. The feeble resistance of the men guarding the supply train was quickly smashed. Fire sent billowing smoke into the sky. Iron swords bit into the tender flesh of women of the camp, for Yahweh did not value Philistine whores. Leaving death and ruin behind them once again, the men of Israel disappeared into the hills.

Galar had started toward the front of the army when the Hebrews struck at his rear. He wheeled his horse, summoned his guard, and rode hard, all the while ordering his infantry to turn and face the new threat. He saw his supply trains smashed and burning, the grain to feed men and horses scattered in the dust, loaves of bread and the fruits of the rich plains mixed with blood.

Galar shook his fist, shouting curses at the pigs of the hills who had, once again, thwarted his plans. His mobile scouting force was gone. His chariotry was destroyed, his horses dead. It would take an army of wheelwrights and craftsmen to put his chariots right, and even then there would be no horses to pull them. He had the infantry, but no food was left to feed them. Once more he would have to explain to the lords of the cities how the mighty Philistine army had been bested by a barefoot rabble of Hebrews.

With gall backing up into his throat, Galar ordered his officers to turn the army, to take it back to the plain.

"If Abner were here with the main body we could strike through the infantry and destroy Gath itself," David said.

"But Abner is *not* here," Jonathan said.

"We have smitten the Philistine severely," Eri observed, "but we do not have the strength to drive through to the plain, even though we have destroyed the main units of Galar's cavalry and chariotry."

"You speak true, my friend," David said.

"There are those whose families will have nothing to eat this winter unless they go home now to gather their crops," Jonathan said.

David nodded. "Gibeah," he said sadly.

"Do you think our general has remembered that he is a married man?" Eri asked, winking at Jonathan.

CHAPTER NINETEEN

The victorious Eri rode into the compound surrounding his home to the sound of hammers on anvils and the smell of burning charcoal. The forges were working. A servant took his horse. He controlled the urge to run across the grounds to the house, but he did walk more rapidly than usual.

When he entered the house he sensed a strange emptiness. It took him a moment to realize why. Not once in the years since he had made Baalan his wife had she failed to greet him at the door. He walked to the kitchen, where he found the weeping housemaid sitting on a stool. Her face was bruised. One eye was swollen shut. She started in fear when he entered.

"What in God's name has happened to you?" Eri asked.

The girl wept even louder, gasping out words.

"I can't understand you," Eri said harshly. "Control yourself. Where is your mistress?"

"Gone." The girl sobbed.

Eri seized the girl by her shoulders and shook her. "Where? Where has she gone?"

"They took her."

"Who took her, damn you?"

"Men. Men who hid their faces. They took Sunu, as well. I tried to stop them—"

"When did it happen?" Eri demanded.

"Last night, just after dark."

"And Sarah?" Eri asked, feeling a tiny twinge of guilt. Until that moment he'd been so eager to see Baalan and his son that he'd forgotten Sarah and the new child that he had not yet seen.

"She is with Aiah," the servant said.

"Her baby?"

"A girl."

Eri left the weeping girl sitting on her stool and ran from the house to Mered's. A servant opened the door at his pounding.

Aiah met him in the entryway and escorted him through to a shaded balcony where Sarah sat. She was dressed in white. Her hair was flowing free in dark, perfumed waves. Her face brightened with a smile.

"You're all right," Eri said.

"I am well, husband," Sarah said. "And—"

"What do you know of Baalan and Sunu?" Eri asked.

Sarah's smile faded. "I was going to tell you, husband, that you are the father of a beautiful daughter, but if you are more interested—"

"Hush," Eri said sharply. "There is no time for that. What of Baalan and Sunu?"

It was Aiah who spoke. "My husband is of the opinion that Baalan's Ammonite relatives came for her."

"What makes him think so? Did he see them?" Eri demanded.

"No," Aiah said.

"Did anyone see?"

"Only the servant," Sarah said sullenly.

"They came in darkness," Aiah said.

"Where were you?" Eri asked Sarah.

"I was here, with Aiah. She, at least, is kind to me."

She glared at Eri defiantly. "I think that it was slave traders from over Jordan who took the Ammonite whore and her whelp."

"You speak of my son," Eri said. "Have you no shame?"

Tears flowed from Sarah's eyes. "How I suffered to give you a child, and all you can think of is the Ammonite."

It was at that moment that Mered came out of the house onto the balcony. "Ah, Eri," he said, "please accept my congratulations. Sarah has given you a beautiful little daughter."

Eri had never been particularly fond of Mered, whom he considered an ineffectual leader. He tolerated him only because of Aiah's kindness to Sarah. Even though God had not given Mered the wisdom of the judges, Eri was surprised by Mered's callous disregard for Baalan and Sunu.

"Of course, it's bad news that your slave woman has been taken," Mered said.

Eri took a quick, angry step forward, controlling himself with an effort. "What do you know of this, Mered?"

"Only what the servant in your house was able to tell me," Mered said.

"And what action did you take?"

"I reported the incident to the king's guard," Mered said.

"And?"

Mered shrugged. "I fear, my friend, that Saul has concerns more pressing than the loss of one slave."

Eri turned to Sarah and said, tight-lipped, "Get your child, woman."

Sarah's lips twitched in a fleeting smile. Eri followed her into the house and, when she had the baby in her arms, guided her to his home. Once there he turned her to face him.

"You are not to enter the house of Mered again," he said.

Sarah's face hardened. "Aiah is my friend."

"And I am your husband."

She thrust the baby toward him. The sudden movement made the infant wail. "Act like my husband, then," Sarah said. "At least look at your daughter."

Eri took the small, warm bundle into his hands. The child's face was contorted with crying, eyes squeezed tightly closed, toothless maw agape.

"There, there, little one," Eri said, touching the red little face with one callused finger. "Hush, little one."

The baby's wailing quieted. Eri said, "You have done well, Sarah. She is, indeed, a fine daughter."

Sarah put her hand on his. "Don't worry about Baalan and Sunu," she said. "You have us. We can be happy now. I'll give you a son. I promise you that I will."

"Why do you say that we will be happy—*now*?"

She backed away. "The child knows her father. She has stopped her crying."

"Were we not happy before?" Eri asked.

"Yes," she said, "but—"

"Baalan tended you as if you were a baby," Eri said. "There were times when you were as helpless as this new one, and she was always at your side."

"Only to curry favor with you," Sarah said. "You were blind to her deceits, Eri. You don't know the tricks she used."

"I have always loved you. You have always been my first wife."

"I don't care what you say, I'm glad she's gone," Sarah said.

A terrible fear began to grow in Eri that there was more to Sarah's words than the fact that her mind was that of a spoiled and selfish child. He handed her the baby.

"Call the servant," he said. "Have her put our daughter to bed."

He waited until the girl had come and gone and they were alone. "How did it happen that you were not at home last night?" he asked.

"Baalan was being hateful to me," she said. "I went to be with my friend, Aiah."

She had never lied well. He took her arm, led her

to a couch, and sat her down. They both turned around as someone rushed into the room.

"Thank God you're here," Urnan said. "I just now heard about it."

"What have you heard?"

"Only this. The captain of Saul's guard said that Mered told him that the wife and son of Eri the smith had been abducted."

"That's all? Has there been no effort to find out who took them and why?"

"I'm afraid not," Urnan said.

"I was just talking with Sarah about it," Eri said, giving Urnan a meaningful look. "I think she is going to be able to tell us something." He took her hand and said coaxingly, "Are you, Sarah? Are you going to be able to tell us what happened to Baalan and Sunu?"

She shook her head sullenly.

"You're upsetting her," Urnan said, giving Eri a warning look.

"He has always loved the Ammonite slave more than he loves me," Sarah said. Tears formed and slid down her cheeks.

Urnan sat beside her and put his arm around her, and she leaned her face against his shoulder and wept. He motioned for Eri to leave. Eri went to the door but halted just outside it.

"You are going to be at ease now, Sarah," Urnan said. "I am here. I will not let anyone bother you. You're going to rest, and think of nothing. You're going to let the sweet peace of sleep come over you. I am here. You are safe."

Eri leaned against the wall and listened to his father's soothing voice. Once he had to shake his head as he felt the onset of sleep, but he was instantly alert when Urnan said, "You can come in now, Eri." He moved quietly back into the room.

"Sarah is resting," Urnan said. "She is at peace, and nothing will harm her and no one will condemn her. She wants only to help us find Baalan and Sunu. Isn't that right, Sarah?"

Sarah's voice was flat. "No. I do not want to find them."

"Why, Sarah? Why don't you want to find them?"

"Because I have no son. Because Baalan's son will be my husband's heir."

Urnan looked up at Eri and shook his head sadly.

"Sarah," he went on, "how did it happen that men came for Baalan and Sunu?"

"I don't know," she said.

"But you do know," Urnan said. "And it's all right if you tell me." He paused and said even more softly, "You do know, don't you?"

Sarah nodded.

"Did you ask someone to send men for Baalan and Sunu?"

"Yes."

"Whom did you ask?"

"I didn't ask."

"But you talked with someone?"

"Yes."

"Who?"

"Aiah and Mered."

Anger darkened Eri's face. He reached for his sword.

"And Mered offered to have Baalan and Sunu taken away?" Urnan asked.

"Yes."

"Where were they to be taken?"

"Over Jordan." Sarah paused. "I didn't want them to be killed."

Eri tensed as pain shot through him. To think of Baalan dead, to think of his son dead, was sorrow enough, but to realize that the tragedy had been brought about by Sarah, the girl he had loved so deeply for so long, was almost more than he could bear.

"And have they been killed?" Urnan asked. Was this what the shade of Shelah had meant when she said that one he cared for would be lost?

Eri held his breath.

"No. They were to be sold into slavery to passing nomads once they had been taken over Jordan."

"Sleep now, Sarah," Urnan said.

She allowed him to lower her to the couch, snuggled down, and was still.

"First I will kill Mered," Eri said, "and then I will go after them."

CHAPTER TWENTY

David was eager to get home to his bride, the beautiful Michal. Moreover, since he was young and desirous of praise for his efforts, he hoped that his success against Galar's army would, at last, restore the affections of his father-in-law.

David was young and naive in some matters, wise beyond his years in others. He had not forgotten how Samuel bade him to kneel before him, how the prophet anointed his head with scented oil. He had been only a boy, and at the time Samuel's gesture was meaningless. It was only later that he came to understand that he, David, the shepherd boy of Judah, would be king of all Israel.

But he had no ambition to replace Saul on the throne, and he deferred to Jonathan as Saul's heir. He was loyal to Saul, to Israel, and to his God.

Although he was a young man with the fire of love in him, his sense of duty took him to the throne room as soon as he arrived at Gibeah. He approached the king respectfully. "Sire, we met the enemy near Beth-shemesh, and once again we sent him back to his cities on the plain with his tail tucked between his legs like a cur."

"You make the defeat of a Philistine patrol sound quite grand," Saul said sourly.

"Not a patrol," David said. "The Army of the Five Cities, commanded by Galar himself."

David launched into an excited account of the battle, detailing the numbers of horsemen and chariots. He did not notice the changes that were overtaking Saul, the way his dark eyes flashed with anger as he listened. Not knowing the turmoil in Saul's mind, he truly believed that his father-in-law, his king, would share his pride in Israel's army and rejoice that God had once again given his people victory. He looked upward toward the high ceiling, trying to remember the exact number of the Philistine dead, when he saw something move. Silently, without warning, Saul had grabbed a ceremonial javelin from the wall and hurled it at his son-in-law.

David's first impulse was to strike back. His hand went to the haft of his sword, but his blood cooled as quickly as it had been heated when he saw Saul slumped on his throne, his face slack.

"Twice now you have tried to kill me," he said, looking directly into Saul's anger-glazed eyes.

"Leave me," Saul growled.

At his home, Michal, soft, warm, and perfumed, came into David's arms, but his joy in seeing her, in holding her, was diminished by his hurt and confusion over the king's hatred for him. Soon, however, all thoughts of Saul were driven from his mind by his wife's kisses.

In the early evening he awakened from the most untroubled and complete sleep that ever comes to a man, the serene peace that follows the act of love. Michal was sitting on the couch beside him, beautiful in her nudity. He reached for her, and she came into his arms.

"It will be dark soon," she said.

"I do not have to see you to appreciate your loveliness."

"I do love you, David."

"For which I thank God."

"Nevertheless, you must go."

He pushed her away and looked at her. "Why?"

"Because my father is going to send men to kill you during the night." The words, spoken in a whisper, hung in the air like drifting spores on a still summer day.

David held his wife close and gave her one last, lingering kiss.

"You must go," Michal whispered.

"May God annihilate the devils that have possessed the king," David said.

"Go, please."

He left by way of a window, dropping lightly onto the paving stones of the courtyard and slipping away into the shadows as four men approached the house. He recognized one of them. Of late Saul had gathered about him men whom once he would have driven from his camp as unworthy. As David hid in the shadows and watched, Doeg the Edomite, as hairy as the apes of Kush, pounded on the door. David caught a glimpse of Michal's lovely face, lit by the glow of an oil lamp, when she opened the door. When Doeg and his men rudely pushed past Michal, he leaned forward and his hand went to this sword, but he knew that Saul would not allow harm to come to his own daughter.

God would also protect Michal, but God required action from his people for the good of Israel. So it was a keen sense of duty that prevented David from going back into his home to test his sword against Saul's assassins. Instead he made his way to the gates of the citadel and was allowed to pass without question. He was, after all, the man who had killed Goliath, the man who had crushed the mighty army of the Philistines.

"How dare you enter my home?" Michal demanded of Doeg.

"I am here on orders from the king," the Edomite

said. His eyes were too small, his nose too large. His arms reached almost to his knees, and in one hand dangled a short, gleaming blade. "Where is David?" he demanded.

"Go back to the king," Michal said with great dignity, "and tell him that I do not allow mercenaries to invade my home."

One of Doeg's men pushed past Michal and threw open the door to the bedchamber. "He is here, Doeg," he whispered. "And he sleeps."

The remaining two men, both of whom had seen David in action against the Philistines, hung back. Doeg rushed into the bedchamber. David's body made a definite form under linen bed coverings. The Edomite ran across the room, lifted his blade, and, holding the hilt with both hands, plunged it into the shape under the bed coverings. He cursed. Something was wrong. He threw back the coverings to see goat-hair pillows arranged in the shape of a sleeping man.

Doeg stalked back into the other room. Michal smiled at him.

"Where is he?" he snarled.

"Are you so eager to find my husband now that you know he is not asleep and helpless?"

"Go to the king," Doeg told one of his men. "Inform him of what has happened here."

"You will leave my house," Michal ordered.

Doeg nodded. "Yes, perhaps that is best. We will take *you* to the king." He reached out to grasp Michal's arm. She clawed his face with her nails, leaving four red streaks along his cheek.

"Touch me and you will die so unpleasantly that your passing will become legend," she said.

"Witch," Doeg spat out. But he made no attempt to touch her again. She walked haughtily ahead of the mercenaries across the courtyard.

When Doeg entered the throne room, Saul was slumped on his throne. "He is dead, then," Saul said in a flat voice.

"No, lord," Doeg said. "He is fled, and your daughter aided him. She told us he was in his bed, but when we went in, there were only pillows under the robes."

"Where is he?" Saul asked quietly.

"So you did order this get of a jackal to invade my home," Michal said, striding across the room.

"Defy me, girl, and you will join the man you call husband in death," Saul said.

"Will you kill all those who love you?" Michal asked. "In God's name, Father, think what you are doing."

"Go from me," Saul said. "I will not suffer the presence of any who sides with traitors, even if you are of my own blood."

Michal hesitated.

"Shall I have my men remove you by force?" Saul demanded.

By morning, news of the events of the night were general knowledge. Mered was the first to gain entrance to the king's chamber, but he had no opportunity to speak before Urnan entered. The smith of Shiloh was the only one of Saul's old advisers who was still welcomed.

"Which of you will speak?" Saul asked sourly. "It is not merely to see my face that you seek me out so early."

"I have heard of David's treachery," Mered said. "It is evident, lord, that he has friends at court, friends who warned him that, at last, he was to get his desserts for his sins against you."

"What are those sins, Mered?" Urnan asked. He had persuaded his son not to search out and kill Mered for having Baalan and Sunu kidnapped. The right time would come for Mered to be punished. Now, as he faced the man, he tried to conceal his anger.

"Was it a sin against Saul and Israel when David slew the Philistine giant when no other man in Israel dared face him?" Urnan demanded. "Is his loyalty to Israel and to Israel's king a sin?"

"You try me sorely, Urnan," Saul said.

"Perhaps Urnan's opinion of David is colored by

the fact that his own son, Eri, has become David's personal armorer?" Mered asked.

"Eri makes arms for the Army of Israel," Urnan said. "When last I saw David in action he fought with that army."

Mered ignored Urnan and turned to the king. "You have made a beginning, sire. The attempt to punish David for his ambition failed last night. Now you must order not only David's death but the death of all those who support him."

Saul's face darkened.

"Do you support David, Urnan?" Mered asked.

Urnan touched his sword. "Let him who questions my loyalty to Saul and to Israel test his truth against mine."

"It is in my mind that Mered speaks wisely," Saul said. "David's ambition must be punished."

Saul's left cheek had taken up a rhythmic tic, a sign Urnan recognized as a precursor to one of the king's uncontrollable rages.

"Where is Eri?" Saul asked. A tear formed in one eye and rolled down into his black beard. "To think that he with whom I played tricks on the Dagon priests would desert me."

"He has not deserted you," Urnan said. "His wife and his son were stolen from his home. He has gone in search of them."

"And Jonathan?" Saul asked, looking at Mered.

"With his great friend, I would assume," Mered said.

"With his friend, Eri," Urnan said. "The prince has gone with my son to help in the recovery of my daughter-in-law and my grandson."

"They have all turned against me," Saul said, hanging his head. "All are against me."

Suddenly the king lifted his head and roared like a wounded lion. His eyes were fiery when he looked at Mered. "Give the order in my name," he shouted. "David must die, he and all those who stand with him."

Urnan backed slowly out of the chamber as Mered smirked at him in triumph. Although Urnan would not sit idly by and see Eri slain as an enemy of the throne, he knew that it was hopeless to try to convince Saul otherwise while he was in the grip of his devils.

He had to find Eri and warn him of Saul's decree. Perhaps, he thought grimly, he shouldn't have talked Eri out of killing Mered immediately.

CHAPTER TWENTY-ONE

For a boy approaching official manhood the great river that was the heart of the Two Lands could be a temptress, a siren whose song was formed of colors and smells and changing light. Kaptar had thought that he knew the river. He had hunted fat ducks in the marshes near the Southern City. He had seen the stealthy stalking of the crocodile and had, with a boy's casual bravery, sought out the nests of the great beasts in the reeds and the mud to watch the young emerge from their eggs and, peeping belligerently, scramble toward the safety of the water.

He knew the river as one who dwelt on its banks. To experience it while floating on it in a small boat was new to him. Great herons stood, melancholy and alone, in the shallows. The hunting dive of the fish-eagle fascinated him. Small jewels of beauty flashed past the boat as bee eaters flew low over the water. Swallows on gray wings flitted and twittered.

In the rich, green belt of cultivated land, farmers

chanted as they turned a thousand waterwheels. Horus, the hawk, sent his harsh cry downward from his dominating flight. Boats with white sails joined the struggle against the Nile's current or sailed northward riding the flow.

By the time he had sailed two days south of Waset, wonderful sights temporarily pushed aside thoughts of his mother's marriage. Aboard the dhow on which Kaptar was a passenger were two crewmen in addition to the captain, a weather-browned, sun-wrinkled man who, although he was no older in seasons than Kaptar's uncle Kemose, had aged prematurely. His name was Seti. He took delight in the name. On the first day he announced, "My mother named me for a great king in the hope that I would do great things like my namesake." He threw back his head, gazed into the cloudless dome of sky, and roared with laughter.

"I surprised her, didn't I?" he asked, winking at Kaptar.

To drink there was the water of the Nile. The staple of the crew's diet was the tough, chewy bread of the Egyptian countryman. Kaptar had tasted such bread before, and he always wondered if sand and grit were baked into the dough on purpose. Seti's teeth showed signs of being worn down by the constant crunching of sand, and the older crewman, an evil-faced ruffian called Nof, suffered terribly with his worn and rotted molars. A potent demon had taken up residence in one tooth, causing it to throb constantly and to swell Nof's jaw as if he held a large stone in his cheek.

The third member of the crew was a young man of no more than twenty summers. The gods had blessed him with the inability to realize that life was sometimes an ordeal. He, Messes, had only enough wit to enjoy everything—the heat of the sun, the chill of a night wind, the ache of his huge, tired muscles. He noticed little outside his immediate surroundings. He seemed a docile type, but when a cat wandered on board the dhow one night he displayed frightening cruelty. To most people, the cat was a sacred animal. To Messes, it was a living thing to be tormented into agonized howling and convulsive attempts to escape a slow, terrible death. When the animal was too weak to yowl at the indignities being performed on its dying body, Messes threw it into the river.

"That one," he said, laughing wildly, "will not be preserved for the ages by the fat priests. That one's spirit will not find the afterlife."

"That one," Seti said sadly to Kaptar, "I must acknowledge as my son."

Messes laughed. "I want his pretty sword," he said, pointing to Kaptar.

"I think that he will cut off your seeds and make you a eunuch if you try to take it," Seti said.

Both Messes and Nof took every opportunity to go ashore to seek out beer, a woman, or, preferably, both. In the day, if the wind was favorable and the dhow was moving southward without effort, they slept. At such times Kaptar took his turn on the sweep, steering the dhow up the broad, lazy river.

"You are not the son of a poor man," Seti said one afternoon when they were the only ones awake.

"My father was an armorer," Kaptar said, "as I am one of the Children of the Lion."

Seti laughed. "An armorer, and not yet a man?"

Kaptar extended his blade. "This I fashioned."

Seti took the sword and examined the fine workings on its hilt. "Excellent work indeed," he said. "A weapon that would make a king's son proud." He handed the sword back. "Tell me, young sir, what crime has forced you to flee Waset?"

"Not my crime, but my mother's," Kaptar said. "She married a Libyan."

"The gods of the Two Lands weep," Seti said.

"I felt like weeping myself," Kaptar said. "I would have enjoyed killing the Libyan more than weeping, but—" He shrugged. "I left."

"For what?"

Kaptar shrugged again. "I did not think except to put Waset behind me." He gazed out over the water to the green fields along the banks and to the shimmering yellow desert beyond. "My purpose now, Seti, is to see as much of this land as I can, to know its grandeur and its beauty. I want to talk with the common people and get to know them. I want to see the works of the great kings. I have heard that beyond the First Cataract is a temple the likes of which is not seen in all of the Two Lands north of it."

Seti nodded. "The temple of the great Ramses," he said. "Four stone giants cut into the rock of a sheer cliff. It is said that they guard against the passage of the black hordes of the far south."

"You have seen this temple?"

Seti nodded. "More than once. I will see it again, for, the gods permitting, I will trade with the black Nubians of Kush before returning to Waset."

"But what passes for law and order in this land today does not extend past the cataract."

"Those who live there welcome goods from the north." Seti chuckled. "Unless they happen to be in an evil mood and value blood more than the luxuries that I offer them for their gold."

"I think that a good sword arm might be of value to you if you encounter Nubians in a bad mood," Kaptar said.

Seti laughed and felt the well-developed biceps of Kaptar's right arm. "I warrant that arm, young as it is, can wield a good sword."

Late on a day of heat the river began to roar. At first it was nothing more than a whisper, so that Kaptar thought it was only the wind, but there was little wind. By twilight, when Seti directed the mooring of the dhow along the bank, the sound was like distant thunder. It lulled Kaptar to sleep, and when he awoke the dhow was already in midstream, flying before the winds that accompanied the rising sun. All that day they fought the strengthening current and rested early by tying up on the shore of a palm-dotted island on the east side of the river. Dates and fruit from the luxuriant vegetation made their evening meal.

"Here the sun god ruled," Seti said, as darkness came to the river. "And here Isis blesses those who pay her honor. Pray to her, young one, and she will answer you."

"I see no temples," Kaptar said. "I hear no priests chanting praise to Ra and Isis."

"But you believe in the resurrection of Osiris, surely," Seti said.

"I have seen the ceremony celebrating his death," Kaptar said carefully. "And his new life as well." Kemose paid public homage to Amon, god of Waset, while telling Kaptar about a host of other gods, including one introduced to him by Kaptar's father, Urnan, who spoke of the One God, of the God of Abraham. Kaptar was in no hurry to commit himself.

The dhow was under way with the sun, and was soon negotiating twisting channels where black rocks reared up from the blue water, turning it to white foam. To Kaptar the torrents seemed an impossible barrier, but Seti steered the dhow skillfully into a channel and grabbed a line from a group of men standing barefooted on the rocky shore. Using stout poles to keep the hull away from rocks worn smooth by the onslaught of thousands of years, Seti and the crew pulled the dhow through white water into channels that seemed too wild, too narrow. But, at last, the dhow reached calm water, the workers on the shore accepted the return of their line along with payment for their labors, and the land of Kush stretched out before them.

At first the land looked the same. True, the strips of arable soil along the banks were not as wide and rich as they were below the cataract. The desert crowded down upon the river as if threatening to dry up its flood with an ocean of sand, but the villages seemed to be prosperous, the cattle fat, the people industrious. All that soon changed. Villages lay desolate, mud-brick walls collapsed, waterwheels smashed, cropland abandoned to bake and crack in the sun. The chaos that came with the breaking up of the empire had hit the land south of the first cataract.

"The black savages have been here," Seti said.

"We must turn back," said old Nof, his voice distorted by the pain of his swollen jaw. When he spoke a smell of rot and decay arose from his mouth. "There will be no one left alive here."

"We have come far," Seti said. "At the first sign of danger we will turn back." He waved his hand toward a destroyed village. "Let us not forget that the Nubians will have new loot to trade for our cargo."

"There is no gold in a place such as that," Nof said.

Nevertheless, Seti pushed on. "Tomorrow," he told Kaptar, "you will see the stone giants of Ramses."

The two temples seemed to rise from the water's edge. The four giant images of the great Ramses sat in pairs on either side of the dark entrance to the rock temple. Peeking from between the sets of giant legs were statues of the great king's family.

"By the gods," Kaptar said. "They are taller than the statues of Amenhotep at Waset."

To the north of the great statues was a smaller cliff temple.

"That one is dedicated to the goddess Hathor," Seti said, "and to Ramses' queen, Nefertari."

Kaptar had eyes only for the great temple. On the thrones that held the giants were carved row upon row of figures, clearly prisoners, testimony to the victorious wars of the king. Above the king's face were lines of hieroglyphs and a row of baboons greeting the rising sun.

"The temple does not honor the king alone," Seti said. "The Great One built it to praise Amon, god of Waset; Ptah, god of On; Ra, the sun god." He chuckled. "And, of course, Ramses, god of all Egypt."

Kaptar was proud of his Mesopotamian blood, proud to be marked by the lion as a metalworker, like Cain, but he was half-Egyptian, and it grieved him to see the temples deserted and abandoned. The stone giants were shin-deep in sand. The ravenous desert was reclaiming its own.

Nof and Messes were unimpressed by the temples, concerned only with catching a nap and, at the end of the day, with choosing a mooring site for the night so that they could prepare the evening meal. Just before sunset Seti agreed that it was time to stop. He steered the dhow to the bank, where Messes leaped ashore to secure lines to two stout palms. He had tied only one when, with a deadly hiss and an audible impact, an arrow struck Seti in the hollow at the base of his throat.

"The savages . . ." Nof gasped.

Kaptar reacted instantly. With a slash of his sword he severed the line that held the dhow to the shore.

"Quickly!" he yelled to Messes.

The muscular young man leaped for the gunwale, missed, and splashed into the water. While Nof pushed the dhow away from shore with a long pole, Kaptar reached down for Messes and was almost dragged into the water before Messes clambered aboard.

Another arrow hissed by Kaptar's ear.

"Keep down," he ordered. He did not have to speak twice.

The dhow was picking up momentum as the current moved it away from the bank. Kaptar crawled to the side of the fallen Seti.

The arrow had pierced all the way through to sever Seti's spinal cord. "He's dead," he told the others.

"I told him we should turn back. It's too dangerous here," Nof said.

Messes was kneeling beside Seti's body. He made a sound deep in his throat that caused the hair to stir on the back of Kaptar's neck.

"He's dead," Nof said. "Stop that noise."

Messes rocked back and forth, still groaning, his head bobbing up and down as if in prayer.

"Quiet," Nof said roughly.

"What are we going to do?" Messes asked.

"We'll bury him when it's safe to go ashore," Kaptar said.

"But he's bleeding all over the deck, and I'm the one who has to clean it up," Messes said.

"Help me," Nof said, lifting the dead man's legs.

Messes reached under his father's body with his powerful hands. Before Kaptar realized what they intended, the two men had swung Seti over the gunwale.

The body made a surprisingly small splash as it went into the water.

Shocked by this disrespect for the dead, Kaptar leaped to the rail. Sensing movement behind him, he whirled just in time to fall away from a wild swing of Nof's arm. In the crewman's hand was a wooden pin used for tightening lines, and the heavy club grazed Kaptar's head. A thousand suns burst inside his skull.

"You can have the sword now," Nof said to Messes.

The words came to Kaptar from a world away. He struggled to raise himself on one elbow. He saw the powerfully built son of Seti start toward him. He didn't know how his sword came into his hand. It seemed as if his arm was moving as slowly as a turtle seeking the sun on a muddy bank, but he felt the blade strike solid flesh, heard a scream of pain. The blow to Messes' leg sent him sprawling to the deck. The dimwit screamed again as he clutched his leg, blood running between his fingers.

Nof whirled one of the push poles at Kaptar's head. Again Kaptar seemed to be moving with a turtle's slowness, and it seemed that there was only one way to escape being smashed by the heavy pole. He rolled over the gunwale. Water closed over his head, and in the eerie silence he could hear his own blood coursing through his veins. He kicked for the surface. The coolness of the water cleared his senses. He took a deep breath and saw that the dhow was drifting off downstream. He raised his head to orient himself, then set out toward the nearest bank. He had learned to swim, and swim well, in the pleasure lakes of the royal family. He swam slowly, conserving his strength, and came ashore far downstream of where the dhow had been attacked.

He felt his feet touch bottom, swam a few strokes farther, and stood with his toes sinking into Nile mud. Something bumped into him. In the growing darkness he imagined the sharp teeth and strong jaws of a crocodile. He struggled toward the bank in chest-deep water, but the weight still rubbed against him. He looked down to see the shaft of an arrow protruding from Seti's neck.

He forced down a scream and ran frantically into the shallows and far up on the bank before he stopped and turned around. He could see that Seti's body had lodged a few paces downstream against a mudbank. The crocodiles would find it there and carry it to their underwater lair to ripen.

Seti had been kind to him. If the crocodiles tore apart his body he would not live in the hereafter. Kaptar ran into the shallow water and pulled the body to the bank. When it was safely on dry sand he rested; then, little by little, he dragged the dead man across the sandy beach and into the cracked mud of a once-cultivated field. A sound behind him made him freeze and sent his hand toward his sword. A rawboned donkey, emerging from a field of sere weeds, stopped to stare at him.

"Good fellow," Kaptar said, holding out his hand as he walked toward the animal. "Good boy."

The donkey stood stock-still, then nuzzled Kaptar's hand. "Well, you were someone's pet, eh?" Kaptar whispered when he saw a halter and reins. "Help me, fellow, and I'll try to find you a home."

He led the animal to Seti's body. The donkey stood obligingly still as Kaptar, mustering all of his strength, lifted Seti and draped him across the donkey's back.

He found a pathway up the low cliffs and led the laden donkey to the top, where soft desert sand poured over the edge of the rocks in tiny, dry rivulets. Scooping up the sand with his hands he dug a hole and buried Seti.

"God of the dead be with you," he said, as he pushed sand over the body. "It is the best I can do, my friend."

The sun-heated sand would desiccate the body tissues and preserve Seti's bone and his mummified flesh almost as well as all the magic of the priests in the house of the dead at Waset.

"May you find peace, my friend, and live a life good and sweet in that other world."

He did not ride the emaciated donkey, but led him down to the river. He could only guess how far it was to the last occupied village they had passed, but he had no doubt that he would reach it. There was water aplenty, enough water to give the gift of life to Egypt over the millennia. There were palm trees laden with dates, and fat quail came to the riverside to drink in the evening. With his tree-climbing skills and accuracy with small stones he had both fruit and meat for his evening meal.

He slept that night curled in a hollow in the sand. The earth held its heat until the early morning hours, when he awoke shivering with cold. There was, as yet, no hint of dawn.

"No need to wait," he said to the donkey, and they set off down the riverbank, walking slowly. Quite suddenly the oddly serene faces of the stone giants of Ramses appeared, eerily real and yet unearthly.

In the gray light of dawn the images of the great king wore a static, fatalistic look. Behind him, to the east, the sky warmed and the red flush of the rising sun gave color to the stone faces. They changed as if by magic, smiled, and flashed for one brief moment with the stuff of life. The transformation lasted no more than four heartbeats, and then the river and the rocks of the cliffs became distinct in the steady light of day and the stone giants were once more simply stone.

CHAPTER
TWENTY-TWO

Unaware that Saul had ordered Eri's death, Eri and Jonathan followed the trail of Baalan's kidnappers northeastward into the vale of the Jordan. Although the river was a relatively small one, steep banks allowed for few natural fords. The route of the Ammonites had been easy to follow, for strangers were rare in the hills of Israel. When the two friends went down into the rich, green Jordan Valley it became clear that Baalan's captors would have had to cross the river at one of two places. Eri chose the one farther to the south, since it seemed unlikely that Ammonites would travel northward toward the land of Gad.

"When Joshua crossed the Jordan it was an event no less miraculous than the parting of the waters of the Red Sea," Jonathan said when he and Eri had crossed the river and halted on a rise overlooking the dense green trees that lined the narrow river. "Somehow, today, it doesn't seem so impressive."

"Look," Eri said, pointing to a thin column of smoke that arose from a grove of trees.

They left the horses a safe distance away. As they crept into the copse, swords in hand, they heard low voices. Suddenly a small voice, reedy, childish, rose to audibility.

"Wait until my father and my grandfather come," said the voice, and Eri's heart leaped. The brave voice was his son's. But his face went dark when the sound of a sharp blow rang out.

"Don't strike my child," he heard Baalan cry.

He motioned to Jonathan to go to the left and circle behind the men, who were congregated around a fire in the center of the grove. Jonathan nodded and moved ahead. Eri circled the camp from the other direction. He counted seven Ammonites. Two men were roasting a lamb over the fire; two were sprawled on the ground sleeping. Baalan sat with her back against a tree. Chains dangled from her wrists as she cuddled Sunu to her breast.

Eri guessed that a tall, rather dirty man who stood over Baalan with a sneer on his lips was the one who had slapped Sunu.

"Be grateful, woman, that I do not give you to my men as a toy," the tall man in the filthy robe said. When Baalan spat at his feet, he laughed. "Keep that up, slut, and I just might let them take you in spite of the fact that you would not be of much value after they finished with you."

Sunu jerked out of his mother's arms and kicked the tall man on the shin. The Ammonite lifted his hand.

Eri stepped into the clearing. "I heard my wife tell you not to strike the boy," he said.

The tall Ammonite whirled, reaching for his weapon. Eri leaped forward, leading with a broad sweep of his sword that left the Ammonite with a gaping hole in his throat. He whirled and with his backswing opened the stomach cavity of a second man. On the other side of the clearing Jonathan gave his distinctive war cry, a bellow that seemed to fill the glen as the remaining Ammonites scrambled for their weapons. Jonathan quickly dispatched two men. The sleepers were scrambling to their feet. The man who had been basting the roasting lamb picked up a flaming stick from the fire and hurled it at Eri. Eri deflected it with his sword and, as the cook leaped to his feet, drove his blade deep into the man's abdomen.

"Father, behind you," Sunu cried out.

Eri jerked his blade free, ducked as a blade whistled over his head, turned, parried the Ammonite's backswing and, with two quick slashes, killed him.

The last of the men, seeing his fellows so easily slain, tried to flee. Jonathan drew his dagger and threw it at him. The blade buried itself in the man's back. The runner took only three more steps, then stopped and fell to the ground, his limbs twitching. It was over quickly. Seven men were dead.

"You see, Mother," Sunu said, holding Baalan's hand, "I told you that my father would come for us."

Eri knelt in front of his wife and son, took the boy in his arms, and reached out to touch Baalan's face.

"If you had not come," Sunu said, "I would have killed them myself." He drew a little dagger out from under his tunic. "I would not have let them hurt my mother."

Jonathan withdrew the pin holding the chains on Baalan's wrists. She flung them away.

"We're going home," Eri said, reaching out to draw Baalan to him while still holding Sunu with his other arm.

"To share a house with the one who arranged this?" Baalan asked.

Eri frowned. "You know?" he asked.

"She laughed when she saw me bound and gagged and carted away. She said that I would remember my place when I was in slavery over Jordan, and that never again would I be in a position to put on airs and aspire to a position above my station in life."

"I loved her once," Eri said.

"I know," Baalan said soothingly.

"But this treachery against you, you who cared for her so tenderly, is too much to bear."

Baalan shook her head, not knowing what to say.

Nor did Eri. Sarah had been such a beautiful girl, and his heart had leaped with joy when she agreed to be his; but shortly afterward she had become a burden. Baalan, who had come into his house as a slave, had given him only loyal service, love, and joy. His first thought was that he would take his daughter from Sarah and send the mother away in disgrace.

"She is not herself," Baalan said. "We must understand that she is still troubled by the terrible things that happened to her."

"Did terrible things not happen to you?" Eri asked. "Did not your family sell you into slavery to be the servant of any man who had the money to pay the price that was set upon you? You did not let that color your life forever, did you?"

Baalan shook her head in agreement.

"And I. I saw the Philistines rape and kill my mother. I wore the slave collar and watched my father being dragged away from me. Did that give me an excuse to retreat from life and claim that whatever wrong I do cannot be blamed on me but on the terrible things that happened to me?" He shook his head. "No," he said firmly. "She will be held accountable for her actions."

They set up camp upstream from the scene of slaughter, taking the Ammonites' half-cooked lamb with them. Eri built a fire and Baalan put the meat on a spit of green wood. Soon they were all eating hungrily.

They met Urnan at midmorning the next day as they traveled back toward Gibeah. He was greeted with much enthusiasm by his grandson, who insisted on telling in one long burst of words how his father and Jonathan had slain scores of Ammonite bandits to rescue him and his mother. The smith listened patiently and fondly. It was only when Sunu paused for breath that he said, "Thank God I found you before you reached Gibeah."

"What is wrong?" Jonathan asked.

"The king, urged on by Mered, has given orders

that David is to be slain on sight, David and all who support him."

"Then has he passed the death sentence on me?" Jonathan asked, his face pale.

"No, not on you," Urnan said.

"On Eri?" Jonathan asked in amazement.

Urnan nodded.

"I should have killed Mered a long time ago," Jonathan said. "Who is more loyal to Saul than Eri?"

"David has fled," Urnan said.

"Where?" Eri asked.

"My guess is that he has gone to Ramah, where he might claim the protection of Samuel," Urnan said. "I suggest that you do the same."

"I will go to the citadel," Jonathan said grimly. "I will speak with my father."

"Walk softly," Urnan said. "The devils that possess the king have been active."

"And what of my daughter?" Eri asked.

"Mered and his wife have taken Sarah under their protection," Urnan said. He raised one hand when he saw the anger in Eri's face. "I know. Mered deserves to die, but he has the ear of the king, and he has told Saul that Sarah is estranged from you because of your disloyalty to Saul. She and the child will be safe, at least for the time being."

"Until one of us kills Mered," Jonathan said softly.

"I'll keep an eye on them," Urnan said.

"You're going back?" Eri asked. "The king isn't rational; isn't there a chance that he will condemn you because you are my father?"

"No, I'm safe enough, and perhaps I can leaven the advice that is given to Saul by people like Mered."

Urnan took a leather bag from his pack and handed it to Eri. From its weight and irregular shape Eri guessed that it contained silver ingots.

"You'll need this," Urnan said.

"I'm grateful," Eri said.

"I'll keep the forges running," Urnan said. "If this fight between Saul and David isn't settled soon, we'll need all the armament we can produce. Galar is not a stupid man. When he hears of dissension within the army, he'll strike."

"If my father continues this senseless persecution of David, half the army, perhaps more, will side not with the king but with David," Jonathan said. "Let us pray to God that we can prevent a permanent division of the Army of Israel."

The guards before the gate of Saul's citadel greeted Jonathan and Urnan eagerly. Inside the walls they were approached by a young officer.

"How is it with the king?" Jonathan asked.

"He is calm," the officer said.

"And David?"

"He has fled."

Saul did, indeed, look quite calm. He lounged on his throne eating a melon. "Where have you been?" he asked without emotion.

Mered was standing behind Saul in the shadows. Half a dozen of Saul's so-called advisers were scattered around the room.

"I want to speak to my father alone," Jonathan said. "Leave us." He directed his gaze at Mered, who shifted uneasily.

"It is I who give the orders here," Saul said.

Mered's pouting lips spread in a smirk.

"Of course you do," Jonathan said. "Your permission, Father, to address you in privacy."

"Leave us," Saul said, waving a hand. He tossed the melon aside. It broke into several pieces on the stone floor. A servant ran forward. "Not now," Saul said calmly. He looked at Urnan. "You will be a part of this private conference between me and my son?"

"If I may," Urnan said.

"If I cannot trust you—" Saul paused, frowned, and cast a baleful glare at Jonathan.

Mered was the last to leave the throne room. Saul watched him go, then said, "We are alone. Speak."

"Father," Jonathan said, falling to his knees, "I implore you in the name of the One God to reconsider your death sentence against David."

Saul frowned. "Where is he?"

"I know not," Jonathan said.

"Liar."

"I have never lied to you, Father. If I had to guess I would say that David is on his way to Bethlehem, to be safe among his own people in Judah."

"He will not be safe anywhere," Saul said fiercely, "no matter where he flees."

"No man has been more faithful to you," Jonathan said. "No man, save only you, has done more for Israel. You have treated him unfairly, Father. You heed the advice of the wrong people."

Saul leaned forward. "You are my firstborn son," he said, his voice deceptively soft. "It is you I want to sit on this throne when I am gone, but as long as the son of Jesse lives the crown will never rest on your head."

"If seeing Israel divided, if seeing the tribes fighting among themselves is the price I must pay to be called king, I will gladly forgo it," Jonathan said.

"Saul," Urnan said, "David acknowledges your son as the rightful heir to the throne. He will be as loyal to Jonathan as he has been to you."

"You, too, old friend?" Saul asked sadly. "The Judahite has bewitched you, too?"

"Father, it is said that you have condemned not only David, but others of my friends," Jonathan said.

"I do it for you," Saul said.

"Then I ask you not to," Jonathan said. "You would see Eri dead? The son of your friend, my friend, the man who put iron weapons into our hands and fought at my side against the Philistine?"

"Try me no further," Saul said.

Urnan touched Jonathan's arm, for he saw the madness glinting in Saul's eyes.

"It is not right, Father. It is not just to turn on men who have given you their allegiance, who have fought bravely for Israel."

Without a word Saul rose, walked slowly to the wall, and took down a long, iron-tipped ceremonial javelin.

"Enough, Jonathan," Urnan whispered.

Jonathan took a step forward and thrust out his chest. "Would you kill me, Father, because I talk reason to you?"

Saul balanced the long spear expertly. He drew back his arm. His robe fell aside to reveal his powerful biceps. Urnan took a deep breath.

"Do you ally yourself with my enemies?" Saul asked, his voice harsh and hard.

"Never," Jonathan said.

"Then forswear your misguided friendship with David."

"David is not your enemy," Jonathan said heatedly.

As Saul launched the javelin directly at Jonathan, Urnan drove his entire weight against the prince. They fell to the floor together. The javelin swished past Jonathan's head, blunted its tip against the stone wall, and crashed to the floor.

Urnan rolled to his feet. Saul stood mutely, arms at his sides.

"Come," Urnan said, taking Jonathan's hand and pulling him to his feet. Jonathan started to speak. "Not now," Urnan cautioned, "not now."

Jonathan nodded, bowed to his father, and backed out of the throne room.

"Where will you go?" Urnan asked as they left the palace.

"I don't know. I am a man divided down the middle."

"Stay here in Gibeah," Urnan said. "Perhaps together we can do something to lessen the influence of the evil ones."

They fell silent as a common soldier approached. "Prince Jonathan?"

Jonathan nodded.

"A message," the soldier whispered. "He will meet you at the place you know well."

"He?" Jonathan asked.

"I must not speak his name here," the soldier said.

Jonathan nodded. The soldier hurried away. "He has not fled to either his people or to Samuel," Jonathan said. "I must go to him and warn him that the situation is hopeless, that he will surely be killed."

Urnan nodded his agreement. "Be careful," he said.

"And you. What will you do now?"

"I will stay here for a while, but soon I must go north to oversee a mining operation. There's a little village called Endor near Mount Tabor." He smiled with fond memories of Jerioth.

"I'll tell David that Eri has gone to Ramah," Jonathan said. "God go with you."

"I will take my chances," Urnan said, "and leave God to use all His powers to protect Israel, lest she be divided before Galar's army."

CHAPTER
TWENTY-THREE

It seemed to Kaptar that all the world stood in awe of the past grandeur of the great king. After the magical moment when the first rays of the morning sun gave brief life to the huge, serene faces, there was a hush. Even the river ceased its gurglings along the sandy beach, and the silence of eternity wrapped the boy in an unseen cocoon.

He had never felt more lonely. He turned away, unable to withstand the insistent stare of the four giant memorials to Ramses II, and walked toward a second, smaller temple also carved from the solid face of the cliff. Red sand, already beginning to warm in the morning sun, covered the terrace before it and clogged the entrance almost to the top. On either side of the doorway were six smaller statues of Ramses and his queen, Nefertari. The queen's head was adorned with the plumes and disk of the god Hathor. She was posed with her daughters, the king with his sons.

"Ramses, the Strong in Truth, the Beloved of

Amon, made this divine abode for his royal wife, Nefertari, whom he loves," the hieroglyphs cut deeply in the stone proclaimed.

The names of Ramses and Nefertari were always mentioned together. Kaptar ignored a quick rise of bitterness. He knew from hearing his mother talk about Urnan, his father, that they, like Ramses and Nefertari, had loved each other. The Libyan had robbed them of that happiness, had not allowed Kaptar to know his father, and now his mother was married to the very man who had separated her from the husband with whom she had merged souls.

Thinking of the world he had left, so very real, so more immediately pressing than that of the quiet, abandoned temples, brought him back to reality. He heard the lap of wavelets on the sand of the riverbank, the sigh of the wind around the cliffs, the call of a waterfowl. He returned to the larger temple. The insidious sand of the desert was challenging Ramses' claim to immortality, blocking the entrance almost as completely as it did at the Nefertari temple. Leaving his donkey behind, Kaptar scrambled up the slope. Grains of the desert poured over the crag and rained down not only on the head of the Ramses statues but on Kaptar as he crawled over the top of the mound and slid into the gloom of the interior.

There was enough light coming in the opening to see statues of Osiris on either side of the door. Each image carried a corn measure on its head as a symbol of plenty. As Kaptar's eyes adjusted he saw that he was in a huge hall divided by three rows of statues supporting the roof. The walls, dimly lit, were covered with colorful hieroglyphs. Kaptar moved closer to a wall and saw the figure of Ramses in a war chariot in the act of shooting an arrow at the enemies of Egypt. Around him were the dead, the earth strewn with them, and the wounded begging for mercy.

"Ah, great king," Kaptar said aloud, "how the Two Lands need you now."

His voice echoed eerily. Sensing the black emptiness behind him, he turned swiftly. The depths of the temple were lost in the darkness. The echoes died and now even the silence seemed ancient. As Kaptar strained his eyes, his peripheral vision played tricks on him. Things moved just at the edge of his sight, but when he turned his head they were gone.

"Great king," he cried again, and the words were taken up by a deeper, more resonant voice speaking words he could not understand. It was as if the gods of Egypt had stepped down from the walls and were calling to him out of the darkness. His heart thudded. He couldn't swallow. He touched his small sword, but he knew that even a sharp iron blade was of no avail against the spirits of the dead. He turned, poised for flight, and out of the corner of his eye he saw a flash at the base of one of the columns. Anger replaced panic. He ran lightly, his footsteps padded by the sand that lay on the floor, to approach the pillar from the rear.

A figure smelling stale and old crouched there. Kaptar lifted his sword, but did not strike.

"Who are you?" he asked.

The gray-clad figure gave a gasp of surprise and started to run. Kaptar reached out and seized a handful of fabric. He heard a ripping sound, but the robe held. There was a struggle. Kaptar was the stronger, although he was only a boy, and when the two adversaries fell to the floor he was on top.

"Mercy," said an old, trembly voice. "There is nothing left here worth stealing."

"I came not to steal," Kaptar said. He grabbed the man's shoulder and turned him around to see the face of an old man, sere, wrinkled, desiccated by the desert almost as if it had been buried in the sand. "Who are you?"

"You're only a boy," the old man said.

"Man enough to hold you," Kaptar said.

"True, but it is not necessary, after all, to hold me, young sir. If it is true that you come not to do mischief I will not try to escape you."

Kaptar pushed himself to his feet, then took the old man's fragile arm and helped him up. His robes were those of a priest of Amon.

"Your name, sir," Kaptar said.

"I am Ikkur, high priest of the temple of Userma`atre`."

"Give me your hand," Kaptar said.

He took the priest's hand and arm and gave the secret sign of identification of the Amon priests at Waset. The old man lifted his head and cackled happily.

"At last someone has come," he said. "I gave up hope long ago, thinking that the barbarian hordes had destroyed the Two Lands." He bent and kissed Kaptar's hand. "Thank the gods."

Kaptar pulled his hand gently away.

"But you are no priest," Ikkur said.

"I am the son of Tania, princess of Egypt, nephew of Kemose, high priest of Amon at Waset."

"Gods be praised," Ikkur said. "But where are the others? Where are the workers to restore this holy place to its glory? Where are the soldiers to drive away the savage Nubians?"

"Sadly, I am alone," Kaptar said.

"Then all is lost?"

"Not all," Kaptar said. "Upriver, as you fear, there is chaos and savagery, but my uncle Kemose rules Upper Egypt to the First Cataract."

"And the old land of Lower Egypt?"

"In the hands of, or at least under the influence of, foreigners."

"The Peleset?"

"No. These people came from the western deserts, from Libya."

"You lie," the old man said. "The western deserts are fit only for goatherds. None such could conquer one of the Two Lands."

"They did not conquer the delta by force of arms," Kaptar said, "but by breeding like mice in a granary. At first they were few, and they were tolerated by the rich landowners as a source of cheap labor, but they came in greater numbers, and they bred, and in their countless thousands they infested the land. They did the jobs that no Egyptian wanted to do. They were willing mercenaries in the army and errand runners in the royal courts. And little by little everything that was Egyptian was submerged, for, like water, culture seeks the lowest level."

"My, how learned you sound," the old priest said.

"I have had good teachers," Kaptar said.

"So you are alone. That means, I suppose, that you're hungry."

"I will not take your food. Later I'll hunt. There are waterfowl on the river and perhaps a gazelle on the edge of the desert."

"Come," the old man said. He lit a torch and led Kaptar into the deep darkness toward the rear of the temple. In the sanctuary, at the feet of the gods of Egypt, Kaptar ate cold meat by the light of an oil lamp.

"In return," Ikkur said, "you have a story to tell me."

So it was, that deep in the heart of a mountain where the eternal darkness was disturbed only by one flickering oil lamp, Kaptar told of the events of the past decades in Egypt's history, and of his father, his mother, his uncle, his desperation when his mother married the Libyan.

"Has it ever occurred to you that the princess Tania had good reasons to marry the Libyan?" Ikkur asked.

"For Egypt?" Kaptar asked, his voice rich with sarcasm. "That's what she said."

"Was your mother in the habit of lying to you?"

He thought for a few moments, then shook his head.

"Could it possibly be that she was telling you the truth?"

"It shames Egypt for a princess of the blood to marry a foreigner," Kaptar said.

"Unless by doing so she serves your uncle, the ruler of Upper Egypt?"

Kaptar was silent for a long time. "I should have talked with her," he said at last. "I should have asked her. Even if Kemose had sworn her to secrecy she would have given me some hint."

"I would say that it is not too late," the old priest said. "Perhaps you have traveled the wrong way?"

"No," he said slowly, pondering his words, "for I have seen the greatness of empire." All at once the path of his life seemed clear to him beyond his boyish plan to kill Musen. "When I am a man I will lead an Egyptian army up past the First Cataract, and I will return to Kush the glory that was known in the times of the great kings." As he spoke he remembered words he thought he'd heard his uncle speak as they celebrated around the campfire after he killed the lion. The next morning he had assumed it was the wine that made him imagine the words, but now he thought his uncle had truly spoken them and that he might have been right. Perhaps he, Kaptar, would be the king who saved Egypt.

"I think you just might," Ikkur said, "but I fear that it will be too late for me to cheer your triumph." He chuckled. "In the meantime, I am tired, and sleep calls me."

Kaptar slept under a musty-smelling robe and was awakened by the touch of the old priest's hand on his shoulder. He opened his eyes to the darkness of the netherworld.

"Sit up," Ikkur said.

Kaptar obeyed. Ikkur put his hand on the boy's chin and pushed. "There," he said. "Watch."

"How does one watch total darkness?"

"Be patient."

Kaptar listened to his own heartbeat. The darkness was unbroken. The air was stale. Suddenly a long, level beam of liquid sun flashed down the length of the temple to penetrate the darkness like a molten arrow, to reach into the tiny sanctuary at the far rear of the temple and fall like gold from the heavens on the altar at the feet of the gods of Egypt.

"The great king lives," Ikkur whispered.

The light faded. Kaptar sat, stunned by the experience. After a time Ikkur lit the oil lamp and shared his breakfast of dates. By the flickering light he took papyrus from an alcove and sat on the floor, groaning as he assumed the position of a scribe. He wrote laboriously, using the ancient ceremonial hieroglyphs.

"Shall I read it to you?" he asked, when he was finished.

"I need no help in reading the priestly signs," Kaptar said proudly, taking the papyrus. He read aloud:

" 'To the Great Prince, may he live, Kemose, High Priest of Amon. Let it be known that the boy called Kaptar has acquitted himself well in the abode of the god Userma`atre`, Ramses the King, may he live forever. Be advised, Great Prince, that a boy who fears not the spirits of the dead and will attack a shade from the afterworld is worthy of great things. Guard his future in the name of our god, Amon.' "

Kaptar smiled and looked at the old priest. "Come with me, Ikkur."

"These old legs would not carry me through one day."

"I'll go down to the village," Kaptar said, "and get a boat. Then I will come for you."

"You are kind, young prince, but no. I have been here since I was no older than you, and the gods speak to me here. I will lie down one night and join them, and here in the darkness and the heat of the desert they will preserve my earthly body. My *ka* will worship with the soul of Ramses, and with the *kas* of his queen and the young princes and princesses. I will pay tribute to beautiful Beketmut, who stands by the king's left leg in front of the temple, and Merytamun the mystical, and—" His voice trailed off. "But you do not need for me to call the roll of the spirits that inhabit my abode."

He took Kaptar's hand. "Go with the gods," he said. "And do as you have said you will do. Restore Kush to the empire. If when you come you discover my bones here in front of the altar of the gods, remember me and treat them with respect."

"I will, Ikkur," Kaptar said. "I promise you that I will."

CHAPTER
TWENTY-FOUR

Ahimelech, the high priest of Yahweh at Nob, had a distinguished guest. He considered the visit of David to be a gift from God, and he had opened the stores of the temple to give the hero of all Israel the finest food and drink. That it was a drain on the temple's resources to entertain David's followers was the price to be paid for the honor of hosting the man whom Samuel had anointed king of Israel.

David had not fled the wrath of Saul alone. After his meeting with Jonathan, during which each pledged his love and friendship, David spoke to his tightly knit band of warriors, telling them that they were free to leave his service and remain with their families.

"That Saul, the king, hates me does not mean that you must give up your loyalty to Israel," he had said, "for I myself will never do that."

To a man they had followed him, and during the march to Nob, more men joined them.

On a pleasant morning Ahimelech found his guest

seated on a garden bench outside the temple looking at the view. In the distance the Judean hills were smoky with morning mist. Jerusalem, the little village named for a Canaanite god, Shalem, perched like a jewel on the ridge overlooking the Kidron and Hinnom valleys.

"It is a fair place," David said as Ahimelech approached.

"A hive of heathen idol worshipers," the priest said.

"One day we will change that."

The priest nodded. One day, he felt, God would at last fulfill his pledge that all of the Promised Land would belong to the Chosen People.

"Son of Jesse," Ahimelech said, "I have something for you if you will come with me."

David took a deep breath, tore his eyes away from the view, and followed. Since leaving Gibeah and his beloved Michal he had suffered from a lassitude against which he seemed to have no defense. He had prayed, asking for guidance, but there had been no answer. He felt guilty for having allowed so many men, the elite warriors of the Army of Israel, to accompany him. He was intimidated by the prospect of having to provision them, and he was undecided as to how to employ them. If anyone had asked he might have said that he would go on fighting the Philistines, but the statement would not have carried conviction.

He had done what no other man dared do. With the help of God he had played a part in freeing the land from the savagery of the Philistines. To what avail? To be almost skewered, twice, by Saul's javelin? To be condemned to death by the man whom he would have been pleased to call father?

Gradually he became aware that the priest had stopped in a small room. He focused his attention and recognized the armor of Goliath hanging on the wall. When the priest took down Goliath's massive sword, he took it with both hands. Not even Saul, who was larger and stronger than most, could have wielded it in battle.

"This weapon, the sword of the giant whom you slew, is yours," Ahimelech said.

"It will be of small use to me," David said with a laugh. "To carry it to battle would exhaust me, and I would have no strength left to fight."

"God will give strength to you," the priest said.

"The place for Goliath's sword is here," David said firmly, "where it can be seen, where it can remind all that God was with me and with Israel on that day."

"The sword is for the king of Israel," Ahimelech said.

"Then have it delivered to Saul."

"It was not Saul whom Samuel anointed in the house of Jesse in Judah."

"Saul is king," David said heatedly. "I will hear no more of such talk."

"God has lifted the crown from the head of Saul and placed it on yours," the priest said. "So it is written, so it was prophesied long ago."

"I acknowledge your gift," David said, "even while I question the wisdom of the priesthood in turning from the king who freed most of Israel from the Philistines."

Nevertheless, when the small army marched away from Nob, the sword of Goliath was stored with the baggage, well oiled and carefully wrapped in a sheepskin.

One day an advance patrol returned escorting Eri, Baalan, and Sunu.

Eri cut short the joyful greetings. "The king has moved swiftly," he said. "His troops block all roads leading southward to Judah."

"You have seen them?" David asked.

"I have seen many men lying in wait," Eri said, "so many that I didn't dare try to pass, even though I was a man alone with his wife and son."

David thought for a few moments. "Where are you going?"

"The armories in the Wilderness of Judah. Although Saul has put a price on my head I will not stop doing my part to keep Israel armed."

"I expected the king to try to block our route, which is why I marched southwest toward Gath. How in

God's name did he manage to post men on roads this far to the west?"

"You must remember that Saul taught the fighting men of Israel how to move quickly while he was alone in the battle against the Philistines," Eri said.

David called his captains to him and gave orders to reverse the march. The route was long, and with each day there was danger that Saul's army would appear, but God was with David as he marched toward the northern end of the great Salt Sea.

From just northeast of Gath David's army countermarched past Bethlehem to the north beyond the great Salt Sea. More than once it seemed that the blood of brothers would irrigate the dry hills, for Saul's minions had moved out of Gibeah in force, forsaking the old fight against the Philistines to slay David. Each time, however, David avoided conflict by moving swiftly. To his men it seemed that God had given him intimate knowledge of the land, for he moved his small army along obscure routes.

With a picked company of Saul's followers in pursuit, David marched southward into the land of Moab and in the rugged, arid lands to the east of the Salt Sea, always eluding those who followed. It was the glacial winter of David's soul.

Doeg the Edomite returned to Gibeah as exhausted as his men, only to find the king in a fury. All had fled the throne room except Urnan, the one man courageous enough to brave Saul's rages.

"Where is his head?" Saul demanded of Doeg. "Where is the head of the man who defies me and seeks my throne?"

"He will trouble you no more," Doeg said. "We have driven him from Israel far to the east into the land of Moab."

"And what is to keep him from marching back?" Saul bellowed.

"Your army, sire, will be on constant alert."

"If my army was incapable of finding and defeating

a force that it outnumbered five to one how can I expect it to do better in the future?"

Doeg saw the madness building in Saul's eyes. "Had it not been for the priests we would have taken him," he said quickly.

Saul froze and stood motionless, glaring balefully at the Edomite.

Doeg continued. "Ahimelech and the priests at Nob gave him sanctuary and provisioned him."

Saul's face hardened with determination. "We march," he said. "Prepare the troops."

"The objective, sire?"

"Nob," Saul said.

Doeg saluted and turned smartly on his heels. He had thought to tell the king that the army was exhausted and needed at least three days' rest, but if the king merely wanted to go to Nob to reprimand the priests for aiding David, the king's own guard would be force enough.

"You will come, Urnan," Saul said.

"As you wish," Urnan said.

Saul left his citadel with the rising sun, marching at the head of the elite guard with Doeg and Urnan at his side. At the end of the march he positioned his forces before Nob and ordered a good night's rest. With the morning he personally inspected the guard and addressed them in a loud, ringing voice.

"There before you lies Nob, where my enemy was given comfort. A nest of traitors." He looked out over his men, studying their faces. He saw only stern loyalty among the handpicked men.

"Some of you were with me in the land of the Amalekites. You will remember that Samuel ordered every living thing to be destroyed. In the name of God he ordered me to spare nothing, no woman, no child, not even the cattle of the field. You will remember that I spared the life of the Amalekite king, and gave to the men of the army the choice specimens of Amalekite cattle as legitimate spoil. For that my reward was to be ostracized by the priests."

He paused dramatically. "Now the priests, not con-

tent with their insidious undermining of me in the name
of the God who is also my God, have actively opposed
my will by allying themselves with the man whose only
goal is to wrest the throne from me and my family. Will
we allow them to go unpunished?"

The guard roared as one. "No! No! No!"

"It was Samuel himself who set the precedent,"
Saul cried. "He showed no mercy to the Amalekites. Let
us show no mercy to those who have declared themselves to be our enemies. Let nothing living remain in
Nob."

A hoarse battle cry went up from the guard. Officers began giving orders and positioning the troops.

Urnan found Saul standing on a crag looking out
toward the city. "Saul," he said, "the people of Nob are
of the seed of Abraham."

The king turned his face and looked Urnan full in
the eye. He had been weeping. "It was not easy for me
to give that order," he said.

"Easier to rescind it," Urnan said.

Saul shook his head sadly. "I cannot."

Not for the first time, Urnan wished he could have
gone to Jerioth for a glimpse into the future. He drew
his sword and held it before him in salute. "I have been
your friend," he said. "I have, more than once, risked
my life serving you and your honorable goal of a united
and free Israel. I have been willing to die in that cause.
But I am not willing to shed the blood of the people of
Nob."

For a moment Saul's eyes flashed dark and angry,
then softened. "Of all men you have been most loyal,"
he said. "If you have no stomach for this fight I will not
reprove you for it."

Urnan watched the slaughter from the crag. There
were no armed men in the city to offer resistance. The
king's guard swept down upon the town with no walls.
Urnan could hear the cries of terror and the screams of
agony. It was over within minutes, and the victorious
guard congregated around the temple.

Urnan entered the town to find slaughter and

waste. He paused, sickened by the sight of a family who had died together, a woman, a man, two small children lying with arms and legs mixed in a bloody pool. At that moment he was within a heartbeat of turning away to follow David and Eri into Moab. It was his duty to his son and his family that kept him there. He had promised Eri that he would look after Sarah and the girl child.

When he reached the temple he saw all the priests of Nob, fourscore-and-five of them, grouped on the steps in front of the temple. Before them stood Saul and the royal guard. Many of the soldiers were splattered with blood, and their swords still dripped red.

The king stepped forward and lifted his voice. "You see, priests, the price of treason. Your leader once told me to slay all men, women, children and sucklings, oxen, asses, and sheep. So it is that Samuel himself has taught me how to deal with my enemies. Think on that as you die." Then he turned around and said, "Officers, finish the job."

Ahimelech stepped forward. "How dare you?" he demanded. "We are men of God and—" His voice was drowned out as Doeg the Edomite bellowed an order.

Not one man in the ranks made move to obey.

"Sire," the captain of the guard protested, "they are priests of Yahweh. They are servants of the One God."

"They are traitors," Saul bellowed. "Kill them."

The young captain fell to his knees and clasped his hands. "Sire, I cannot," he said, with tears in his eyes. "I cannot lose my soul by dipping my hands into the blood of the servants of God."

"Is there no one who will obey me?" Saul shouted, lifting a tortured face to the heavens.

Doeg the Edomite ran up the stairs and with two swings of his sword, forward and back, felled two priests. A moan went up from the remaining holy men, but they made no attempt to run.

"Men of Edom," Doeg cried out, lifting his sword. "With me."

A dozen men ran up the steps, and the bloody work

began. The priests panicked and fled, only to be hunted down one by one by Doeg and his men. By evening the stench of death lay heavy over the ruined town, and the guardsmen turned their attention to taking the spoils of war.

In twilight Saul sat beside a fire, his head hanging. Urnan, still sick at heart, offered him meat. The king shook his head and pushed Urnan's hand away.

"You saw?" Saul asked.

"I saw," Urnan said.

"Was I so wrong in punishing those who betrayed me?" the king asked, looking up.

"You were wrong," Urnan said. "So very wrong."

Saul was silent for a long time. "And yet you are still with me."

"I have pledged my loyalty to you," Urnan said. "Just as David and my son vowed their allegiance to you."

"Don't speak his name in my presence," Saul said, his voice cold and harsh.

"Saul, I beg you, stop this persecution of David. Think of what you have accomplished. The Philistine is driven out of the land and a united Israel could move on his strongholds on the plain. But with the Army of Israel fragmented, divided by civil war—and surely you must realize that will be the ultimate outcome—Galar can invade Israel at his leisure. And there will be no one to oppose him."

"It is David who chose civil war," Saul said.

"I have not seen Hebrew bodies left behind David's march."

"Be with me, Urnan," Saul said softly. "Oppose me not."

"You have often said that you value my advice," Urnan said. "I am with you. I do not oppose you, but if I am to be at your side I must speak my heart. I will not voice words simply because I think that is what you want to hear."

"I am tired," Saul said. "I am so tired."

"I'll call your armor-bearer," Urnan said.

Saul had selected a young man of his own family,

the son of one of his brothers, to take David's place as his armor-bearer. The boy was slim and youthful, but strong of limb. His name was Jaalam, after one of the sons of Esau. He helped the king remove his armor and laid out his bed.

"Sleep well," Urnan said.

"Come to me in the morning, old friend," Saul said. "Be my conscience. Speak to me from your heart." He laughed. "Perhaps I will not heed your advice, but I will listen."

Urnan was silent, but he knew he had no choice but to do as Saul asked. As long as there was one small chance that he could influence the king away from his enmity for David, as long as there was a possibility that he could break through Saul's ramparts of jealousy and fear, he would stay at his side.

Urnan was preparing for sleep when Jaalam approached. "Excuse me," the young armor-bearer said, "I intrude on your rest."

"No, no," Urnan said. "Sit with me, boy." He had talked with Jaalam before, for both were always near the king.

"I am troubled," the boy said.

"This day will not be recorded as a great one for the people of Israel," Urnan said.

"I wonder if I should do more," Jaalam said. "I stood silently and made no protest when the king gave the orders to destroy a city and all living things in it. I watched without protest as priests of God were butchered by the Edomites."

"One looks after one's own head."

"But you protested," Jaalam said. "I have observed you, Urnan. You are not a dedicated Yahwehist, and yet only you spoke out beforehand against the slaughter. You are not even Hebrew—"

"The mother of my son was."

"—and yet you are the only one who has the courage to tell the king that he is wrong."

"The king is a man, and beset by the uncertainties of being a man," Urnan said. "Be loyal to him, for he is still the best hope of Israel."

"It is rumored that Samuel anointed David as king. And David has proven himself to be a great warrior."

"True," Urnan said, "but consider this. If David had the best interests of Israel at heart, would he have weakened the army by taking many of its best fighting units with him when he fled?"

"It's hard to know who is in the right, isn't it?"

"As a Yahwehist would say, God alone knows, and His will be done."

"Amen."

"You'd best get your rest. The king awakens early."

The boy laughed. "That I know well." He rose. "What will happen, Urnan?"

Urnan shrugged. "Again, only God knows."

"I pray that the king and David will be reconciled." Jaalam's voice became stronger. "Together they would make the Philistine turn tail. Together they would drive the enemy to the plain, and into his cities, and then, like Joshua, they would bring the walls of the strongholds tumbling down."

"Yes, God does move in mysterious ways, doesn't He?" Urnan was glad, after he spoke, that the boy did not catch the sarcasm in his voice.

CHAPTER
TWENTY-FIVE

It seemed to Kaptar that he was, indeed, under the protection of the god Amon as he traveled back down the Nile from the great temple of the second Ramses. He carried the letter written by the old priest of the temple close to his heart, and he paid his passage on trading dhows with coins given to him by Ikkur. In return he had given Ikkur the donkey. The journey was much swifter than the upriver voyage had been.

The first thing he saw, as his native city came into view, was the tall, gold-gleaming spire of one of the great obelisks erected by the mighty Thutmose. He took that to be a sign. He had told the old priest in the temple of Ramses that one day he would come back up the Nile with a mighty army and restore the land of Kush to the empire. To be reminded of one of Egypt's most successful conquerors was a good omen that one day he would follow the example of the hero.

When he got off the dhow, he waved his thanks to the captain and crew of the vessel, then made his way not toward the palace but to the temple. It was as if he were drawn there by a need to drink in the glory of the great kings. He stood beneath a tall pylon and read the names of towns taken by the great Thutmose during his expedition to the land of the cedars.

Kaptar had read the account of the triumphs of Thutmose many times, but he had never felt such a closeness to the god-king. Never before had the words filled him with so much inspiration. His heart soared as he read how Thutmose invaded a great city far away: *". . . they fled headlong to Megiddo in fear, abandoning their horses and their chariots of gold and silver, and the people hauled them up, pulling them by their clothing into this city . . ."*

He imagined a future time when artisans and craftsmen would be carving the deeds of Kaptar in stone, when he would order his architect to add to the great temple pylons and halls and columns to match those of Thutmose and of Ramses himself.

True kings, unlike the Asiatic barbarians, did not waste whole cities. They spared those who yielded, and instead of seeking destruction they reaped the spoils of war, just as Kaptar would carry back the gold of Kush one day to the Southern City. And one day poets would write of Kaptar, as they had of the immortal Thutmose, words of praise spoken by Amon himself:

> I have come, giving thee to smite the eastern
> land,
> Thou hast trampled those who are in the
> districts of God's-Land
> I have made them see thy majesty as a
> circling star,
> When it scatters its flame in fire and gives
> forth its dew.
> I have made them see thy majesty as a
> soaring hawk,
> Seizing that which he seeth, as much as he
> desires.

Kaptar entered the temple, and in the sanctuary he prayed to Amon, thanking the god for his safe return to Waset, asking forgiveness for pride in his grandiose dreams but promising to build to the greatness of Amon if, indeed, those dreams were allowed to come to fruition.

It was only then that he went to the palace, where word of his presence in the city had already reached Kemose. He was admitted to the presence of the high priest and prince of Egypt immediately. When Kemose came down from his golden throne to embrace his nephew, Kaptar sighed in relief.

"The gods have preserved you," Kemose said, "for which I thank them."

"I, too, thank them," Kaptar said.

"Now, where have you been?" Kemose demanded, his face darkening.

It appeared that he was not to escape so lightly after all. "I saw wonderful things, Uncle," Kaptar said. "I slept in the great temple of the second Ramses, and in the morning the sun lanced the darkness with a jeweled shaft of light—"

"That I have seen," Kemose said. "What I do not understand is how and why you came to see it."

Kaptar dropped his head, unwilling to voice his feelings about his mother's marriage.

"You have not asked about your mother," Kemose said, not unkindly.

"She is well?"

"She is well," Kemose said. "She is concerned about you, of course, but she does her duty."

"And just what is her duty, Uncle?" Kaptar asked.

"If you have not come to that by yourself, you are not my nephew," Kemose said harshly.

Kaptar flushed. "I have thought—"

Kemose motioned him into silence. He glanced around at the servants, courtiers, and petitioners who crowded the room. "We will speak of that later," he said. "I want you to go to the scribes and have them write to your mother immediately of your safe return. You would do well to formulate an apology to her."

"I obey," Kaptar said.

Kemose smiled again. "I want to hear all about your adventures. You will dine with me."

"This is for you," Kaptar said, taking old Ikkur's letter from his tunic.

Kemose read it quickly, then smiled. "That old reprobate is still alive?"

"Just," Kaptar said.

"You impressed him favorably, which is much to your credit."

"He thought that I headed a relief expedition to rescue Kush and the temples from barbarity," Kaptar said. "I would lead such a force, Uncle."

Kemose nodded. "We will talk of that later, as well. I must attend to matters of state. Go now to your correspondence."

"As you wish."

"By the way, your mother is with child."

The words lashed into Kaptar like a whip of thorns. His heart ached with the thought of his mother bearing the mixed-blood child of a Libyan. His emotions burned like acid. He ran from the throne room. Why had he not gone with his mother to the delta? She was alone, one woman amid the churlish, cowardly people of the court of Paynozem and the swarthy, barbaric Libyans. In her time of greatest need he had deserted her.

Suddenly a feeling of peace came over him. His pulse slowed. It was as if Amon had spoken. He went to his quarters and made his preparations. With evening, when he joined Kemose for dinner, he knew what he had to do.

"Uncle," he said, "I must go to my mother. With your permission I will leave tomorrow."

"Let's not be too rash in our decision," Kemose said. "If it is wise for you to join your mother you should do so as a prince of Egypt, and to arrange such a formal visit requires time."

"I bow to your wisdom, but I feel that I must go to her," Kaptar said.

The voice of the high priest was soft but firm. "You will do what is best for Egypt," he said.

Kaptar nodded. "I want to do what is best for my country, for I have seen the glory of the great Ramses, and of Egypt herself, devastated by the savages. I have seen temples to the gods being covered slowly by the red sands of the desert. You well know that I have read the deeds of the great kings, and that I, like you, long for a return to glory and honor for the Two Lands. I am willing to do whatever is required of me. Tell me what I can do to restore unity to Egypt, to bring back her honor, and to recover her empire."

Kemose swelled with pride. When he spoke his voice was husky with emotion. "Perhaps your time to do all of that will come. Now, however, you can best serve by supporting your mother in her decision to give Musen an heir."

"An heir with a claim, through her royal blood, to the throne of the Two Lands?" Kaptar asked.

"Hear me," Kemose said. "I will begin preparations for your visit to the north. There you will give your mother your love and understanding, for she is helping Egypt in her own way."

"I will obey," Kaptar said, "although, in the name of Amon himself, I do not understand."

A messenger was sent down the river to inform not only the Libyans but the court of Paynozem that Kaptar, son of Tania, prince of the Southern City, would journey to the delta under the flag of the high priest of Amon. In the meantime, as the change of seasons came and with it the yearly gift of the river in the form of floods and new silt for the fields of the farmers, Kaptar contented himself with his studies.

The flood was abating when he was informed that an answer had come from Paynozem, stating that a visit from Prince Kaptar would be welcome. He made his preparations. He was looking forward to seeing his mother as he waited for the smaller of the two royal barges to be made ready for his trip down the Nile. As it happened, the royal barge would not leave its moorings. The voyage to the north would be postponed, to be made at a later date under entirely different circumstances.

CHAPTER
TWENTY-SIX

In the hush of the evening the smoke from a hundred campfires scented the still air. David's small army was camped in a vale in Moab. Eri lounged against a boulder watching Baalan tending a roasting leg of lamb. Sunu, all boy and hungry, could not wait. He touched the sizzling meat gingerly with his finger, then yelped with pain and thrust his finger into his mouth.

"Ummm," he said. "Good."

From the other side of the camp David's golden voice blended with the wondrous music of his harp, filling the twilight with exquisite beauty as he sang a prayer to the One God.

"Make haste, O God, to deliver me; make haste to help me, O Lord. Let them be ashamed and confounded that seek after my soul."

Tears wet Baalan's cheeks. Even Sunu was quiet as David continued his song, then ended it with gently diminishing intensity. The chords struck by his agile fingers lingered echoingly as the western sky flared with the last futile efforts of the setting sun.

"Go now," Eri told Sunu, "and tell the general that food is ready."

Sunu did a creditable imitation of a salute and dashed off. He returned hand in hand with David.

"I impose on you too much, Baalan," David said.

"You are always welcome at our fire," Baalan said.

"Still," David said.

"Stop protesting and eat," Eri said.

David accepted a portion of the lamb, touched it with his fingers, and said, "Ouch."

"It burns," Sunu said, "but your fingers will taste good."

David put his fingers into his mouth. "So they do, little one."

The army had turned northward again after eluding Saul's pursuit. The soldiers walked. Donkeys were used as pack animals, and there were a few captured Philistine carts with their high, broad wheels to carry bulky equipment like Eri's forge and tools. As the only armorer Eri was in constant demand, and at each stop his shop was set up quickly to allow him to repair and sharpen weapons.

David's intention was to make his way back around the northern end of the great Salt Sea and gradually move south into Judah, where he would be among his own people. "If we have to fight our way through Saul's army, so be it," he told Eri.

Eri shook his head sadly. "Saul was my friend," he said, "faithful and just to me, a lad who loved his God and a good laugh at the same time."

"What he did at Nob was sheer savagery," David said. "A wanton slaughter worthy of the Philistines themselves."

It was as if David's vow to fight if necessary had been a prediction, for the path of his army was blocked by Saul at almost every turn. Eri grieved as he sharpened weapons that had been dulled on the armor of men of the same blood. But there was something about

David that demanded loyalty and overrode all other considerations. Eri justified fighting against his mother's people with the firm belief that he was engaging in a divine crusade.

David's army grew. Men died, but they were replaced, often by veterans of Saul's own forces. And in those sad days when once again the descendants of Abraham fought among themselves, there came important news. It was carried by a grizzled warrior who had watched David fight Goliath. The man had taken the first opportunity to desert Saul's army and join David. He approached the general as he was having his evening meal. David leaped to his feet and clasped the warrior's arm.

"Pekah," he said with genuine warmth. "You are most welcome."

"I came as soon as I could get away without losing my head, lord," Pekah said.

"We will fight together for Israel," David said.

"We will fight Saul," the old soldier said.

"I pray not."

"You are his only enemy now," Pekah said, then paused. "Samuel is dead."

David turned away to hide his tears. The others were silent, understanding his sorrow. He did not, however, vent his feelings with the traditional gestures of bereavement. He could not wail aloud, not with a hundred men within sound of his voice, and to rend his clothes would leave him naked, for he had no others.

"They say that it was news of what Saul did at Nob that killed him," Pekah said. "And for a time many feared another slaughter, for hordes gathered at Ramah to lament the prophet's death, and their loyalty to the prophet angered Saul."

"Pray God, no more killing," David whispered.

"The king is determined to kill you, lord," Pekah said.

David's face hardened. "Then we must do our best to frustrate him."

*   *   *

At last they arrived in Judah, and the army was swelled by members of David's own tribe. At Adullam, near Bethlehem and the little valley where Goliath fell, David built his stronghold and waged war with Israel. His force was desperately small, just over four hundred men. Saul's army outnumbered him vastly. So he found himself fighting the same kind of war that the young Saul had fought against the Philistines. He survived by knowing every fold and bend of the land and staying one step ahead of the remorseless pursuit, slowing those who would kill him with deadly, lightning-swift raids.

One day, after a spirited clash with one of Saul's forces, with men dead and the moans of the wounded heavy in the night, David spoke softly to Eri. "Our luck will not hold forever. It needs only one mistake on my part, one small misstep, and we will find ourselves surrounded. I won't have that, my friend." He sighed. "If it is God's will that I perish by Saul's sword, so be it, but I will not sacrifice all these." He waved his hand to encompass the whole camp and its men. "You know that Saul is merciless. Remember Nob and imagine what would happen to your wife and your son should we fall into his hands. We must find a way. It grieves me that my people, who were eager to ally themselves with Saul to fight the Philistines, now fight against the man who once led them."

"Saul can't live forever," Eri said. "With Jonathan on the throne this foolish fighting will end."

David shook his head sadly. "You do not know, even though your mother was of us, how vengeful we are. Even God said that we are a stiff-necked people. If we allow this struggle with Saul to develop into full war between Judah and the rest of Israel, the priests and the people would cry out for our blood even if my friend Jonathan were on the throne."

He rose and, hands behind his back, began pacing back and forth. Around them the army was bedding down. A horse snorted. A man sang, and although his voice could not match that of the master musician,

David, the sound had a melancholy beauty that quieted the talk of others.

"We must find a way," David said. "We must."

"He is dead," Saul bellowed. He was striding around the throne room. "If he was so beloved of God, if God spoke to him and to him alone, why is Samuel dead?"

No one spoke. Urnan watched the king sadly.

"God did not favor him any more than me," Saul shouted. "So why do the worthless people flock to Ramah to pay homage to him?"

One by one the retainers and hangers-on sneaked away from Saul's rage. When only Urnan was left, the king, as if angered by having lost his audience, picked up a pitcher and shattered it against a wall.

"Why do you not desert me, too?" he bellowed at Urnan. "Do I not frighten you as I frighten all the others?"

"If Samuel was only a man, are you more?" Urnan asked.

Saul halted his pacing and cocked his head. His face wrinkled and a bellow of laughter surged out. "My old friend," he gasped. "You do have a way of sobering me."

"Samuel is dead," Urnan said. "Perhaps now is the time to make peace with the priests."

Saul ran his fingers through his beard, lost in thought. At length he shook his heavily maned head. "No. There is the blood of the priests of Nob between us. And soon another hairy one in long robes will inform the world that God has spoken to him. No. We have come this far without them."

"And if Galar strikes?" Urnan asked. "What then?"

"I fought the Philistine alone for years," Saul said. "The Army of Israel is more powerful than it has ever been."

"And it is divided, expending supplies and energy in the search for David."

"In search of an army of traitors," Saul said, glowering at Urnan.

"For four hundred men with their women and a few children," Urnan said. "Saul, in God's name, it is time to call a halt to this civil war."

Saul's eyes flared. With a visible effort he calmed himself. "You are my friend," he said, turning away.

"I despair," Urnan said.

"*You* despair?" Saul whirled around to face Urnan again. "*You* despair?"

Urnan sighed. He would never bring the king to his senses.

Saul sat and let his head sink into his hands. Urnan's attention was drawn to the door, where Mered stood watching the king. It was the shifty way the fat-lipped officer looked at Saul that hardened Urnan's resolve. He had to escape Saul's court and the sickness that bred there.

He wasted no time. He made his preparations, mounted his horse, and set out toward the north on a journey that had been long delayed. He traveled fast, for, somewhat to his surprise, his urgency grew with the passage of each day.

Endor was the same, a quiet and peaceful little town within sight of the mountain that towered tall and blue and the sacred high places of the ancients. Urnan remembered the way to the house of Jerioth. The witch was tilling her small garden. Her robes were tucked high to expose her mature, shapely lower legs. Her bare feet were darkened by the soil. Her splendid, dark hair was covered by a hood against the sun. He pulled Ramses to a halt and watched her. Even at labor she moved with feminine grace.

Sensing his presence, she straightened from her work, turned, leaned on the handle of her tiller. He dismounted and walked toward her.

"You said you would return," she said.

"It was not for lack of thought of you that I waited so long."

"It doesn't matter," she said. "You're here."

Once, as was the custom of hospitality, she had

washed his feet. On this day he insisted on doing the same for her. The dark soil of the garden clouded the water in the pan. She giggled girlishly, embarrassed but flattered nonetheless. When he came into her she lifted herself with eagerness to meet him, and their mutual need consumed itself with fiery haste, leaving them breathless and damp as she lay in his arms.

"Why have I waited so long?" Urnan asked. "Why am I such a fool?"

"You are not a fool," she scolded. "Your work on behalf of Israel is more important than our happiness."

Urnan muttered an oath. She gasped in shock. "Nothing is more important than this," he said. "Especially not the bloody folly of kings and prophets."

He found himself telling her everything. She listened attentively as she dried the perspiration from their bodies. He told her of the situation at court, of Saul's rages during which he seemed to be possessed by devils. He spoke of the king's determination to kill David even if it meant leaving Israel open to destruction at the hands of the Philistines.

"I have tried," he said. "God knows that I've done everything in my power to convince Saul of the madness of this war on David. He can think only of establishing a dynasty, and he has convinced himself that David is a threat to that ambition. If I could only make him see that David is content—or at least he *was* content—to see Jonathan on the throne. If I could only convince him that David is not the enemy, that the enemy is still the Army of the Five Cities."

"Bring him to me," Jerioth said. "Perhaps I can show him."

Urnan shook his head. "If he leaves Gibeah at all it is to march with his army to the south to follow some rumor of David's presence."

"There will be a way," she said.

"If there is, then I will find it," Urnan said.

Mered wasted no time in taking advantage of Urnan's absence. The day after he left, Saul demanded, "Where is Urnan? Find him and send him to me."

"He is not in Gibeah, lord," Mered said.

"Where is he?"

"Lord," Mered said, "if he had not the courtesy to tell you, I'm sure that he would not inform anyone else of his intentions."

"When he returns send him to me," Saul said sullenly.

"I hesitate to mention it," Mered said. "In fact, I merely repeat the gossip of others, but it is said that he has gone to join David."

"Nonsense," Saul bellowed. "He is my friend."

"His son is David's armorer," Mered said.

Saul's face became pinched.

"You may have forgotten, sire, that Eri, who has become a traitor to you, holds valuable property in Gibeah."

"I have not forgotten," Saul said. "The forges he constructed continue to work for me, as they should."

"There is his house, lord, and his personal possessions."

"I had assumed," Saul said, "that his house was occupied by his wife, the woman whom you have befriended."

"Not so, lord," Mered said. "The woman Sarah and the daughter deserted by Eri live with me and my wife in my house."

"You are to be commended for your charity toward the poor woman."

"It is, lord, an additional expense, of course."

Saul nodded.

"And she is a woman of little experience in fending for herself. I fear that her welfare will be my affair from now on. It would ease my situation if I were to be given title to the house and its furnishings. The proceeds from the sale of the property would allow me to keep the woman and the child comfortably."

"Draw up the papers," Saul said, "and I will sign them."

Within the hour Mered had the deed ready for Saul's signature. He spent the rest of the day talking with various rich men of the town, and by nightfall he had concluded a sale that netted him more silver ingots than could be carried by one man, and his pastures were enriched by more than a score of fine sheep ready for shearing.

He waited almost a week to complete his plan. Sarah was no longer of any use to him, no longer a source of information, through Eri, about the movements of David and the army. He had no intention of wasting further time or money on her and her brat. It was the duty of her husband to keep her, not his.

He bided his time until he found Sarah alone in her room. The baby was sleeping. The young mother, dressed lightly in a blue robe, smiled when Mered entered. She was, Mered was reminded, a toothsome morsel of young womanhood. He was a man who did not believe in waste. He intended to drive the woman from his house; where she went was her affair. But why not have something in return for all that he had done for her?

"Have you had a good day?" Sarah asked brightly.

Mered acted immediately. He seized both her arms and lifted her from her seat. His lips searched for hers, and so stunned was Sarah that she did not, at first, resist. His tongue pushed into her mouth, and she cried out, the sound muffled by his ardor. One of his hands went to her buttocks, and his fingers wrapped around the tender curve, squeezing the softness. The other hand closed over a breast swollen with mother's milk. She flinched at his roughness.

"Please, please," she gasped as she managed to free her mouth for a moment. "Please, no."

He thrust his hand between her legs, and she jerked back, falling on the couch. Mered fell atop her. His engorged manhood pushed against her stomach. He began to rip at her robe, lifting it, thrusting his fingers into her most intimate parts as he pulled up his own clothing with the other hand.

"No!" she screamed. She clawed at his eyes, making him bellow with anger. The sound of his open palm against her cheek rang in her ears, and she lifted her knee to smash into his genitals. He bellowed once more and slammed his fist into her face. But fear gave her strength. She pushed him from her and he fell, landing on his hands and knees. She leaped up and ran, but he caught her robe, ripping the sheer material and pulling the garment from her shoulders. She tried to hide her bare breasts, but he seized her.

"Spawn of evil," he hissed at her. "Female dog. Whore."

"What have I done that you treat me so?" she asked through her sobs.

"Where is your gratitude?" he whispered hoarsely. He slapped her once, twice. She went limp, and he let her slump to the floor, where she lay with her breasts exposed.

He rubbed himself gently, for the ache in his groin was painful. Determination glinted in his eyes as he exposed himself, fell to his knees on the floor, and ripped her robe away.

She fought, but he was too strong for her, and in the end she swooned so that as he took her she was limp and pliant. He finished quickly and, with a snort of disgust, freed himself of her, leaving her where she lay. He was standing over her when she regained consciousness.

"Whore," he said, "you will leave my house."

Sarah tried to pull her torn clothing to cover her nakedness.

"Shameless wench," Mered said, "I will not have the likes of you in my house."

"I want Aiah," Sarah moaned. "Where is Aiah?"

"Do not profane the name of that good woman with your filthy lips," Mered said. Suddenly he realized what he had done. The penalty for the rape of a married woman was death. Aiah loved the girl, and he was not sure how his wife would react. Sarah must not be given the chance to appeal to Aiah.

"Get up, whore, and find yourself some clothing," he ordered.

Sarah, as if in a trance, obeyed. While she dressed, Mered called a servant and gave orders.

"Prepare the child for travel," he then told Sarah.

Sarah wept, but she went unprotestingly with two of Mered's male servants.

"Take her to Gilgal," Mered told them. "Leave her there."

"It is far to Gilgal, master," one of the servants said.

"Go," Mered said. "Quickly."

It was a hot day and the road was dusty. "As you said, it is far to Gilgal," one servant said to the other. "Better to leave her body in the fields for the carrion birds, take our ease for two days, and return, telling our master that we did as he said."

"We could, first, take our pleasure of her," the other said.

"And will you then kill her?"

"I have killed women before," the man said. "I was with Saul in the land of the Amalekites."

"Did you kill sucklings there?"

"That I did not do."

"Who, then, will kill this woman's suckling?"

"Not I."

"Nor I."

They shared a sigh.

It was far to Gilgal, and in the days that it took to reach the city the woman drew deeper and deeper into herself. She spoke only when ordered to do so, and she spent her evenings holding her child close to her breast. They reached Gilgal late in the day, just before sunset. Mered's men took Sarah and the child to the market-place and left her, then traveled by moonlight to put distance between them and the woman.

In the deserted marketplace Sarah looked around in puzzlement. She sat on a stone bench beside the village well and spoke in whispers to the child. "Don't worry, little one, Eri will come for us. Don't cry, my baby, soon we will be back with Aiah."

A man approached and stood looking down at her.

"Can you find Eri for me?" she asked.

"I know no one by that name," he said. "What is your price?"

"I must go home," Sarah said.

"Yes," he said, "there, I assume, you will have a place for the child to sleep. But you have not told me your price."

"My price?" she asked.

"Are you of dim wits, woman?" the man demanded. "You offer yourself on the bench of the prostitutes, do you not?"

Shame flooded Sarah's face. She leaped to her feet and clutched the baby close as she ran. She ran until she was panting for breath, and when she stopped she found herself in a narrow, dark alley. The night closed in about her. She came to a sheltered doorway and curled up, warming the baby with her body. She slept fitfully and awoke in the dawn, dampened by dew. She shook with the chill, but the baby was warm, for she had cupped it to her breast all night. In a daze she walked the streets of the town. She saw no familiar face. She could not find the way to her home, or to the house of Aiah. She hungered, but it did not occur to her to beg. At the end of a long day of wandering the streets she found another doorway.

By the end of the second day her milk was threatening to dry up. She was no longer hungry, but she feared for the child. She made her way to the square and sat by the well. When a man approached she forced herself to smile.

"You're new," he said.

"Yes."

"Your price?"

"Food and a place to sleep."

She insisted on eating first, and then she nursed the baby. The price she paid for food and lodging made no impression on her, for it was as though the woman who heaved and labored under the thrusts of the stranger was someone else, a lost soul who had no connection with her.

CHAPTER
TWENTY-SEVEN

The palace of the Libyan lord Buyuwawa in the city of On was an imposing structure erected in the classical style of the great kings. Like all the foreigners in the past who had gained a foothold in the ancient land by force or by breeding, the Libyans admired all things Egyptian except the Egyptians who were in positions of rule and power. The buildings that housed Buyuwawa's family and his regional administrative complex had been built largely with materials pillaged from monuments to great Egyptians of the past, so that now and again, in some dark corner, one might encounter a fragment of an inscription to a king or a noble long dead.

Although the old man, Buyuwawa, still adhered to some Libyan customs, his son, Musen, dressed as an Egyptian, spoke Egyptian, ate Egyptian food, fancied himself to be a scholar of Egyptian history and art, and through his wife hoped to blend his Libyan blood with the best blood of the Two Lands.

Musen named his son Namlot. When the infant

had safely survived the first few critical weeks of life Musen ordered the mother, Princess Tania, to present the boy at the temple where Musen was high priest.

With her train of attendants, Tania, her son in her arms, was carried through the streets in a gold-bedecked litter chair. Musen was waiting. He wore rich ceremonial robes heavy with gold trim. His pectoral was beautifully beaded with lapis. To see his arrogance—he was a priest dressed as a king—made Tania smile wryly.

"Try as he might, my little one," she whispered to the baby in her arms, "the foreigner will never be what he desires to be most, one of us."

Priests struck up sacred music as Tania moved solemnly toward the sanctuary. There Musen anointed the baby and intoned ancient Egyptian charms over him. To listen to him one would never suspect, Tania thought, that he was a product of a barbarian nation and that the gods of the Two Lands would never bless him.

"Little one," she whispered, "he and his kind will pass, as the pretenders who tended sheep passed, as the Syrians passed, and you will erase his name and the names of all his kind from the walls of the temples, and their tombs will be emptied of their stolen riches."

Tania would have preferred a more traditional name to Namlot. She had asked her husband to call the boy Menes, or Seti, but the Libyan had insisted on an Egyptianized version of a Libyan family name.

No matter, Tania thought. She had done what had to be done, and now all was in the hands of the gods of the Two Lands.

Musen was grateful to Tania for giving him an heir. When he was tender with her, Tania was tempted to forget her thirst for vengeance. Her first son was now officially a man, and his father, Urnan the smith, was long gone. Tania was no longer a young woman. It was tempting to relax, to accept Musen's attentions and enjoy life as the wife of a powerful and wealthy man, but in the end she could never forget that Musen was an invader.

Tania had to admit that Musen was devoted to Namlot. She smiled proudly when he played with the infant, when he praised his son's dark beauty and the strength of the infant's grip on his finger.

"It is the hair of my fathers, in which is the darkness of the Libyan desert nights," Musen would say proudly. "And look at the eyes. Libyan eyes."

Although it was the custom for royal mothers to have their infants wet-nursed by fecund slave women with infants of their own, Tania insisted on nursing Namlot herself.

"I appreciate your devotion to our son," Musen said when Namlot was four months old, "but isn't it time that you resumed your duties to me?"

"What I do for you can be done by any slave girl," Tania said. "Plant your seed in that little harlot you favor and leave me to give health and strength to Namlot."

"You smell of baby vomit and milk," Musen said. "Have you no pride?"

"This is my pride," Tania said, lifting her son.

As the weeks passed, Musen became more sullen and ever more demanding. Tania laughed at him, her tongue sharper than ever. When Namlot was eight months old and still nursing, Musen came into the nursery one night to find Tania lying on her couch with the baby sleeping at her bare breasts. She did not bother to cover herself.

"It would be polite if you announced yourself before entering my room," she said.

"It is my house," Musen said, "and this is your room only so long as I allow it."

"I remind you, husband, that I had a house of my own long before I met you, a house much more comfortable than this, and that I have no need for you or the wealth you have stolen from true Egyptians."

"Before you met me you were whoring with a common workman, the smith."

"Whoring with Urnan was a pleasure," she said with a smile. "There was a *man*."

"One day, woman, you will push me too far," Musen said, standing over her. "The boy is old enough to take solid food, and to be given into the care of a wet nurse. You will do so immediately. Before your womb becomes sere and useless you will bear me more children."

"I promise you that my womb will never swell with your seed," Tania said.

"You will come to my bed within the month whether or not you are still nursing the boy," Musen said.

That night Tania visited the temple of a minor god, a small temple tended by a cult of priestesses who worked magic with goose quills and potions to prevent the arrival of a child when it was inconvenient or dangerous.

"Mother," Tania said, handing the high priestess a golden statuette of Isis as payment, "is there a way to excise forever the chance of bearing children?"

The priestess nodded gravely. "Yes, but it is rarely used. We perform the procedure on some temple servants who could not go about their duties with swollen bellies."

"That is the service that I ask of you."

The priestess hesitated. "No, Lady, it is both painful and dangerous. I could not risk your health and your life."

"You must," Tania said.

It was painful, but Tania accepted the pain as the price she had to pay. For six days after the high priestess performed an agonizing operation inside her vaginal cavity, Tania lay near death's door. During that time Namlot was given to the care of a wet nurse, and this, at least, pleased Musen.

When Tania was on her feet once more, looking gaunt and wasted, Musen was considerate of her, but when she was blossoming with health again he called her to his chamber. Once more she lay perfectly still in Musen's bed, depriving him of the satisfaction of mutual passion. Aware of what he was missing, his heart ached.

When, some months later, Tania's belly was still flat, Musen questioned her.

"I told you once, husband, that your seed would never swell in me," she said.

"Are you using the magic of those witches of the temple to prevent my seed taking root?" His eyes flared with anger. "I forbid you to do anything to prevent bearing my child."

"I will do nothing more to prevent it," she said with a little smile.

It was not until months later, when she still showed no signs of being with child, that Musen remembered her words. He led a squad of soldiers to the temple, and soon the high priestess was experiencing pain that she had never thought possible. She talked quickly and eagerly before she met her death at the point of Musen's sword.

Musen found Tania in her favorite garden playing with Namlot. He ordered the boy to be taken away and faced her, his features expressionless.

"Why did you do it?" he asked.

"Before I can answer, you must tell me what it is that you fancy I did," she said with a little smile.

"The witch of the temple told all before she died," Musen said.

"I see." Tania rose and walked a few paces away.

"You knew that I wanted more children."

"You wanted more children with the blood of kings in their veins," she said.

"I thought that in that wish, at least, we had common cause. You are not averse to having one with your blood sit on the throne of Egypt?"

"Yes, in that we have agreement."

"But if, may the gods forbid, anything should happen to Namlot—"

"Nothing will happen to Namlot," she said. "He will be a king or he will sire kings."

"But why did you do it?"

He was surprisingly calm. She was puzzled and disappointed. She had eagerly looked forward to seeing his hurt and anger when she told him that she was incapable of bearing more children. She needed to see his anger.

"Because the thought of giving life to the seed of a desert barbarian sickened me," she said.

"If only that bothered you," he said, "then there is no reason why you should object to this." He moved swiftly, seized her loose tunic, and ripped it away, leaving her naked. He lifted her and threw her down roughly on a couch. She laughed and made no protest, but when he came into her she was as still as the Sphinx.

"Move, damn you," he grunted. "Prove to me that you are alive."

"I am very much alive in the arms of the right man," she said.

He hit her across the face with the back of his hand. His knuckles left red spots. Her eyes became slits. To forget the pain she promised herself that she would slip a dagger into his heart while he slept. Better yet, she would pour boiling wax into his ears and his mouth.

It was not until later, when she was alone, that she decided death was too easy for him. She knew that he was helpless to resist his craving for her body. When next he came to her room she was ready for him. He discovered her writhing and moaning under the huge, sweating bulk of a Nubian slave.

Silently he approached the couch. He killed the Nubian with one mighty swing of his sword. The black man's head hung by skin and flesh only. As blood gushed down on Tania's naked body, she laughed.

The sound maddened Musen. He jerked the dead Nubian away, let the body fall limply to the floor, and lifted his sword.

Tania did not plead. She smiled up at him, watched the blade descend, and died with the knowledge that she had won.

The sword rose and fell, rose and fell. Musen stood back at last, panting, his arm aching with his exertions. The couch was a gory pool of blood. Tania's eyes were open, but the glaze of death filmed them. He lifted her severed head by her long, black hair and hurled it across the room. It struck heavily and bounced twice when it hit the floor.

But Musen was not finished. He worshiped the same gods that Tania had. His beliefs were her beliefs. Ever since he and Tania had arrived in On, workmen had been constructing a royal tomb where he was to have shared eternity with her. As a princess of Egypt she had lived her life on earth knowing that when death came for her, her body would be treated in the house of the dead to survive the ages, her internal organs would be preserved in decorated jars so that her body would be complete in the afterworld, and her *ka* would live comfortably in the elaborate tomb that was being prepared for her.

Smiling, Musen summoned several trusted slaves and directed them to place Tania's various parts in woven baskets. Then he supervised as the baskets were carried to a spot along the Nile where it was known that huge, hungry crocodiles hunted. Piece by piece Tania's body was fed to the river and its creatures. He laughed wildly as a crocodile seized one of her shapely legs. Now Tania's *ka* would be caught forever between death and the afterworld, and she would know no peace.

At last Musen stood on the bank of the river alone. There was no sign of the hungry crocodiles. Tania's body was hidden in their underwater lairs, where her flesh would ripen to the consistency they preferred. Then she would be no more.

"You told me once, *Princess*," he said aloud, "that since I am not Egyptian I could not properly appreciate the Egyptian concept of eternal life, but at least I know what that concept meant to you. May your *ka* be damned forever."

Back in the palace, he washed off Tania's blood, then took Namlot in his arms. "So, my son," he whispered. "You and I are alone. But don't fret, little one. You are my son. You carry not only the tainted blood of your whore mother but the blood of Libyan chieftains. And this I promise you. You will be Egyptian, and you will change the history of the Two Lands."

CHAPTER
TWENTY-EIGHT

The arrival of a wounded and exhausted man in David's camp attracted little notice. Men came and went. Judean warriors joined David's army, stayed to fight one or two battles, then went home to tend their flocks.

"Lord David," the man whispered when he saw him. He prostrated himself.

"Rise," David said. "I am neither lord nor king that you should throw yourself down in the dust before me."

"Great general, help us," the man gasped.

"Give him water," David said.

A servant leaped to obey. The newcomer drank gratefully.

"Now speak," David said.

"The Philistines," the man said.

"Yes, yes," David said impatiently.

"They rob our threshing floors," the man said, "and besiege us behind our walls."

"Where?"

"Keilah, lord."

"And where is Keilah?" Eri asked.

"In the foothills," David said, "near the Philistine plain."

"Help us, lord, or we perish," the man begged in a throaty, tearful voice.

"Give this one food," David told his servant. "And a place to sleep."

"Help us," the man said.

David ate his meal in silence, then went into his tent. Eri and Baalan heard his voice rise in prayer. When he came out he seemed pensive.

"We face discovery by Saul at any moment," Eri said. "Not a day goes by without the possibility of a fight. For my part, I'd rather dull my blade on the bones of Philistines than on my own people."

"We are but six hundred," David said.

"From what the Keilahite said I would guess that the forces that surround the town are nothing more than the garrison of a frontier blockhouse," Eri said.

"It is not the Philistine that I fear," David said. "At Keilah we would be exposed to the full force of Saul's army."

"We go in quickly and get out quickly," Eri said. "And while we're there we can take some Philistine supplies."

David nodded. It was becoming increasingly more difficult to feed the army. They were not an occupying or invading force that could live off the land by plundering. It was an army in its own land. Although the inhabitants were in sympathy, and tended to be generous, it was a hard land, and the herds and orchards of the hill country were not sufficient to quarter even a small army.

"Shall I tell the officers to prepare to move?"

David looked toward the darkening sky, noted the emergence of a handful of bright stars, heralds of the glory of the night, and nodded.

It was as Eri had guessed. A bored Philistine garrison commander, having had enough of sitting in safety behind the walls of his frontier post, had taken it on himself to go adventuring. His two hundred men died swiftly at Keilah. The people of the walled city greeted David with joy, but one man left the city mounted on a sturdy donkey and rode hard toward the north.

"Lord King," he said to Saul, "it is rumored that there is a price in silver on the head of your enemy, David."

The king glowered as he nodded.

"Then I claim the prize, lord, for even now David and his six hundred enjoy the hospitality of Keilah."

Saul marched in full strength. When word came to David that the Army of Israel was on the move, he readied himself to leave Keilah.

"We will not turn you over to Saul," the elders and the priests of Keilah's small temple promised.

Eri gave a bitter laugh. "When Saul stands outside the walls and shows his strength," he told David, "they will open the gates to him. No matter their promise, they will deliver you into Saul's hands."

"I fear you are right," David said.

Once more they marched, and behind them came the army of Saul. Three thousand men followed David's six hundred into the wilderness, through Ziph and Maon into Engedi, where the men of David took refuge among the rocks of the wild goats. There David, Eri, and a half-dozen of David's aides found shelter in a large cave. Late in the day a sentinel, posted high on a crag, reported that units of Saul's army were near.

"We're safe here," David said.

As he prepared himself to rest, a soldier came running into the cave. "General," he said, "a small party approaches. They march under the banner of Saul."

David and Eri hurried to the entrance of the cave to watch in astonishment as the king and a party of six men climbed slowly up the narrow path toward the entrance to the cave.

"In God's name," Eri said, "he's coming here."

"This is your chance to right all the wrongs he has done you," said one of David's officers.

"Let all men hold their arms," David ordered.

"The king seeks the dry comfort of our cave," Eri said. "Shall we share it with him?"

David laughed, but there was no mirth in the sound, only bitterness. "I think it would be more prudent for us to give the king possession. After all, there are other dry caves that will shelter us."

"If we move now they'll see us," Eri said.

David nodded and motioned them back into the cave. He ordered his aides to gather their belongings and hide in the tunnels that led deeper into the mountain. He and Eri stayed and watched from behind a rock as the king entered. Saul was accompanied by Abner, his army commander, and by Mered.

"Shall I send a man to the main camp for your food, lord?" Mered asked. His voice echoed through the cave.

"No, I'm tired," Saul said. "I want only to rest."

A man spread blankets for Saul's bed. Hearing the king sigh as he began to remove his armor, Mered leaped to help.

Eri's hand reached for his sword; it itched to slice off the pouted lips of the toady who had sold Baalan and Sunu into slavery.

"But you are hungry, all of you," Saul said. "Go down to the camp and eat."

"No, I will stay with you," Abner said.

"Nonsense," Saul said.

"It would not be wise to leave you alone," Mered said.

"Do you think that I can't take care of myself?" Saul demanded.

"The traitors could be near," Mered said.

"Leave me," Saul ordered harshly. He nodded at Abner. "You, too, cousin. Let me rest."

When the others were gone, Saul lay with one arm thrown across his eyes to block the light from the cave's entrance.

"General," whispered David's aide, who had come back to join them, "kill him now. End this war between brothers."

David drew his sword and crept forward.

Eri's mind was in turmoil. He and Saul, boys together, had tricked the Dagon priests of the Philistine cities into returning the sacred Ark to Israel. They had grown up together. Eri admired Saul, for it was Saul and Saul alone who had stood tall when Israel was at the mercy of the Philistines after the disaster at Ebenezer. Saul had freed Israel. But David, who was creeping closer to the sleeping king, was Eri's companion and a beloved friend.

Eri opened his mouth to cry out a warning to Saul as David knelt beside him. The king's bare throat was exposed. Eri could see the pulse pounding there. He forced back his words and held his breath.

David grasped his sword tighter and inched it toward the king. With one rapid stroke he cut a large swatch from Saul's robe. He thrust it into his tunic, turned, and motioned toward the entrance of the cave.

"I thought to kill him," David told Eri when they were safely hidden in another cave. "I thought to bring down my blade across his neck and with one blow end the war between Israel and Judah. But I could not. I heard the voice of God saying, *David, he is my anointed,* and I could not."

David fell to his knees, lifting his hands in prayer. "Saul, Saul," he whispered. "Why do you seek my death?"

Next morning the sun was behind David as he showed himself high on a crag overlooking Saul's main encampment. "My lord the king," he cried out.

Saul, who had arisen early, whirled around, his eyes searching for the source of the voice. Beside him an archer drew his bow and aimed an iron-tipped arrow, ready to shoot.

"Hold," Saul ordered.

"My lord the king," David called out again.

"Is it you, my son David?" Saul asked.

"My father," David cried, in a voice filled with sorrow, "why do you listen to those who tell you that I desire your hurt? What evil has my hand done you?"

All around, archers were readying their arrows. Saul motioned for them to hold their fire.

"We can kill him now," Abner whispered.

"And leave his army intact," the king whispered. He shouted up to the crag, "I have sinned against you, my son David. Return to me." Then he whispered to Abner, "Send the troops of my left to circle behind him."

"Saul," David called down, "look to the skirt of your robe."

The king looked down and gave a startled cry.

David waved the swatch he had cut from the king's skirt. "Let this be my evidence that I bear you no ill will, Saul. I had the chance, but I did not slay you."

"Ah, my son David," Saul said. There were tears in his eyes. "I have rewarded your services with evil."

Mered spoke into Saul's ear. "He will cut off your seed after you. He will be king and Israel will be his."

"May God bless you," Saul shouted to David. "Come to me and we will perform great deeds together."

Eri saw that David's cheeks were wet with tears. He heard David utter a quick but earnest prayer of thanks. "I think that God has softened Saul's heart," David said to him.

Eri was silent. Suddenly a soldier appeared and saluted. "General, Saul's left flank is moving forward. Before the sun is halfway to midday he will have surrounded us."

For a moment David stood stunned. His face was pale.

"May God forgive him," he finally said.

Backing away from the edge of the cliff, he began giving orders. The six hundred moved rapidly. Men on both sides died; many more were wounded.

That night David prayed until a crescent moon faded into the west. When he finished, Eri was sleeping warmly at the side of his wife. He awakened, instantly alert, at the touch of David's hand on his shoulder.

They walked away from the sleeping camp. "One day I will die at Saul's hand," David said gloomily. "He will not leave off pursuing me, and even if we continue to evade him he will lay waste the land of my people."

"You saw what happened when you tried to reason with him," Eri said. "To surrender to him would mean death not only for you but for God knows how many others."

"I have prayed," David said. "There is only one thing left to me. I will save both Judah and Israel from war and blood."

"How will you accomplish this miracle?" Eri asked.

"I march with the sun toward Gath," David said flatly.

It flashed through Eri's mind that David intended to end the civil war among the seed of Abraham by sacrificing himself and his army against the strong walls and the heavily armed defenders of one of the Philistine cities. Had that been David's plan, perhaps he would have followed him.

"I have sent a messenger to Achish, son of Maoch, king of Gath, offering him my services as a mercenary. His answer was one of welcome. And he will accept all those among my men who will follow me." As David spoke he stared up at the sky, not at Eri.

Eri was stunned. For a long time he could not speak.

"Will you come with me, old friend?" David finally asked.

Eri's answer was quick, but not as quick as the flood of memories that prompted it. In his mind's eye he saw the rape and death of his mother at the hands of the Philistines, saw his father stumbling and falling, dragged along behind a Philistine's horse. He remembered how savagely the Philistines had fallen on the house of Sarah's adoptive father, and how the massacre of her family had robbed Sarah of her mind and him of her love.

His voice was firm. "Much as I love you, David, I cannot become a tool of the Philistines."

David nodded sadly. "But you do understand why I must do so?"

"Each man must follow his own path as God shows

it to him," Eri said, "but is it God whose voice tells you to pass over to Gath, to join the enemy of all the people of Israel and Judah?"

"I can only pray that it is," David said. He clasped Eri's arm. "What will you do? You can't go back to Gibeah."

"I'll take my family to the wilderness, to my hidden armory," Eri said. "We'll be safe there, and the Army of Israel will need arms when Saul turns his attentions once more toward the plain."

"God go with you," David said.

"I promise you that I will never raise my sword against you," Eri said.

"Nor I you," David said.

"I would that you would make the same vow for all of the nation of your fathers."

"That vow I do not have to voice, for it is part of my soul."

CHAPTER TWENTY-NINE

The Army of Israel marched into the land of Benjamin and slowly dispersed, each man going to his own home, to his own flocks, orchards, and fields. There was no enemy to threaten Israel. The man whom the king called traitor had fled the hills and now resided with his army in Ziklag, a city given to him by Achish, the son of Maoch, king of Gath. There were rumors that Galar, the great general of the Philistines, was training new recruits for the Army of the Five Cities, but the Philistines had been beaten so often by Saul and David that no man considered them to be a threat. Should Galar march, veterans of the wars agreed, the army could be assembled quickly.

Only Saul and a few of his advisers seemed to be concerned that David was alive, and that the Philistine cities were still strong and powerful. As the season passed, Saul continued to be obsessed with his distrust of David. He had put Mered in charge of keeping a record of David's campaigns for the king of Gath.

"He has not been idle," Mered said. "My men report that after his invasion against the Geshurites and the Gezrites, he moved on to smash the Amalekites."

"It seems to me, cousin," said Abner, "that he serves Israel still, for he smites our old enemies, those who were on the land when Moses led the nation out of Egypt."

Saul said nothing, but his eyes flashed with anger.

"He leaves neither man nor woman alive," Mered said. "He takes the sheep and the oxen, even the asses and the camels." He looked at Abner balefully. "And while it is true that he smites the old enemies, he takes time, now and again, to strike in the south of Judah, in his own land, where he metes out the same punishment that he gave to the others." Turning to Saul, he continued, "Lord king, I leave tomorrow, with your permission, to see for myself the damage that this man does to his own country."

"Go, then," Saul said.

But it was not to the south of Judah that Mered journeyed. His destination was a Philistine frontier blockhouse on the edge of the plain. By sheer luck he arrived at the same time as General Galar. The general, who was inspecting the garrison, frowned in displeasure when Mered was announced.

"The gods have guided my footsteps, General," Mered said. "We are well met, for I have information for you."

"Speak, then," Galar said, wrinkling his nose as if the Hebrew traitor smelled bad.

"Your chance for the ultimate defeat of Saul has come," Mered announced. "Because of Saul's attempts to kill David, Judah is alienated from Saul. The army is dispersed. The priests of Yahweh hate Saul and prohibit him from worship."

To Galar something about that situation did not ring true. It was not like a Hebrew to abandon his people, his country, and his own God.

"I have talked with Achish, who is high in praise of his mercenary," Galar said. "But tell me, Hebrew, were

you me, would you want this David's army behind you
when you faced the army of Saul?"

Mered smiled. "Lord, were I you, with my army
between the men of Saul and the men of David, I would
divide my army and attack in both directions."

Urnan rode south from Endor whistling a merry
air. He arrived at the citadel of Saul to find the king in a
black mood, untalkative, discontent. So he left and rode
to the house of his son, which he found occupied by
strangers who told him that they had bought the house
from Mered. He made his way to Mered's house and
inquired for Sarah. A servant escorted him to a shady
veranda, where Aiah lay on a couch with the pallor of
illness on her cheeks.

"Thank God you've come, Urnan," she said. "I
have prayed for your swift return, but the days and
weeks passed."

"Where are Sarah and the child?" Urnan asked,
feeling uneasy.

"Gone," Aiah said. "I don't know what came over
Sarah. God knows we've been kind to her. My dear husband looked upon her with the same favor that he
would have given to his own daughter."

"Tell me what happened," Urnan said.

"I know only what the servants told my husband,"
Aiah said. "There came a young man inquiring for her.
She admitted him and talked with him, and then, before
the servants could tell my husband, she packed her belongings and left with him."

"You saw this man?"

"Unfortunately, I have been ill," Aiah said. "I knew
nothing of it until I recovered. Mered, bless him, had
already sent men to search for her, with no success."

"She left, just like that, without saying a word to
you or Mered?"

"She told one of the servant girls that she was going
to marry the young man with whom she went away."
She wiped a tear. "I miss her so, Urnan, but, God willing, she's happy with her new husband. It was shameful,
you know, the way your son discarded her."

Urnan said nothing. He could believe, since he knew Aiah to be a kindly woman, that she knew nothing of Mered and Sarah's plot to sell Baalan and Sunu into slavery.

"Rest well," he said.

"Please find her, Urnan," Aiah begged. "Find her and come to tell me that she is happy."

At court Urnan learned how David had become a scourge of the south and heard rumors that Galar was massing his troops.

"Has this marshaling been witnessed by reliable eyes?" Urnan asked Saul.

"By our most trusted spies," Saul said.

"Then, sire, I suggest that you send a messenger to David to implore him to return to Judah, there to muster his fellow tribesmen to join us in the fight."

"You try me, old friend," Saul said, without rancor. "You know I will not beg David for his help."

"I will," Urnan said. "I'll beg him on bended knee not to fight for Achish and the Army of Gath."

"We beat the Philistine without David more than once. We will do it again." Saul rose from his throne and came to put his arm around Urnan's broad shoulders. "I've missed you. Will you march with us?" His voice was oddly vulnerable.

Urnan nodded, and Saul squeezed his shoulders again.

"I have a suggestion," Urnan said, "if I may presume to advise you."

"You may as well; everyone else does," Saul said.

"There is a woman whom I'd like for you to see," Urnan said.

"A woman?" Saul's heavy eyebrows rose.

"She has an uncanny way of helping you to see inside yourself, my friend."

"When I look inside myself," Saul said, "I am sometimes dismayed."

"Will you trust me in this?"

Saul nodded slowly. "Where is this woman?"

"In Endor."

"Then perhaps I will humor you, for the Philistine seems to be gathering his forces at Shunem. I have sent my heralds to gather our army. Abner is already on the march, toward Gilboa."

"If there is time, then, when we reach Gilboa, we will continue on to Endor," Urnan said.

The army grew on the march northward. By the time Saul approached Gilboa he was at the head of not only his palace guard, but a growing, enthusiastic, and undisciplined mob of an army, and he was beginning to worry. Many of the veterans who had pursued David and who had fought at Michmash were gone. In their place were raw recruits, some of whom couldn't have hit a bull at ten paces with the bows they had inherited from their fathers.

"I fear, Urnan," Saul said, "that our trip to Endor must wait. Just look at these." He waved his hand disdainfully at the masses of straggling infantry. With Urnan at his side, he left the formation and rode ahead to where Abner had pitched his tents under the Gilboa hills. Sere and barren ridges towered over the encampment.

"The enemy?" Saul asked of Abner.

Abner led Saul and Urnan to the top of a hill. Below them the Philistine army was spread out as if on review. Squadrons of chariots rumbled across the floor of the valley. Thousands of heavy infantry in their kilts and ribbed helmets marched back and forth in smart precision.

"This army against raw recruits who have seen blood only when they butcher their lambs," Abner said.

"My God," Saul whispered. Fear rose up in him in a wave, fear not for himself but for Israel. For that moment all madness was driven from him by the realization that he had allowed his nation to be drawn into a situation of grave peril.

"Samuel," he said aloud, looking up toward the heavens, "look down upon us and see how low we have fallen. Ask yourself, prophet, if some of the blame is yours."

He lowered his head sheepishly, then looked at Urnan. "I am not accustomed to speaking to the dead, but I wonder what the old man would say, could he see this."

"Would you like to know?" Urnan said.

Saul looked at him sharply. He himself had drafted the decree to banish those who claimed to have a familiar spirit through whom they spoke with the dead.

"Perhaps you should know," Urnan said. "Surely, in the face of this force, the priesthood would not hold back their blessings and their support. You can question the shade of Samuel himself."

"You speak of a witch."

Urnan nodded.

"You have seen this woman?" Saul asked.

"She has a genuine gift."

Saul laughed, but the fear was acid inside him, eating at his stomach. "And so I, who do not believe, I who forbade all such activity, I am to go seeking the services of a witch? Am I to do this foolish thing, Abner?" Saul asked.

The army commander waved a hand in the direction of the Philistine hordes. "We need all the help we can get, cousin. If you can get the shade of old Samuel to relent and call down God's blessings on us, what can be the harm?"

Urnan and Saul, dressed as countrymen, rode into Endor that night on two sturdy donkeys. The witch stood in front of her small house, wearing beaded sandals and flowing blue robes.

"I have brought a visitor," Urnan said.

Jerioth gazed at Saul without smiling.

"I ask you, woman," Saul said, "to divine with your familiar spirit to bring up the man whose name I will whisper to you."

Jerioth looked questioningly at Urnan. "You know that the king has banished those who speak with the spirits. How is it that you lay a snare for me, to cause me to be exiled?"

"By the name of God you will not be punished," Saul said, before Urnan could answer.

"He speaks the truth," Urnan said.

"Come, then," Jerioth said.

In the dimness of her sitting room she spoke her charms and prayed her prayers. Saul gathered his cowl around his face, as if wanting to hide his shame from the world. Urnan sat in a far corner, making no move, no sound, watching the face of Jerioth.

"Give me the name," she said.

"Bring up the shade of Samuel," Saul whispered.

From Jerioth's incense burner came a puff of smoke. The air moved. Urnan heard what could have been a voice, but he could not make out the words. Jerioth did. She cried out in fright and reached across to pull Saul's cowl away from his face.

"You are Saul," she whispered. "I am betrayed."

"How do you know who I am?" he asked.

"From Samuel."

Saul looked around, his eyes wide. "What did you hear?"

"It is what I *see*," she said. "I see an old man covered with a mantle. His hair has never known the sharpness of a blade of any kind."

The faint hint of movement in the air solidified. Saul made a stricken sound, fell on his knees, and touched his forehead.

"Why have you disturbed me, Saul?" a deep voice asked.

"Pity Israel, Samuel," Saul said, "if not me. The Philistines make war with a mighty army and only I stand against them. God has deserted me. He does not hear my prayers. Tell me, prophet, what am I to do? Surely He will not desert Israel."

No one breathed as they waited for Samuel's answer. None came.

"I have called you," Saul said, "so that you can make known to me what I must do."

Only then did the shade of Samuel speak. His

words rang eerily in the still room. "What can I advise you if the Lord has departed from you and is your enemy? I told you in life that the kingdom had been torn from your hand, that it was given to David because you refused to obey the word of the Lord."

"Because I spared the life of one man is all Israel to suffer?" Saul asked.

The chill of death settled on them as Samuel's words echoed over and over.

"The Lord will deliver Israel with you into the hands of the Philistines."

"No," Urnan whispered, but Saul was silent, his mouth open, his eyes wide.

"Tomorrow, Saul, you and your sons will be with me, and the host of Israel will be delivered into the hands of the enemy."

Suddenly the room was still. The faint wisps that had been the prophet were no more. Saul moaned as he fell to the floor. Jerioth and Urnan knelt by his side.

"He breathes," Jerioth said.

"He has taken no bread, no food at all, since yesterday morning," Urnan said.

"Help him to a couch," Jerioth said. She disappeared and came back with bread, which Saul refused.

"You must eat," Urnan said. "You must have your strength."

"To what avail?" Saul asked darkly.

Urnan had been cursing himself for bringing Saul to the witch of Endor. "The words of the spirits are not always true prophecy," he said weakly.

"No," Saul said, drawing himself up. "They were just the baleful words of an old man who had come to hate me."

"Will you eat, lord king?" Jerioth asked.

"With much pleasure," Saul said, his face brightening.

Urnan was surprised when the witch slew her one calf and dressed a portion of it for the oven. The smell of roasting meat soon filled the air.

Saul ate in silence but with gusto, and his spirits seemed to be on the rise. When the meal was over he thanked Jerioth and went out ahead of Urnan into the night. As he faded into the gloom, it seemed to Urnan an omen of what was to come.

CHAPTER THIRTY

The richly ornamented barge of Lord Musen signaled its arrival with a trio of horns so that the authorities of the city could be notified. A runner immediately pounded his way through the streets to the palace of the high priest of Amon.

"Lord, a royal visitor comes," he gasped to Kemose.

"What are his banners?" Kemose asked quickly.

"The banners of the lord of the city of On, majesty."

Kemose nodded and turned to his aide. "Send for my nephew."

"There is something else, lord," the runner said.

"Go on, man," Kemose said.

"The barge is draped in the color of mourning."

"Gods," Kemose whispered.

Kaptar had not been far off and came quickly.

"I fear, nephew, that our visitor bears bad news," Kemose told him.

"Perhaps it is only the Libyan," Kaptar, with the optimism of youth, suggested. In that event it was likely that Tania was coming back to them. There was the possibility that the death being announced was that of the child his mother had borne to the Libyan. If that were true he would not weep.

Musen had sent a delegation of priests to carry the news. The glittering court of Waset was drawn up on the docks when the delegation from On exited the barge in solemn pomp, with bent heads and downcast eyes.

It was only after the ritual of greeting that honored Kemose and in return offered hospitality to the visitors that Kemose motioned the chief priest from On to his feet and said, "Give us your sorrowful news, brother."

"It is my sad duty to report to you, great lord—"

Even though the priest rattled off the titles of his mother ringingly and with splendid pronunciation, Kaptar could not bring himself to accept the truth.

"—Great Wife of the Lord Musen of On, the Princess Tania, she has departed us to the abode of the blessed, where the goddess Nut received her with outstretched hands—"

A sorrowful Kaptar left the ceremonial procession and made his way to the temple.

He prayed not to the jackal god of the dead, nor to any particular one of the dozens of gods that swarmed from the ancient past into the daily lives of Waset, but to the memory of the woman who had nursed him, who had comforted him and treated the scrapes and bruises that are the lot of a small boy. He prayed to her and for her in the words of the scribes of old:

"Thou art pure, pure is thy *ka*, pure is thy soul, pure is thy link with Amon."

Now he was alone in the world. Although he had not known Urnan the armorer, his mother had made his father's memory live in his heart, and the beautiful woman who had borne him joined the Mesopotamian armorer as a shade in her son's thoughts, for he had long assumed that his father was dead. His prayers coupled the two who had loved so well and placed them together in the land of the sky, in that afterlife where mortals consorted in adoration of Ra, where lovers could behold Osiris and pay homage to him.

"Make bright my mother," he prayed. "Hold out your hands to her, Nut. Hail, all you gods of the Soul Temple, all you weighers of heaven and earth, all you givers of sustenance, of food and meat in abundance. Hail Ra, lord of heaven. Receive my mother and make her bright."

In On, Kaptar was greeted with proper ceremony and housed in Musen's palace. Musen was most gracious, although he did not act like a man bereft. When Kaptar accepted an invitation to inspect the tomb that was being prepared for Tania, he was surprised to find that the tomb was incomplete, for his mother had mentioned in her correspondence that work had been going on for years on the final resting place for Musen and his wife.

"I have decided," Musen said, as they entered the tomb where workmen were plastering the walls and artists were painting stylized portraits of Tania in the presence of the gods, "that your mother deserves a dwelling place of her own. I am sparing no expense in making it the equal of the tombs of queens."

Kaptar remained silent, thinking it unwise to point out to the Libyan that this poor place paled in comparison with the huge, rock-cut tombs of the ancients in the Valley of the Tombs of the Kings across the river from the Southern City. Nor did he mention that it seemed odd not to inter Tania in the tomb of her husband.

That night Kaptar found himself awake and thinking of what was being done to his mother's body in the house of the dead. He was Egyptian, and it did not seem gruesome to him that his mother's intestines, heart, and lungs had been removed, washed in palm wine, and then stuffed with spices and aromatic gums. Her brain, meanwhile, had been withdrawn through her nostrils by the use of a hooked rod before being dried and preserved, to be interred later with the body. The body itself was soaking in a vat of liquid natron.

Once, he and his uncle had visited the house of the dead at Waset just in time to see a body being removed from the natron vat. The skin of the dead woman, a pale greenish-gray, clung to her bones. Her fingernails and toenails were well preserved, her face, although thin, was lifelike. He had watched the servants of Anubis make slits in the greenish skin into which was stuffed spices and natron. With one final touch, the priests had inserted obsidian eyes into the empty eye sockets.

He envisioned the body of his mother. Rich golden rings adorned her fingers. A golden scarab lay on her breast. She was wrapped in unguent-smeared bandages that had been moistened so that they clung tightly to her body. Her arms were wrapped close to her body; her hands were folded on her stomach. She rested in an elaborate, multilayered coffin, with her internal organs nearby in four canopic jars so that in the afterlife, when her body was revitalized by the gods, all her vital parts would be there.

On the day when the body of Princess Tania was to be taken to her tomb, professional mourners—their great number testified to the love of the husband for the deceased—led the funeral procession beating their breasts and pretending to tear out their hair. In a place of honor Kaptar accompanied Musen to the tomb, where tables had been set up to hold a feast of bread, cakes, baked duck, haunches of beef, vegetables, and beer.

When later the hastily furnished tomb was sealed and given over to the protection of the priests, the professional mourners and the curious hangers-on attacked the tables of funeral offerings, carrying off what they did not eat.

"The son of my beloved wife is welcome to stay with me and his brother in On," Musen said. "There is much work to be done, and I could use a strong right arm." He smiled smoothly. "More than anything else I could use a valued aide whom I could trust."

"Your consideration is appreciated, Stepfather," Kaptar said. "But my place is with my uncle in Waset."

"Your place is at the side of a strong king who wears the crowns of both Upper and Lower Egypt," Musen said. "If an alliance were forged between the two sons of Princess Tania, who share the same royal bloodline as Kemose and Paynozem, who could deny them a legitimate claim to the throne of the Two Lands?"

"Who, Stepfather, would be seated on the throne, and who would stand at his side?" Kaptar asked with a disarming smile.

"The gods will decree that," Musen said. "It is for us to think of the good of Egypt, not of personal ambition."

"I will stand ready at any time to meet with my brother," Kaptar said. "However, isn't talk of a son of Tania on the throne a bit premature? There is Paynozem, and there are his sons. There is Kemose in the south."

Musen spead his hands. "Both Paynozem and Kemose are past their middle years. Kemose has no heir save you. And it is not treason but the unfortunate truth when I say that Paynozem has sired weaklings who think only of their own pleasure."

Kaptar was silent.

"You will find the terms of your mother's will to be fair," Musen said. "She divided her wealth between you and Namlot. Since much of it is invested in holdings in this city it will be necessary for you to remain here to benefit fully."

"I will leave my share in the care of my brother and his honored father," Kaptar said.

"You are wise."

"I would like to have some few personal things from my mother's quarters, something to remember her by."

"Take anything you want," Musen said, waving his hands with expansive generosity. "There are some choice and valuable pieces among her jewelry."

The perfume that Tania had favored still lingered in her quarters. It clung to her bed, to the clothing in her dressing room. Kaptar sat in a gilded chair in front of a dressing table. He picked up her mirror and looked at his image. He could see there an echo of his mother in his eyes and nose. He touched her cosmetics, her paints, her kohl sticks, her bottles of sweet oils.

Then he found her letters. He was surprised to discover she had taken an interested but not overly active part in the diplomatic relations between the Libyans and the court of Paynozem. She had saved all the letters sent to her by Kemose, and it lifted Kaptar's spirits to read words of calm wisdom from his uncle.

At the bottom of the box he found a letter addressed to *"My beloved son, Kaptar."* He read through it eagerly. At first it seemed to hold nothing of import. His mother wrote of her new son, Namlot, and expressed the wish that her two sons would get to know each other. It was only at the very end that she added an odd comment: *"When I have gone to be with the gods, my son, seek me with Amon. Seek me in his temple."*

He shook his head in puzzlement. It was unlike his mother to be so cryptic, but the letter had been written in a city that was not her own, among people who were not of her blood.

A feeling of dread came over him. "Mother," he whispered, "what are you trying to tell me?" He stared down at her jewelry and cosmetics, as if they could bring her back to answer his questions.

For a long while he just sat at the little dressing table. Finally, although he didn't know exactly why, he burned his mother's last letter to him.

Amon was not the major god of the city of On. His temple, resting on the fringes of the desert in the full glare of the sun, was small and insignificant. Only a few priests served their god there, but the man who greeted Kaptar accepted his secret grip of the Amon priesthood with both curiosity and pleasure. When Kaptar identified himself he was taken immediately to the sanctuary, where he was embraced by the high priest of the temple.

"So you have come," said the old priest, whose name was Cefut, an ancient title honoring a god.

"I believe that you have something for me," Kaptar said. "Something left for me by my mother."

"That is true," Cefut said. He gestured, and a

young priest left the room to return with a rolled papyrus in his hand. Kaptar took the roll, noting that Tania's
seal was unbroken.

"She left instructions," Cefut said. "You are to read
the letter here, and then it is to be destroyed."

Kaptar stepped close to an oil lamp, broke the seal,
and unrolled the papyrus.

*What I have done, my beloved son, is for Egypt.
What you must do will also be for the glory of the
Two Lands. When you read this I will be dead,
but your brother, Namlot, lives on if the gods do
not prove fickle. He is your brother in more ways
than one, Kaptar my son. He is the fruit of my
womb, as you are, but he is more. He is Egypt.
Think not of him as the son of a Libyan, for it
was not the seed of Musen nor of any man of the
blood of the usurpers that ripened in me. The
father of your brother, Namlot, was a man of
Egypt, a common man who traces his lineage
back to the time of Ramses the Second. This I
did knowing that one day the Libyans would
rule. This I did while praying to the gods that my
son, Namlot, with the blood of the kings and the
blood of Egypt in his veins, would be or would
produce by the toil of his loins the king who re-
unites the Two Lands. Be with him, Kaptar. Help
him. I think that you are wise enough to know
that the gods favor, at least temporarily, the
growing power of the Libyans. I pray to you that
you will help put a true Egyptian on the throne.*

Kaptar's eyes had filled with tears as he began to
read his mother's words, but then his sadness was dis-
solved in a burst of delighted laughter. So the old priest
Ikkur was right. His mother had been serving Egypt by
agreeing to marry a hated Libyan. "Mother," he whispered, "you have cut off the seed of the Libyans."

"You find your mother's message to be amusing?"
Cefut asked.

"I find it very amusing," Kaptar said.

"For which I praise the gods, since it may leaven the horror of what I have to tell you now."

As Kaptar bowed and waited for the old priest to gather his thoughts, the young priest took the papyrus from Kaptar's hand and held it over the flame of the oil lamp until it blazed and blackened.

"There are new servants in the house of the dead," Cefut said. He raised one hand to stop Kaptar's protests. "I know, you are wondering what this has to do with you. It is important to you because the men who prepared the body that rests in your mother's tomb were killed by the minions of Musen."

Kaptar felt a chill.

"You must know that the woman who lies in the gilded coffin in your mother's tomb was a woman of the town, a prostitute. I know this because the priest who supervised the house of the dead was my brother, and when he saw that the body delivered to him was not that of Princess Tania, he grew suspicious. A servant of his had a cousin who served Musen, a man who helped Musen carry the dismembered body of your mother to be thrown to the reptiles of the Nile."

Kaptar's stomach churned. His legs gave way. What Musen had done to his mother was the horror of horrors. She would never be reanimated in the heavens. Her *ka,* her soul, was doomed to wander between reality and the netherworld forever.

"May the gods curse you, Musen!" he whispered.

Now he knew what his mother had done for Egypt: She had sacrificed her eternal soul. He could do no less than obey her last request. He would do everything in his power to make sure that a true Egyptian, his brother or his brother's son, sat on the throne of the Two Lands.

CHAPTER THIRTY-ONE

The plain of Jezreel echoed with the rumble of chariot wheels, the bawled orders of officers, the tramp of the sandaled feet of kilted and helmeted Philistine infantrymen. In this season of drought, clouds of dust marked their movements. Not since the battle of Ebenezer had the Army of the Five Cities been gathered in such strength.

David's small corps of seasoned warriors, garbed in an assortment of make-do armor and clothing, seemed out of place among the glittering, splendidly uniformed companies of Philistine heavy infantry. He had marched up from the south on the orders of his employer, Achish. He found him at the rear of the Philistine army in the company of kings and princes who watched David's wild-looking, tightly knit unit march up.

Achish motioned David to halt. The prince of Gath was in heated discussion with the other richly clad nobles.

"What are these Hebrew pigs doing here?" the king of Gaza demanded.

"This man is my loyal attendant," Achish answered. "He has served me well for over a year."

A young prince laughed. "I seem to remember that the women of these pigs have a song to which they dance while they brag that Saul has slain his thousands, and David his ten thousands. They are singing, Achish, of the death of Philistine soldiers."

"I have not found treachery in him," Achish said.

"There is always treachery lurking in the heart of a Hebrew," said the king of Gaza. "This man fights well, but I would not want to see him seek his own kind and turn against us in the heat of battle. Send him away. Let him fight his fights in the south against Judah, if he is so loyal to you."

Achish called to David, and the two of them walked together away from the royal tents. "You heard?" he asked.

"I heard."

"You are good in my sight," Achish said, "but the high lords of the cities have decreed that you will not go into battle against Saul with us. Take your men and go back to your city."

David's army marched away from Jezreel in the pale light of dawn, and the heart of each man was light. Although Saul was possessed by devils, no man among them, even David, would have relished fighting with the Philistines against Israel. They returned to find their city, Ziklag, in smoking ruins, all of their women taken along with their sons and daughters. There was little time for weeping. The men were tired from their long march, but they did not falter when David ordered them out in pursuit of an old enemy, the Amalekites, who had wasted Ziklag in their absence.

At the end of the first day of the forced march, soldiers from the advance party came to David with a prisoner, a man dressed in a filthy tunic that David recognized as the garb of an Egyptian.

"He offered no resistance," David was told.

"Who are you?" David asked.

"Lord, I am Sekmut, emissary of Paynozem, may he live, king of Upper and Lower Egypt."

"This is an odd place to find a servant of Egypt," David said.

"Lord, I was on my way to the city of Saul, king of Israel, with messages from my lord Paynozem, when the Amalekites took my traveling party, slew all my servants and guards, and left me to die in this wilderness."

"I fear that you would find Saul occupied," David said. "Are you wounded?"

"Nothing beyond the marks and bruises you see, lord." The Egyptian bowed. "Am I to understand that you pursue those who killed my companions?"

David nodded. "We do."

"I owe them a debt. If you will give me something light to eat, and a drink of water, I can show you to them."

David nodded to his aides. The Egyptian ate hungrily, drank sparingly. Soon he was recovered enough to sit a horse.

The men of the Amalekite raiding party, heavy with loot from Judah and Philistia, were celebrating with wine, feasting, and dancing when the Hebrew came down like a wolf on the fold. After a brief but sanguine engagement, families were reunited and the spoil of the Amalekites recovered.

David said to Sekmut, the Egyptian, "You will return to Ziklag with us. When you have recovered your health, if you still want to see Saul, I will give you escort to him."

"Perhaps, lord David, it is you with whom I should speak of Paynozem's desire to make alliance with Israel," the Egyptian said.

"There is but one king," David said. "He is Saul."

From Saul's camp by a spring on the northwestern spur of the Gilboan hills, there was a splendid view of the plain stretching toward the Jordan. To a man, the men of the city of Jezreel had joined the army, and even as the Philistines made marches and countermarches aimed at drawing Saul down from his high place, others from the far reaches of the nation arrived to give their support to the king. Jonathan was heartened by their loyalty, for there were even a few warriors from Judah among those who came during the final day.

Saul, however, was sunk deep in a melancholy blackness that no one could penetrate.

"It is God who determines the fate of nations, Saul," Urnan argued, "not a witch who professes to speak with a familiar spirit."

"You saw," Saul said. "You heard."

"I heard something," Urnan admitted. "I did not hear the death knell of Israel. Look around you. We are strong. We are as strong as we were at Michmash."

Abner tried to convince him. "We will hold this high place, Saul, and let the Philistine come to us. His chariots can't negotiate the slopes. His infantry will be climbing directly into our ranks of archers."

But nothing could lighten the king's spirit. He lifted his eyes to the distant peak of Mount Tabor, where once the men of Israel had gathered before going to war against the tyrant Sisera. "God was with them," he said, "but Samuel has placed a barrier between me and God."

A newly arrived group of recruits shouted their greetings to the king. "God be with you, Saul," one young soldier said as he bowed. "We come from Gilgal to join you in smiting the Philistine."

Saul paid no attention, continuing to brood. Urnan lifted his hand in greetings. "Welcome, men of Gilgal."

The young soldier studied Urnan for a moment. "You are the smith, Urnan, are you not?"

"At your service, sir."

"A word with you."

Urnan nodded.

"A woman came to my city recently with a young child in her arms. She calls herself Sarah. She speaks of you and someone called Eri."

Urnan's heart leaped. "Eri is my son. His wife's name is Sarah. She was said to have run away with another man."

"This one has no man, but many," the soldier said.

"She takes her place nightly on the bench of the prostitutes with the child in her arms."

Urnan was stricken and could not speak for a moment. "I . . . I thank you."

"The woman has the mind of a child," the soldier said, "and knows not what she does."

Urnan's first thought was that he must go to Sarah. He could only guess at the events that had brought her so low. Perhaps it was too late to reunite Sarah with her family, but there was the child to consider. The little girl was his granddaughter, and Eri's blood.

At that moment a rider thundered into the camp. "Galar marches," he cried. "His front even now approaches the plain."

A great cloud of dust grew on the edge of the plain, and from it emerged the Philistine chariotry. Somewhere in that cloud of dust would be Galar. Was this his chance to take revenge on the man who had killed his wife? Urnan shook his head sadly. He owed loyalty to his king and to the memory of his wife. Sarah and the child would have to wait.

The battle began as Abner had predicted. The kilted infantry of the Philistine army scrambled up the steep slopes into a deadly hail of arrows, and the slaughter was great. When the attack turned, men in goatskin armor leaped down the hill on the heels of those who fled, changing the withdrawal to rout.

At Saul's side Jonathan cried out in joy and lifted his sword. At the signal the war chariots of Israel swept in broad formation toward the enemy's left flank and a mass of heavy infantry.

"Go, go, go," Jonathan yelled. Dust rose from the wheels, and the shrill war cries of the chariot force could be heard over the clash of weapons and the hoarse cries of the wounded. Arrows flew and the wide iron wheels crushed limbs as the chariots smashed the Philistine formation, then turned and, with blood pouring from the wheels, started back to scatter the remaining infantry.

"Look, Jonathan," Urnan shouted, pointing toward

a solid wall of Philistine chariots that had moved in behind the Hebrew force.

"Withdraw!" Jonathan cried, but his voice could not be heard over the din of the battle. Suddenly the smaller Hebrew force was engulfed. Iron wheels clashed. Wood splintered. Horses fell in a tangle of harness, their screams of agony barely heard in the clamor. For a long time dust obscured the scene, and when it cleared, the field was strewn with wreckage and men and beasts. The Hebrew chariotry had been destroyed.

"They come again," Abner shouted as he ran off to position the defensive forces.

"Father," Jonathan said, "Galar has uncovered his right flank. If we move my corps down the slope, there—"

"Go," Saul said, with fire in his voice. "When you turn them we will come down."

Soon a thousand men were moving down the slope. They struck the Philistine right with a fury that pushed back the superior forces.

"Now, men of Israel," Saul bellowed, lifting his sword. "For God and freedom. Now."

Saul led the charge that took the army from the security of the heights. Galar's infantry was caught between Jonathan and the battering ram of men flowing down the hill.

As he followed, Urnan fell heavily and rolled down the slope to crash into a boulder. He sat up, dazed. Men streamed past him. For a time he saw two of everything. When his head cleared and he tried to stand, his ankle gave way under him, and he cried out with the pain.

Below him the sound of battle rose to a dull thunder punctuated by the dying screams of men and animals. From the left he saw the Philistine chariots regrouping. He got to his feet and hobbled down the slope. In the heat of battle, in the dust, Saul and his captains were unaware of the danger.

The chariots smashed into the melee at the rear of Saul's army. Before Urnan could reach the action, men began to stream out of the dust, running up the hill, discarding their weapons in order to flee faster. As he watched in horror a Philistine soldier loomed up before him. Urnan's iron sword found the softness at the Philistine's neck.

The retreat swirled around him, and out of the dust he saw Jonathan emerge, hacking his way through a wall of Philistine infantry. As Jonathan came nearer, the iron tip of a pike penetrated his leather armor and was pressed deep into his flesh by a grinning pikeman. Jonathan gave one cry and fell. Urnan screamed out in protest.

The Philistines pursued the fleeing Hebrews. Urnan, limping badly, his ankle burning with pain, made his way back up the hill. He paused on a ledge and began to seize fleeing soldiers by the arm, urging them to make a stand. Some stood with him.

The roar of the fight below diminished. Out of the dust Saul staggered, his armor-bearer, Jaalam, at his side. Saul's face was red with blood, and his left arm hung loosely at his side. Blood trickled off the end of his fingers.

"We can hold them here," Urnan said.

"With God's help," Saul agreed.

For a while the line held.

Urnan fought in a red haze of pain. His ankle was fire, and his ribs were bruised from the impact of Philistine swords on his armor. One man and then another went down before him until, panting, he could not find an opponent. He looked around. Aside from the dead, both Hebrew and Philistine, three men stood alone: Urnan, Saul, and the young Jaalam. All the others had fled. From the bottom of the slope still another line of Philistine infantry was moving upward.

Urnan limped to Saul's side. The king was seated on a boulder, his sword dangling from his hand. "It's time to go," Urnan said. "They'll be here soon."

Saul looked up. Blood ran from a cut in his forehead. His left arm was useless, and he had taken another wound that, Urnan realized with a surge of despair, would surely cost him his life.

"I go no further, old friend," Saul said, and as he spoke blood ran from the corners of his mouth.

"You must," Urnan said. "We will go into the hills as you did once before. We will rally those who survive to us and—"

"They must not take me alive," Saul gasped. He lifted his sword, but his strength failed. "Take it," he whispered. "Take this sword and let it be the instrument of my passing lest those uncircumcised bastards shame me while I live."

Urnan shook his head. "That I cannot do, lord king."

"You, then, Jaalam," Saul said, turning to his armor-bearer. "Take it and end my torment."

"I beg you, lord, don't ask that of me," the young man said tearfully.

The Philistine infantry was coming nearer. Saul struggled to his feet and, before anyone could stop him, lodged the hilt of his sword against the boulder, the tip at the soft spot in the vee of his ribs, and thrust himself against the keen blade.

"No," Urnan moaned, just as the armor-bearer cried out in what Urnan thought to be sorrow—until he looked up and saw that Jaalam had died at almost the same instant as the king, a Philistine arrow in his heart. Missiles showered down around Urnan.

Almost he stayed to die with the king, but he remembered what he had been told of Sarah, and his promise to Eri to look after Sarah and the infant. And he remembered his vow that someday Galar would pay for the death of his beloved Shelah. He fled, running shamefully with the survivors of Saul's army until he gained the crest of the Gilboan hills and turned toward Endor. In the night he made his way safely through the celebrating Philistine army. So intent were the victors on loot and rapine that they paid no attention to him. He emerged into the quietness of the vale below Mount Tabor undetected and with the morning was knocking on Jerioth's door.

"You're hurt," Jerioth said when she saw him.

"There is very little time," Urnan said. "Listen to me and do not ask questions. Take only what you can carry of food and a warm mantle."

"First I will tend your wounds," she protested.

"We go now or it will be the Philistine who will give the final treatment to my wounds," he said.

She said no more. Within minutes she was ready. Urnan had bound up his swollen ankle with cloth and had prepared a pack consisting of warm wraps and two loaves of bread from the kitchen. Jerioth carried dates and a small portion of cooked meat. She asked no questions until Urnan called a halt to rest when the sun was at its zenith.

"The king is dead, then?" she asked.

"As the shade of Samuel prophesied," Urnan said.

"And as you prophesied, they have come," Jerioth said, pointing back toward Endor, where pillars of smoke were rising into the sky.

"It will be thus throughout the land," Urnan said.

"Where do we go, then?" she asked.

"To Gilgal," he said, "if they are not there before us. And then there is a place, far to the south in the wilderness of Judah, where we will find sanctuary."

A bloodied band of survivors reached Gibeah late in the day following the disaster at Gilboa. Wails of grief assaulted the twilight sky as the word of the death of the king and the defeat of his army spread rapidly through the town that had been Saul's capital. A limping man with a great sword gash in his cheek cried out that the Philistines were coming. Panic followed. By moonlight the people of the town began to flee their homes, although Mered stood in the street and urged them to stay.

"Where will you go?" he asked. "The might of the Philistines is everywhere. Stay here. Give the Philistines their due in obedience and tribute, and you will be safe."

When his own wife appeared carrying a pathetic little bundle of clothing slung over her shoulder, crying out to him to hurry to escape sure death at the hands of the Philistines, he shouted out his anger, ordering her to wait for him in Saul's throne room. Aiah obeyed, although she was sore afraid.

"Fools," Mered raged as families rushed past heading toward they knew not what, toward the hills, toward exposure and hunger and deadly encounters with roving bands of pillaging enemy soldiers. "I, Mered, tell you that you will be safe here."

He stood alone in the street listening to the hurried footsteps of the last to leave. "You'll be back," he shouted, and, since there was no one to hear, he added, "and you will kneel before your new ruler. You will learn to obey me."

For he had been promised by Galar himself that he would be governor of the defeated ones, that he would rule over them backed by the full authority of the Army of the Five Cities.

He lifted his face to the stars and puckered his anuslike mouth for a moment before venting a great, soaring laugh. Let the fools go on their panicked flight to nowhere. Even if many of them died in the hills there would be no shortage of subjects to pay homage to the new governor of the lands of Benjamin once Galar's army had occupied all of the country.

Slowly he made his way to Saul's citadel, which loomed dark and forbidding over him. He found an oil lamp, lit it, and with its tiny flame flickering and guttering walked toward the great room where Israel's first king had held court. His footsteps echoed in the empty corridors. He used the flame of the oil lamp to fire off flambeaus, and in the dim, smoking light he saw Aiah lying huddled on a bench. She was wrapped warmly in her cloak, sleeping soundly.

He sat on Saul's throne and could not halt the joyful laugh that came to his lips. Aiah stirred in her sleep. The great room spread out into shadows, but soon, soon, it would be crowded with those who would fall to their knees to seek his favor.

The throne on which he sat was cold and hard. His ebullient mood faded, subdued by the silence and the emptiness of the citadel. A cracking noise caused him to start and look over his shoulder, but it was only the sound made by wood cooling from the day's heat.

He told himself that it was not for Aiah's company

but for her comfort that he woke her and led her to the king's bedchamber, which he now claimed as his own. He lay on his back next to the soft, warm body of his wife and tried to regain the jubilance with which he had greeted the news of Saul's destruction. A pale, cold half-moon was visible through a window, and from the hills a jackal called mournfully. Sleep was long in coming.

In the first light of a new dawn the glowering hills wore skullcaps of white mist. Those who had fled the town were dampened and chilled by the lowering clouds that blocked the light of the rising sun as if to shield Israel from the eyes of the kilted, helmeted warriors who were, once again, marching victoriously.

Epilogue

~~~~~~

The scholar's words seemed to linger in the air like a bittersweet memory of blossoms long dead. The sun was low in the west, and its evening-red rays glowed on the massive walls of Solomon's temple in the city below.

"It is difficult to believe that the great David fought bloody little wars in the hire of the Philistines," the sloe-eyed girl whispered.

"And against his own people?" another student asked in an awed voice.

"While he was in hiding in Judah he was forced to fight against Saul's army," a male student explained. "After all, Saul was determined to kill him."

"Rabbi," the girl asked in her soft voice, "was it always the ancient enemies of Israel who were David's target, or did he and his partisans truly raid into Judah and Israel, striking the descendants of Abraham?"

The scholar smiled behind his beard. "That question leads us to some interesting studies," he said, "upon which you, in your turn, may shed illumination." He nodded in contentment, for he was proud of his students. "By the by, for you who still doubt that Saul was the Father of Empire, I suggest that you seek The Book of Jashar *and peruse it carefully."*

"It is a difficult book, master," a lad said, "and closely guarded by the priests. Tell us what it says of Saul."

"I would not deprive you of the pleasure of reading for yourself," the scholar said. "I will say only this. You will

find examples of Saul's great personal bravery, and after reading the book you will never doubt Saul's love for his country. Moreover, you will gain new insight into his mastery of politics and his understanding of human nature, qualities that made him a great leader."

"Perhaps he was a caring king," the girl said, "but he was a man nevertheless, a man led into evil by fear and doubt and by that most human of emotions, jealousy. I, for one, can understand that he felt abandoned when Samuel forbade him the worship of God."

"This one has the gift of empathy," the scholar said. "Can you others imagine how Saul felt when he heard the shade of Samuel pronounce his death sentence and the end of all his dreams? He had seen the Philistine host, and he knew that only another miracle from God, such as that which occurred at Michmash, could give him victory. He was sent into the final battle with the curse of God's own prophet on his head, predisposing him to defeat. Perhaps it was his heaviness of heart and his belief that he was to die that led him to make the mistake of meeting the Philistine on the plains where their most effective weapon, their chariot corps, could be brought into play."

"Even after death Samuel had the last word," a young man said.

"Indeed," said the scholar. "For eighteen years Samuel's authority distorted Saul's efforts; nor was Saul free of the prophet's influence during the four years of his reign after Samuel's death. As you say, Samuel had the last word, and that word sent Saul and his sons into battle with no hope of victory. In the space of one day, that brief period of time between the sun's rising and setting, the freedom that Saul had given Israel was lost. Galar's Army of the Five Cities infested the land west of the Jordan. The Rachel tribes of the north, those who had been the heart of the national revival led by Saul, were prostrate before the Philistines."

The sun's disk touched the horizon. The scholar watched a flame sky burn into life. He sighed. "To show the extent of his victory, Galar stripped Saul's three fallen sons of their armor and sent it into Philistia. Saul's armor went into the house of the idol, Ashtoreth. To destroy what *little hope was left in Israel, Galar nailed Saul's body to the wall of Beth-shan in the land of Manasseh to feed the birds of the air. And so beaten were the men of Israel and so indifferent the men of Judah that it was left to the valiant men of Jabesh-Gilead, over Jordan, to rise up and take the bodies of Saul and his sons from Beth-shan by force. They buried the king and his sons with all due honor under a tree at Jabesh and fasted during seven days of mourning, for it was Saul who delivered them from Nahash the Ammonite, who would have put out the right eye of all inhabitants."*

"Shame, shame," several whispered.

"And so the men of Jabesh-Gilead saved honor, but with the Philistines rampaging throughout the lands west of the Jordan, all else seemed lost."

"There was David," said the beautiful, sloe-eyed girl.

"There was David," the scholar admitted. "Obviously, there was David. When next we meet I will ask you to speak to me of this man of Judah, this outlaw who had been fighting a hit-and-run war against Saul and the kingdom of Israel. At the time of Saul's death he was a vassal of the Philistines. Ask yourself how, except by the will of God, such a man could inspire patriotic men of Israel to accept his leadership."

"And what of the armorers, those who bore the mark of the lion? What of Urnan and Eri, and what of Urnan's son, Kaptar, in Egypt?"

"Ah," said the scholar, shading his eyes to see the last edge of the sun's disk sink beyond the western hills. "Each has his own story, and each tale is much too long to begin before darkness makes the homeward path difficult."

Children of the Lion—Book XVIII
THE SHINING KING
by Peter Danielson

Saul, the first king of Israel, is dead. While the Philistines, now free of their old nemesis, return to ravage the land, a bitter power struggle ensues among Saul's followers. One faction is led by David, who was anointed king by the prophet Samuel. He seeks to unite the feuding tribes of Israel and Judah against their common enemy, but he succeeds in this only after more blood is shed and Ishbosheth, the last of Saul's sons, is killed.

Urnan, Eri, and Sunu, Children of the Lion, have pledged themselves to the cause of unity and freedom for Israel. During a foray in the north, Sunu, now a lusty fourteen-year-old warrior, is captivated by the fiery Mara—who, it turns out, is the granddaughter of Saul. Will this defiant princess of Israel give in to her own raging desires? Will the players and events surrounding the two allow them to consummate their love in peace and unite the two families?

Read THE SHINING KING, *Volume Eighteen of THE CHILDREN OF THE LION series, on sale in 1995 wherever Bantam Books are sold.*

FROM THE PRODUCERS OF WAGONS WEST

THE CHILDREN OF THE LION

Extraordinary tales of epic adventure.
A saga that creates anew the splendor and sweeping panorama of desert kingdoms aflame with the excitement and passions of the world's earliest legends.

- ❑ 26912-7   The Children of the Lion .... $4.99/$5.99 in Canada
- ❑ 29082-7   The Invaders .... $4.99/$5.99 in Canada
- ❑ 29495-4   The Trumpet and the Sword .. $4.99/$5.99 in Canada
- ❑ 56145-6   Departed Glory .... $4.99/$5.99 in Canada
- ❑ 56146-4   The Death of Kings .... $4.99/$5.99 in Canada

*ACROSS UNTAMED LANDS THEY FORGED A LEGACY
THAT TIME WILL NEVER FORGET!*

Available at your local bookstore or use this page to order.
Send to: Bantam Books, Dept. LE 5
               2451 S. Wolf Road
               Des Plaines, IL 60018

Please send me the items I have checked above. I am enclosing
$_____ (please add $2.50 to cover postage and handling).
Send check or money order, no cash or C.O.D.'s, please.

Mr./Ms._____

Address_____

City/State_____ Zip_____

Please allow four to six weeks for delivery.
Prices and availability subject to change without notice.   LE 5 3/94